Katie's Rock

by

Kayce Lassiter

HayBurner Publishing
Litchfield Park, Arizona
United States of America

Cover by Bella Media Management

This is a work of fiction. Names, characters, places and incidents either are the product of the author's imagination or are used fictitiously. Any resemblance to actual business establishments, events, locales or persons, living or dead, is entirely coincidental. The publisher does not have any control over and does not assume any responsibility for author or third-party websites or their content.

Katie's Rock by Kayce Lassiter

Published by HayBurner Publishing.

ISBN-13: 978-1490958514
ISBN-10: 1490958517

First Edition: August 2013

Dedication

To my father, Willis, and my brother, Buster, who have both gone on ahead. I love you both very much and always will. Don't forget to hold the back door open.

Acknowledgements

Huge thanks go out to my family and friends who have been my biggest cheerleaders. Every one of you has been right there with me every step of the way, always encouraging, never a discouraging word. I love you.

Also, I owe a debt of gratitude that can never be fully repaid to my mentors and critique partners. Amanda Harte-Cabot, you were the wind beneath my wings and the first to ever tell me I could. To my beloved Butterscotch Martini Girls—Brit Blaise, Judi Thoman, Tina Gerow, Cassie Ryan, Dani Petrone, Kayla Janz, Carol Webb, Lynne Logan, H. D. Thomson, Isabella Clayton, Lisa Pietsch and Samantha Storm—you girls worked with me, shopped with me, laughed with me, cried with me, propped me up when I started to lean, and when all else failed, you drank with me. You girls rock!

Chapter One

"Wow! Would you take a look at those boobs—those are the ones I want!" Kendall, the cocktail waitress, collected empties from a table with one hand and pointed past my shoulder with the other, her eyes as big as saucers.

With a glance toward the other end of the bar, I spotted a redhead in a dress so tight and revealing I had to squint to make sure it wasn't body paint. Her nipples stood at full attention and I could see them from across the room.

I shook my head and shouted to be heard over the band, "Kendall, sometimes you scare the hell out of me…" Slapping at her hand, I added, "And stop pointing. You're gonna draw attention. She'll think we're talkin' about her."

Kendall scrunched up her face, "But we are talking about her." Kendall wasn't an idiot, just one of those people with too much enthusiasm and not enough patience to wait until her brain was fully engaged before she opened her mouth. This could make for some very interesting and sometimes embarrassing moments.

"No, we are not talking about her," I hissed. "You are talking about her. I am not interested in women."

Kendall took another squinty look at the woman before my remark registered. Then she whipped her head around and yelled to be heard over the band, "I'm not interested in women either—I just want her boobs!" Unfortunately, the band took that particular moment to end their song, so the whole bar heard Kendall scream, "I just want her boobs." Really?

With my cheesiest smile pasted across my face, I scanned the crowd and found the entire bar—a packed bar—staring at Kendall…and <u>me</u>. "Good move," I mumbled through clenched teeth as I stepped in behind her.

Kendall's eyes stretched big and round as realization dawned. She sucked in a quick breath and slowly rotated her head one hundred and eighty degrees to take in the bar patrons with their freshly scrubbed, perfectly made up faces all turned in our direction. As she opened her mouth in what I was sure would be a disastrous attempt to rescue our dignity, I reacted with lightning quick reflexes and put her in a headlock with my hand clamped over her mouth.

"Shut up. Don't say a word!" Kendall's lips moved under my hand and there was a muffled squeak. "Not a word or I'll choke you to death right here." My lips began to twitch from the phony smile frozen on my face as I held onto Kendall's head and watched the crowd watch us.

Finally, Kendall nodded and I let her go. Stepping in front of her, I turned my back to the crowd and growled, "If you say one more word, you're gonna be pushing up daisies right where you stand."

She rolled her eyes. "But…"

I grabbed her elbow with my left hand and pointed at her with the other. With my finger an inch from the tip of her nose, I kept my voice low, "No, not a word. I mean it. Not a word."

Kendall huffed as her shoulders slumped. "Okay, not a word."

She finally fell silent and I massaged my forehead to forestall an impending headache as I slipped behind the bar. The band was off tonight, probably all that tequila the drummer put away the previous evening. We'd all pay big time for his night with the bottle unless I could get a little hair of the dog into him. So I poured a shot of tequila, added a lime on a napkin, and thumped an extra salt shaker onto Kendall's tray. "Give it to the drummer. If he doesn't recover fast, I might have to stab myself in the forehead with a fork."

She peeked over her shoulder at the drummer and nodded. "Gotcha! I wondered what was wrong."

At nine fifteen, they were packing in like sardines in a can. I had a kid to support, so it didn't matter what kind of day it'd been, I had to perform or my tip jar would be empty at closing.

I was married once—for almost three years—when my husband left for another woman. Why is it, the smartest women sometimes can't recognize a marriage that's gasping its last breath until it finally goes feet-up? They just beat a dead horse, thinking if they're pretty enough or thin enough or accommodating enough, he'll stay. And why the hell would they want him to stay anyway? Long story short, he left and I wised up.

The bar was a nice place to hide on weekend nights. I could be alone with my thoughts in the middle of a crowd, dance with the music as I slung booze, flirt if I wanted to, sing out loud, toss ice cubes at obnoxious customers, or mindlessly serve drinks, lost in thought. It was like being on stage—when glasses went empty, all eyes were on me and I usually had a good shot at being asked out. On the other hand, if I wasn't interested, the bar was a giant chastity belt. I could flirt all night long, throw them out at closing time, and go home alone.

With a deep breath, I turned toward the far end of the bar and threw my shoulders back as I screwed up the courage to wait on the redhead with the gorgeous boobs—the ones on Kendall's wish list.

As I approached, Willy and MJ took seats a couple of stools away from her. Martha Jean—we called her MJ—was one of the other bartenders and my best friend. She'd dated Willy for about a year now and he'd become like a brother to me. They were the closest thing I had to siblings and they would make the night fun. MJ was easy to work with behind the bar and she would pitch in if the going got too rough.

Suhweet!

Willy and MJ both smiled and waved as I dove into the cooler to get their beers. Willy pointed to the redhead and her date, indicating he'd buy for everyone.

I smiled at the couple and asked, "What can I getcha?"

The redhead was very pretty, tall and willowy and carried herself like royalty. She looked down her nose at me like a scientist examining some disgusting insect. "I'll have a martini. Dry." With a roll of her eyes, she looked away and mumbled, "If you can manage to figure out what that means."

Confidence was one thing, being a bitch was another. I smiled to myself. A country bar could be a rough place for snooty. Great boobs or not, she wouldn't have a good time, but she'd be entertaining as hell to watch.

Why are men attracted to mean-spirited women? Duh! What was I thinking? She was gorgeous. I was no slouch, but I wasn't in this woman's league. My shoulder-length hair was dark auburn and my eyes were almost the same color. At five foot seven and about one forty, I wasn't overweight, but I could use muscle tone. I liked to think of myself as voluptuous, soft. The redhead looked to be about the same weight, but easily two inches taller without the spike heels, making her appear long and graceful. Bright red hair framed a porcelain-like face with big, emerald eyes and real lashes that would turn Snuffleupagus green with envy. Those boobs probably measured two cup sizes larger than mine and, unfortunately, didn't look to be store-bought. With looks like those, she could get any guy she set her sights on. She could fake a personality until he was too hooked to know what hit him.

As I set the martini in front of the woman and looked at her date to take his order, I realized I knew him.

"Oh. Hi, Jake. I didn't recognize you."

He laughed. "Yeah, I'm not surprised. Willy and I were pretty dirty from working outside the last time we were in."

I nodded. "Just a bit, but you clean up real good." Actually, he cleaned up incredibly well. He seemed nice and had a good sense of humor, but I honestly hadn't realized how really hot he was. An extremely striking man at just over six feet, with thick dark hair, he had a hard look about him and carried himself with confidence, like he was used to being in charge. But he had the warmest brown eyes I'd ever seen and one of those great, lopsided grins that melts your insides immediately and makes you wonder what he's up to. In country circles, we call it a shit-eatin' grin.

The words to an old Elvis song ran through my mind...*A hunka hunka burnin' love*...Lord Almighty, I could feel my temperature rising!

Unfortunately, he looked really good with the redhead on his arm. So I dragged myself, kicking and screaming, back to reality, looked into his gorgeous brown eyes, and asked what he'd like to drink.

"I'll have a beer, same as Willy's. How you been?"

I opened a beer and answered, "I've been great. You?"

"Terrific, thanks." Jake paid up and left a large tip. Then he leaned in close as his date twittered in his ear. Man, she was workin' it.

Well, why not? Most women in her shoes would.

After serving their drinks, I leaned across the bar and gave MJ a hug.

She whispered in my ear, "What was that thing with Kendall? I thought she was straight."

I groaned and shook my head. "She is. I think she wants a boob job and she seems to like the set Jake's date is wearing."

Sputtering to contain her laughter, she covered her mouth and ducked her head as I headed down the bar to wait on Mad Harry.

Rumor had it Mad Harry had been in prison for murder. No one knew who he murdered, how he did it, or even how many people he'd supposedly murdered. For two years, he'd come in after work and on Fridays he stayed until the end of the band's first set. He never said much and no one knew where he lived or if he had a family. Harry never danced and only responded with one or two word answers when spoken to. But he'd never caused any trouble, so he was always welcome on my shift.

Mad Harry was fiftyish, handsomely gray at the temples and of Hispanic ancestry—a dark and brooding sort—good looking in a rugged, scary sort of way. He'd smiled once and scared the pants off me. I'd been certain he was going to stuff me in his old pickup truck and take me home, possibly to dismember me and store my body in the freezer next to his dead mother. Or maybe keep me chained in the basement as his sex slave for ten or twenty years. I was always careful not to flirt with Mad Harry, and I never let his beer go empty.

Well, the tequila had done its job and the band was hot. The beer flowed freely and everyone got loose. As the evening wore on and couples headed for homes, hotels, or the backseat of a car, I announced last call and cruised the bar one more time for drink orders and empties.

Willy and MJ ordered two more beers and Jake signaled for another also. The redhead had put away four Martinis and it was beginning to tell on her. Jake stared at her empty glass, clearly reluctant to order another drink.

She leaned into him, hooked an arm around his neck, batted half-lidded eyes, and slurred something which sounded disgustingly like, "Get me one too, pookey."

Jake flinched and pulled back slightly. "Do you think you really need another one?"

She stuck her bottom lip out and touched her forehead to his. “You know, if you’re thinking about getting lucky tonight, you’d better think about getting me another drink.”

Oh man, excuse me while I puke on my shoes!

Jake blushed and pointed to her glass as she swayed to the ladies room on spike heels I couldn’t have stood in on flat ground, stone cold sober, with a stick to prop me up.

I leaned on the bar. “She isn’t driving is she?”

He shook his head and scowled. “No way. That’d be the proverbial accident looking for a place to happen.”

“Okay, I’ll give her another drink if you promise to get her home safe.” I smiled and winked as I added, “But then, the promise of getting lucky makes you a pretty motivated guy, huh?”

Jake winced. “I wouldn’t call it getting lucky. This is our first date and it’s damn sure gonna be our last.”

Well, maybe there’s hope for old Jake after all.

Willy and MJ downed their beers and said they were headed to the local coffee shop for a late breakfast. Jake said he would take his date home and meet them after a bit, if she ever came out of the bathroom.

I picked up glasses and wiped down the bar, stocked coolers, and washed glasses, while Jake waited for his date to exit the ladies room.

After about ten minutes, Jake beckoned me over. “Do you think she’s okay in there?”

I laughed. “Well, she couldn’t have gone out a window because we don’t have one. So, worst case, she's sick from all those Martinis. Want me to check?"

He nodded. "Yeah, I'd really appreciate it."

The first thing I saw in the bathroom was four-inch heels stuck out from under the door of the last stall. "Do you need help?"

There was an echo as she mumbled into the toilet. "No. I think I'm coming down with the flu. Just get out and leave me alone."

I chuckled as I left the bathroom.

Yep, that old proverbial "bottle flu" will get you every time.

Returning to Jake, I broke the bad news. "I'm afraid your date is porcelain-hugging sick."

He stared, apparently clueless as to what to do next.

I patted him on the chest. "Relax. Let's see if she can pull herself together and come out on her own. If not, I'll go back in and see what I can do to roust her out of there."

I was done for the night, so I locked up and pulled two beers from the cooler. Handing one to Jake, I sat on the barstool next to him.

"So, what do you do for a living, Jake?" As long as we were going to have to wait on his date, we might as well be comfortable and get to know each other.

"I'm a rancher. We have a ranch just outside of Ashfork."

"Nice. Who's we?"

"My family. Well, my mom and my brother and I. When my dad passed away, my brother and I took over for him."

"So, how long have you and Willy been friends?"

He smiled. "Long time. We've been best friends since we were ten years old. We went to elementary school and high school together."

Jake was quiet a moment before asking, "How long have you been bartending?"

"Not quite two years, I guess. I used to be a secretary, but my mom was killed in a car accident almost three years ago and when my father took ill within a few weeks of her death, I quit my job to take care of him. Dad hung in there for six months, but he missed mom so bad, he didn't have the will to fight the cancer. I was an only child, so they left me the house and the pickup truck. When I got my head straight and tried to find another job, I discovered part-time bartending paid as much as full-time secretarial work and it gives me more time at home with my kid."

"What about your husband?"

I laughed. "I don't own one of those any more. The one I bought musta been the wrong size. He returned himself to the store and found a new home."

Jake didn't smile or laugh, just furrowed his brow. "Probably hard to make it alone, with a kid. You must be a pretty tough gal."

He'd zeroed in on my biggest fear. Sometimes I'd lay awake at night and wonder if I was tough enough to raise a kid alone. Other women had done it. Why not me? Even if I found a man who would love us both, could I risk depending on him? I'd learned the hard way that a biological tie to your own child wasn't enough to keep a man from leaving. Well, I had no option. Like it or not, we were in this together, he and I—the dynamic duo.

"Well, I'm not taking cruises every year or weekend trips to Vegas, but I do okay. This way I have more time to spend with my son. So here I am, slingin' booze at your favorite neighborhood watering hole."

Jake chuckled and we sat in silence for a few minutes before he looked over the top of his beer and asked, "How come MJ calls you Kat?"

"Nothing mysterious," I answered with a shrug. "MJ likes to give everyone a nickname. My name's Katie, so she shortened it to Kat. Seems more personal that way, I guess."

"Is Katie short for Katherine?"

"Nope, just Katie. My folks believed in keeping things simple."

He chuckled. "What's your last name?"

"Schaffer," I replied. "What's yours?"

"McAllister."

I nodded. "Nice name, Jake McAllister."

"Thanks. I like yours too. It suits you."

Not knowing what else to say, I checked my watch. It had been twenty minutes. "Guess it's time to suit up and go back in."

Jake winced as he looked at the bathroom door. "Yeah, too bad we can't go to breakfast and leave her here to sleep it off."

Laughing, I reminded him, "Oh, but remember, she promised you'd get lucky." I winked at him, "Might be the best night of your life."

A blush crept from his collar to his hairline as he shook his head and looked down at his boots. "You can't be serious. I just want this nightmare to end."

Chuckling, I ran a clean bar towel under the faucet and headed into the ladies room. After a good five minutes of trying to coax the redhead into unlocking the door to the stall, I finally lost patience and crawled under.

It was a snug fit with both of us in the stall and I considered it might be time for a diet. With some effort, I was able to climb over her and unlock the door. Sticking my head out of the bathroom, I asked Jake to come in and help.

He hesitated as he asked, “She’s decent, isn’t she?”

I looked back at the redhead. “Well, her underwear is up and her dress is down, if that’s what you mean.”

Jake winced as he stepped into enemy territory. We each took an arm and lifted her from the floor to a stool in the corner of the bathroom. She was rather nasty as she insisted she didn’t need our help, but I insisted if she didn’t let us, I’d have to call the cops. She didn’t get any less ugly, but she did stop swatting at me as I wiped her face and straightened her dress. Truth be known, she was on my last nerve and much as I enjoyed seeing her make a complete ass of herself, I liked Jake and hated to see him embarrassed—even if he was awfully cute when he blushed.

I stood back and sighed as I surveyed the damage. “Well, she’s about as presentable as I can make her.” Unfortunately, she was still gorgeous, even with her hair a mess, smudged makeup, and her nose running. It simply wasn’t fair. I hated her.

Jake stepped in front of me. “I’ll get her. You hold the door for me.” He put his arm around her waist and lifted her onto her feet. The redhead swayed dangerously as I watched him walk her back to her stool at the bar.

By now, her prince charming looked like he'd swallowed a thundercloud. Those warm brown eyes had turned to steel and you could almost see the sparks coming off them. He wasn't happy and I must admit it did my heart good to see him scowl at the gorgeous creature teetering precariously on her spike heels. I made a mental note to attend church Sunday morning and ask for forgiveness for my sins…because I was racking up a few of those tonight.

Jake moved his truck closer to the back door while I propped up the redhead on her stool. When he returned, Jake laid a twenty on the bar, leaned toward me, hooked his arm around my waist and kissed me on the cheek. "Thanks, Katie. I owe you one."

My heart stuttered and I caught my breath as he leaned close and I caught the smell of soap. Suddenly, my over-active imagination conjured up the image of a damp Jake in nothing but a towel, with his wet hair dripping water onto his shoulders.

I love a man who smells like soap!

I stood there like a fish on a line as Jake shouldered his date off the barstool and half-carried her toward the back door. Mentally shaking off the image of Jake in a towel, I grabbed my purse to follow and again heard the redhead mumble something about getting lucky. The back of Jake's neck turned red as he steadied her through the door. Yeah, old Jake was gonna get lucky tonight, if she didn't pass out on him first.

Why do men always go for the prettiest, skinniest, easiest thing in a skirt? I'm no beauty, but I'm not chopped liver either. So, why is it all the men in my life are either "just friends" or only about three and a half feet tall?

As I followed Jake through the door, I couldn't help but sigh inwardly at how yummy he looked in those snug-fitting jeans. Egads! What was I thinking? My imagination was out of control and if I didn't get it reined in, I might soon find myself reconsidering Mad Harry. Maybe I should try to find a church open tonight. I clearly needed forgiving.

Chapter Two

Saturday morning came early. Dustin was at his dad's for the weekend while I filled in for one of the other bartenders. Working the day shift meant pulling a double. After working late Friday night, it would be a long day, but I needed all the hours I could get while Dustin was away. It helped the finances and kept me busy so I didn't sit around missing my boy. There was a dart tournament at two o'clock and the band would start about nine, which meant the tips would be good and the double shift would go fairly quick.

I opened the bar to the usual Saturday morning Bloody-Mary crowd. The afternoon was busy enough to keep me from getting bored, but slow enough to play a game of pool or two. The day passed quietly and the dart tournament went off without a hitch. No fights, no grumbling, and no stray darts in the back of the head. Life was good.

About seven o'clock, MJ wandered in to see how things were going. She was coming on at nine to help me while the band played, and that was a good thing. With a smile and a little wave, she sat on a stool and ordered a beer. "Hey, Kat, I heard Jake's date bombed last night. What happened?"

I laughed, "Oh, yeah, a real stinker. She ended up sittin' on the bathroom floor with her size sevens stuck out from under the door. It was great!"

MJ shook her head. “I don’t get what Jake sees in that woman. She’s a real bitch and I’ll bet she’s no fun at all.” MJ was all about the fun.

I stretched my eyes open wide and cocked my head at her. “Really? You don’t get it? You’re kidding, right? Did you see her? Drop-dead gorgeous, body to die for? Maybe you need glasses…big, thick pop-bottle type glasses.”

She chuckled, “Well, beauty isn’t everything. There are lots of men out there looking for a strong woman with a good heart and a sharp mind.”

I almost choked. “Oh yeah, and don’t forget good teeth. Yep, you run into those all the time. Come on, they’re looking for a wild woman with no mind at all and big tits…personality optional.”

MJ pursed her lips. “Yeah, now that I think about it, you’re right—they’re all dogs.” We both laughed as she added, “God, we’re witty!”

About that time, Willy walked in, threw me a wave and took the stool on the other side of MJ.

We both scowled at him and said, “Dog,” in unison.

Willy flinched. “What? What’d I do? I didn’t do nuthin’. I just got here.”

MJ and I dissolved in a fit of laughter as he looked back and forth from one of us to the other. He was cute as a baby pig in a dress when he was confused.

At eight thirty sharp, Jake walked through the door looking even yummier than he had the night before. He wore a black felt cowboy hat, a black and white shirt, jeans that showed off a great ass, and boots. As he walked by, I caught the fresh smell of soap again and almost swooned. But I stood straight and steeled myself against the temptation. He was probably here to meet the redhead again, to give her another shot at getting lucky. The image of her feet under the bathroom stall made me giggle. Jake caught me giggling and blushed.

I sooo love a man who blushes easily.

Willy bought a round and as I set a drink in front of Jake, he caught my hand, looked into my eyes and said, "Hey, thanks for the help last night, Katie. I really appreciate it, and I was serious about owing you one."

My heart thudded and my face burned as I nodded and stuttered something incoherent about it all being part of the job. As I stammered out my stupid response, I realized Jake still held my hand. Embarrassed and confused, I jerked it back like I'd been burned with a hot poker.

He blinked twice and half smiled, taking a seat on the nearest barstool. As I fled to the stock room pretending I had work to do, I caught a startled look and a raised brow from MJ. Willy avoided eye contact while grinning like a Cheshire cat and picking at the label on his beer bottle.

I hid in the stockroom for three or four minutes with *hunka hunka burnin' love* running through my mind over and over again as I tried to cool down. But I couldn't hide forever. I'd eventually have to go back out there and act like nothing had happened. Everyone would be clamoring for fresh drinks soon. When I finally stepped from the stockroom, Jake's beer bottle and his stool were both empty.

Whew!

Relieved I wouldn't have to face him right away, I raised the lift gate and swung behind the bar with a smile for MJ and Willy.

MJ squinted and pursed her lips to an "o" shape, silently asking, "What's up?" I ignored it and waited on my other customers, torn between being relieved Jake was gone and wishing he'd come back.

After everyone was settled with a new drink, I worked my way back down the bar. As I reached for Jake's empty bottle, Willy said, "Jake went to pick someone up. He'll be right back. He said to save his seat."

"Oh, okay," I tried to steady myself as my stomach did a little back flip followed by a happy dance. "Guess he's giving the redhead another shot, huh?" I wiggled my eyebrows, expecting to get a laugh.

Willy and MJ shared an odd look and Willy smiled at me. "I don't think so." When I squinched my eyes at him, he chuckled and pretended to be very interested in his beer bottle again.

I looked over at MJ and when our eyes met, she snorted beer out her nose and began to choke as Willy laughed and slapped her on the back.

What the heck?

I looked back and forth between the two and when they had recovered, they both smiled at me. Then they looked at each other and busted up all over again.

I scrunched up my face. "What's so funny?" I looked down to see if my pants were unzipped, but everything was in order. I went back to tending bar, annoyed because I suspected the joke was on me.

Shortly after the band started up, I turned around to see Jake sit back down on his barstool. He had another guy with him who looked like a gorgeous clone. He was about an inch taller than Jake, had the same dark hair and eyes, same chiseled jaw, and was probably a few years younger. I dove into the cooler head first to get Jake's beer, hoping the chill would keep me from blushing. I set the beer in front of Jake and looked at his friend. "What'll you have?" He smiled the same heart-melting smile Jake had.

Holy cow, there's two of 'em!

"Beer, same as my brother."

Brothers. Well, that explains the clone. Wow, talk about a kick-ass gene pool!

I peeked at Jake and he caught me, so I decided to come out bold in order to avoid looking like an idiot. I stood straight, put on my best smile, looked him in the eyes and nodded. "Brother. Oh, good. I thought maybe last night's date soured you on women and you'd switched teams."

Jake blushed furiously, but attitude almost gained him the upper hand when he winked and grinned. "Nope. Moral support while I go for bigger game." Well, he almost rallied—not quite, but almost.

I was slow to catch on to what Jake inferred and he must've interpreted my blank look as shock that he had referred to me as "bigger game". He tried to save himself, but this is where it started to go horribly, horribly wrong. "Oh, I didn't mean bigger game, like in bigger. I meant tougher. You're not bigger. Well, no, you are, but that's not a bad thing. I mean, you're bigger, but it's good. I mean, I like a woman with meat on her bones." With a groan, he put his head on the bar and moaned, "Oh God, just shoot me!"

The lights came on in my brain.

Seriously? I'm his "bigger game"? He thinks I'm fat?

I stood there with my mouth open, probably looking like I should be mounted on a board over a mantle or dangling from the end of a hook. Jake shrunk in his seat and lifted his head to look at me like a deer caught in headlights. Willy, MJ and the brother had collapsed in laughter. MJ had tears rolling down her face and she and Willy leaned against each other for support.

At this point, Jake dropped his head back onto his arms and after a minute, he slowly lifted it again and looked me in the eyes. "I am so sorry. That didn't come out at all the way I had it planned."

"Yeah, no shit," I snapped as I spun away. I had other customers to wait on. I didn't need any favors from someone who was slumming for a good time and I certainly didn't need to be insulted.

What a jerk!

As the night went on, I put on a brave face and waited on my customers like nothing had happened, but I was silently licking old childhood wounds. A chubby kid, I was still occasionally sensitive about my weight. Poor Jake had unwittingly poked a hornet's nest and couldn't seem to figure out how to get his foot out of his mouth.

I felt his eyes on me as I worked and by ten thirty, Jake looked a bit drunk. Two things surprised me—first, he wasn't dripping in icicles from the cold shoulder I'd given him and second, he hadn't left yet. I'd figured as soon as I made it clear I wasn't interested, he'd move on to easier pastures. They always do.

The brother, who introduced himself as David, began to flirt with me at some point and I fell easily in with the banter. I could flirt with the best of 'em, but it was all show and no go. I assumed David was trying to make the best of a bad situation and I could see it annoyed Jake. So I went along for the ride to show everyone I could be a good sport, and maybe to get even with Jake just a tad.

David was awfully cute and the more he flirted, the more confident I became. The drunker and more annoyed Jake appeared to be, the more superior I felt. The evening continued along that vein, with David and I flirting, Jake scowling, and Willy and MJ chuckling and whispering.

Shortly before midnight, a bunch of guys walked in and sat at the table in the back, by the pool tables. The crowd had thinned and I'd sent the waitress home early, so I took their order. I delivered two pitchers of beer and said, "That'll be eight bucks." While one guy fished for the money, another guy at the table began to hit on me. I laughed, took their money, left their change on the table, and turned to walk away. As I turned, the guy who'd hit on me grabbed my hand and tried to pull me back toward him. "Tried" was the operative word here. I tripped over his foot, lost my balance, and wound up in his lap, to my horror and the sheer delight of all his friends. From the look on his face, I don't think I could have told you which of us was more surprised.

As I got my bearings and stood, an arm went possessively around my waist and pulled me to the side, away from the table. I looked over my shoulder to find Jake scowling at the guy whose lap I had just vacated, and he looked sober as a judge.

Jake leaned forward and growled, "The next time you touch her without an invitation, you'll deal with me."

The poor guy stammered out a surprised apology and assured us he didn't know I had a boyfriend, promising it wouldn't happen again. I was about to set things straight and tell him I didn't have a boyfriend when Jake nodded at the guy, took me by the hand, and led me back to the bar. He raised the lift gate and guided me behind the bar before I could even think to react. I followed, dumbstruck, and watched as he returned to his stool and his beer, never making eye contact with me.

Anger rose up from somewhere inside.

Who the hell does he think he is? What gives him the right? Well, I'll give him a piece of my mind!

I took one step in his direction and MJ lunged past me, snagging my elbow. "I need to talk to you in back. Now." She flipped up the lift gate and practically dragged me toward the office. I followed reluctantly, without a clue what could be so important and hoping Jake didn't leave before I could give him a dose of "what for" when I returned.

The jerk!

When we got to the office, MJ planted her hands on her hips and smiled as I scowled and asked, "What?"

She shook her head. "You can be so stupid sometimes. Can't you see Jake likes you? And he's a really nice guy."

I stared at her like she had grown another head. "What are you talking about? Are you crazy? The guy's a sleaze ball. He likes skinny little redheads who put out on the first date and he told me I'm fat. Who does that?"

MJ licked her lips and laughed. "Okay, I'll agree he didn't handle the whole 'bigger' thing very well, but he doesn't think you're fat. He tried to give you a compliment and stuck his foot in his mouth, and now he can't find a way to get it out. He told

Willy he's never met anyone like you and he came back tonight to ask you out. Ya gotta give the guy credit, he stuck his foot in his mouth big time, but he still didn't turn tail and run. He's hung in there all evening and waited for you to come around. He knows how to take his medicine. And he's cute as hell."

I just stared. "What the hell are you talking about?"

MJ chuckled and shook her head, spun me around, and pushed me out the door. "Give the guy a chance. He's probably the last decent unattached guy around."

I walked slowly back to the bar, eyeing him as I went. He quietly picked at the label on his beer bottle. As I lifted the gate and MJ and I slipped back behind the bar, he looked up and our gazes held for a minute, long enough for me to see he was still gorgeous—and still a bit drunk. Maybe not as drunk as I'd previously thought, but well on his way.

At that moment, David leaned across the bar and smiled as he said, "Crowd's thinning. Is the bartender allowed to dance?"

I looked at MJ. She scowled, looked around the bar and shrugged as she waved me on. "I'll watch the bar…you go."

As David took my hand to lead me onto the dance floor, Jake made a noise that sounded suspiciously like a growl. David must have heard it too because he chuckled as he put his arm around my waist and pulled me close. "My brother doesn't share well."

"Nothing to share." I gave him my most flirtatious smile. We danced a couple of fast two-steps and as I started to say I had to get back to work, the band moved into a slow song. David held tight to my hand and pulled me into his arms, insisting I stay for one more dance.

As we danced close, I caught a glimpse of Jake at the bar. His gaze was glued to us as we moved about the floor and his eyes looked like black steel marbles. You could almost feel the electricity in the air. From the dance floor, I could see the muscles work in his jaw. Taking a perverse pleasure in his discomfort, I laid my head on David's shoulder and snuggled into arms that seemed more than ready to pull me close.

The song ended, MJ gave last call, and I reluctantly left the dance floor and started to clear tables on my way back to the bar. As I set a load of dirty glasses on the bar above the sink, I noticed Jake's beer was empty. He was driving, so it wasn't a good idea to serve him any more beer. Feeling a bit guilty about ignoring him all night over something so silly, I slipped behind the bar, poured a cup of coffee and set it in front of him. "Cream and sugar?"

He shook his head. "No, black's fine, thanks." He grinned and my heart did a stutter-beat as it absolutely melted into my shoes.

When I turned to walk away, he cleared his throat. "Uh, wait a minute." I turned back. "I'm afraid I made a mess of things earlier and I'm not sure how to fix it. Any chance you'd let me buy you breakfast after you close up?"

I stared at him for a minute before I replied, "It'll take more than breakfast to make up for what you said, but it's a start. I'll drive."

He flashed me his wonderful, crooked smile again and the twinkle returned to his eye when he winked. "Okay, breakfast tonight and breakfast again in the morning."

I narrowed my eyes. "Don't push your luck, buddy."

He put his hands in the air and grinned as he shook his head. "Just wanted to see exactly how much groveling I'd have to do."

"You'll be groveling for a long time, Mister. Get used to it."

He grinned again and nodded. "Okay, it works for me."

I do like a man who knows how to take his medicine with a smile, and it was a really great smile.

As I washed up the last of the glasses and MJ encouraged the last of the customers to hit the parking lot, David called me over to the end of the bar. He reached across the bar and took one of my hands in his. "Go to breakfast with me, and maybe take me home with you after?"

What is it with these two? They share a brain too?

I looked into his eyes. He looked so much like Jake—the same brown eyes and the same smile, but he seemed to have a sunnier disposition than Jake.

Why doesn't my heart stutter the way it does when I look into Jake's eyes? It doesn't seem to be quite the same chemistry. Maybe it's the age difference.

I smiled. "You're a damn cute one, you are, and any girl would be lucky to have breakfast with you. But I think there's a bit too much age difference between us for me." I winked and laughed as I waved him away. "You go on now. There's gonna be plenty of sweet young things at the coffee shop waiting for some handsome young buck to sweep them off their feet. You don't need an older woman like me slowin' ya down."

David blinked and looked from me to his brother and back again. Then he smiled that cockeyed smile, leaned across the bar, and whispered in my ear, "Okay, but you let me know if he doesn't treat you right and I'll kick his ass!"

I blushed hotly as he planted a quick kiss smack dab on my lips and headed for the parking lot. A quick peek at Jake confirmed he hadn't missed a bit of it. The muscles in his jaw were working again and he stared hard at his brother's back as he raised the coffee cup to his lips.

Slightly unnerved, I turned away and grabbed a towel as I prepared to finish wiping down the bar. I took two steps and tripped over the rubber floor mat which had, somehow, managed to get curled up in one corner. I fumbled for a couple of steps, reached out to grab the bar and missed, turning my body to one side and sitting down hard on my butt. I looked up to find MJ staring down at me and Willy and Jake looking at me from over the top of the bar.

MJ blurted out, "Wow! That musta been some kiss!" I threw the bar towel at her.

My aim has never been good. So when it missed MJ, the wet towel hit Jake square in the side of the head and sent him muttering and cursing back onto his bar stool. That elicited a howl of laughter from MJ and Willy.

Well, so much for breakfast.

I sat on the floor for a bit, nursing my wounded pride, until Willy came around the end of the bar and held out his hand to help me up. I let him pull me to my feet and turned to apologize to Jake, when I got hit right between the eyes with my own bar towel. I scooped up a handful of ice to throw at Jake, which sent him running across the bar with his hands in the air, pleading for a truce.

Having rallied enough to soothe my injured pride, I granted the truce and MJ and I began to close out the registers while Willy and Jake brushed off the pool tables and stocked the beer coolers.

With everything done, we went out the back door and locked up. Willy said they'd meet us at the coffee shop, so Jake and I waved and headed out across the parking lot.

Jake followed me to my truck without a single complaint, which surprised me because most cowboys are real hardheaded about letting the "little woman" drive. When I asked him about it, he shrugged and grinned. "I let David take my truck. It seemed like the quickest way to get rid of him."

As I unlocked the doors and we got in, he chuckled. "A truck girl…I should've known."

I threw him an annoyed look to let him know he had not yet been completely forgiven. Jake smiled, but had the good sense not to let me hear him chuckle again.

Chapter Three

The coffee shop was packed. All the locals were there and half of them were my customers. We were greeted loudly and invited to join the group at one of the larger tables in the center of the restaurant where Willy and MJ had parked themselves. As I sat in the empty chair next to MJ, I noticed David on the opposite side of the table a few seats down. He nodded and I smiled in return, as Jake positioned himself in the empty chair to my right.

We ordered breakfast and were waiting for our food when some of those who had arrived earlier finished eating and began to drift out. As seats emptied, we all shifted toward one end of the table and, eventually, David sat directly across from me. Jake seemed unusually quiet, so I made an effort to include him in the conversation, but he didn't have much to say. Shortly before we finished our breakfast, he excused himself and went to the men's room. He didn't return.

Thirty minutes later, I found myself alone at the table with David. I called the waiter over and asked if there was a window in the men's room. Not understanding the implication, he frowned and said there was no window, so I asked if he could check and see if there was someone lost in there. He came back laughing and said my "husband" was in the men's room, praying to the porcelain god and had made him promise he wouldn't tell me.

Oh, man, this isn't my day!

David shrugged. "Looks like it's just you and me, Slick." He winked and grinned over the top of his coffee cup.

I sighed and shook my head. "What is it with me and men? Why is my luck always so damn lousy?"

David reached across the table and took my hand in his as he smiled easily. "It doesn't have to be lousy. Maybe you're picking the wrong guys."

Is it too late to switch brothers? He's awful cute and he is sober. That's a definite plus.

Then I thought about Jake and felt a tug at my heartstrings. "No," I told him as I withdrew my hand, "my mother always taught me to leave with the guy who brought me to the dance. But it was a nice try, and a very tempting offer."

"Well, I'll be around. If you change your mind, you let me know."

"How do you and your brother get along so well, if you hit on his girlfriends?"

Surprise registered on David's face for a second before he jerked back and grabbed at his heart with both hands and in a voice straight out of a King Arthur movie, said, "Oh, she doth wound me to the quick! Fair maid thinks I'm a mere cad."

I laughed and shook my head. "Oh, you are so bad, so very bad."

He gave me that shit-eatin' grin as he leaned forward and looked into my eyes. "Jake and I have never wanted the same woman—until now. I figure I'd better give it my best shot because something tells me it might be the only shot I get."

My face grew hot as I stared at David.

What the hell do I say to that?

The waiter rescued me when he showed up with the coffeepot and asked if we wanted refills or dessert. I nodded at the coffee, declined the dessert, and asked the waiter if he would please check the bathroom to see if "my…uh…husband" was still indisposed.

A few minutes later, the waiter returned. "Yes, ma'am, he's still polishing the porcelain."

"Do you think you could act as a forward scout and make sure the coast is clear before I suit up and go in there to haul him out?"

He laughed. "Absolutely. I would be happy to escort you into no-man's land. Follow me."

When the waiter emerged, he confirmed the coast was clear, so I took a deep breath and plunged ahead (no pun intended). Jake sat on a chair he'd pulled up in front of one of the toilets with his head in his hands, looking rather green around the gills.

I cleared my throat. "Well, here I am again. I seem to spend most of my time around you rescuing someone from the bathroom."

He groaned and scooted his chair forward as he reached back and slammed the door behind him. "Go home. Let me die here alone, and in peace." Then he threw up again.

Yikes.

I picked his hat up off the floor and left before the sound of retching became contagious. On the way out, I ran into the waiter and asked what time they closed. When he told me they were a 24-hour coffee shop, I told him to bring us more coffee and asked him to take a wet towel to my "husband" and tell him I had his hat and I'd be at the table when he was ready to go.

As we waited for Jake to emerge from the men's room, David and I talked and he filled me in on more of the details about their lives on the ranch.

"We have a family-fun ranch in Northern Arizona, just outside Williams. When dad died a few years ago, mom couldn't run it alone, so Jake and I both moved back and split up the responsibilities. We each have a section of land and our own house. I'm full-time at the ranch and I run the day to day operations, overseeing the cowboys and the stock. Mom, her name's Nell, is chief cook, housekeeper, nurse, and camp counselor. Jake runs the marketing end of the business and spends most of his time in Phoenix working with suppliers and customers."

It was an easy conversation and my mind often returned to the question of whether David might be the better choice. He might not be a whole lot younger than me, maybe not more than five or six years, and he was awfully charming and very handsome.

Certainly seems to be a lot less trouble than his brother.

But then I would listen to those stupid old heartstrings again—stupid, confused heartstrings.

About an hour had passed when Jake finally emerged from the bathroom looking much worse for the wear. He walked to the table, picked up his hat, ran his hand back through his hair, and jammed the hat down on his head. I couldn't help but smile at his predicament, but he took one look at me and growled, "I told you to go on home and leave me here."

"Oh, no, you don't get off that easy. Are you kidding me? How can I make you miserable if I don't stick around? Besides, David and I have had a really nice chat."

With that, the dark thunderclouds returned to Jake's eyes as he turned to scowl at David. "You're still here too?"

David grinned, tipped his hat back on his head, and leaned back in his chair as he stretched an arm across the back of my chair. "Yep, just entertaining Katie while you were indisposed. We wouldn't want her to sit here all alone—someone had to keep the wolves from the door."

If I'd thought Jake's look couldn't get any darker, I would have been dead wrong. He clenched his jaw and shot his brother a very sharp look. "That's the fox guarding the henhouse." Jake stared at his brother for a moment, looking like he might throw a punch any minute. Where was this going?

In an effort to avoid an ugly scene, I jumped up, grabbed my purse, and put on my most innocent smile. "Do you want to go home now, sweetie, or would you like a piece of pie or some really greasy chili before we leave?"

Jake groaned, clutched the back of a chair and swayed as the blood drained from his face. When he had steadied himself, he looked into my eyes, took a measured breath and said, "Let's go." I waved goodbye to David and heard him chuckle behind us as we headed for the door.

Jake paid the bill like a gentleman and we walked out the front door and down the sidewalk. I was rather full of myself for having averted a scene and as I bounced past him in the parking lot, he reached out, grabbed my arm, and pulled me to him. I was horrified at first when I thought he might kiss me after he'd just thrown up in the bathroom. But he simply needed a crutch to get to the truck, and I was it. I chuckled against his chest, wrapped one arm around his waist, and slid myself up under his left shoulder. He leaned against me as I helped him to the truck. My heartbeat kicked up a notch.

It's been a long time since a man leaned on me. Feels nice...warm and snuggly.

When we reached the truck and I began to dig in my purse for the keys, Jake leaned back against the truck and pulled me with. I was amazed he still smelled like soap. He hugged me tight as he planted a kiss on the top of my head. "Thank you". I hugged him back and we stayed that way for a full two or three minutes, until he groaned and said, "I'm gonna throw up again." While Jake made his way to the other side of the truck, I settled back against the driver's door to wait.

About that time, David came out of the restaurant and grinned as he saw me waiting for Jake. "It looks like it's going to be a long night for big brother. You'd better let me drive him home."

With a quick peek toward the other side of the truck, I agreed. "Yeah, you're probably right. I'd rather have him throw up in his truck than mine."

David threw back his head and laughed. "That's my girl, always the practical one."

Something about the way he said "my girl" rattled around in my brain and the blood rushed to my cheeks. To cover my embarrassment, I fumbled in my purse for my keys again. When I finally fished them out of a side pocket, I looked up to find David standing very close, quietly watching me. Startled, I tried to step back, but the truck against my back prevented me from moving more than a couple of inches.

David slowly smiled and winked as he reached out and gently ran his hands down my arms. "You drive safe, okay?"

All I could do was nod.

He turned and started for his truck. "Come on, Jake, you're goin' with me."

Jake straightened and settled his hat on his head. "Okay. You go get the truck while I say goodnight." Then he reached in his shirt pocket and popped something in his mouth as he walked toward me. He looked into my eyes and shook his head, clearly embarrassed. "Sorry. Guess this wasn't such a good idea. I don't drink very often. I hope you'll forgive me for ruining your evening."

"You didn't ruin my evening," I told him. Playfully, I poked him in the ribs as I added, "Actually, you were quite entertaining."

Jake scowled over his shoulder as his brother pulled up behind my truck and waited for Jake to get in. Then he returned his attention to me. I watched as his lips pulled to a thin line and he responded, "Okay, I guess I deserved that."

I smiled as he kissed me on the cheek and turned to leave. "I'll see you later," he said as he turned back to look at me over his shoulder.

I breathed deep as the smell of Spearmint and soap followed him.

Will I really see him again? When?

Chapter Four

The phone rang about ten o'clock Sunday morning. I answered, "Hello."

"Hello." It was a man's voice, one I didn't recognize. "I see you got home okay last night." My stomach jumped.

It's him. How did he get my number?

I didn't want him to get too confident, so I asked, "Who is this?"

He chuckled. "I guess you don't recognize the sound of my voice without all the retching in the background."

"Jake? How did you get my number? I'm certain I didn't give it to you last night."

"I called Willy to get it this morning. I had to promise to throw myself in front of the bullet if you decided to shoot him for it." After a moment's silence, he asked, "Well, what's the verdict? Will I live or die by your hand?"

Another moment of silence and I replied, "I don't know. The jury's still out."

He chuckled. "Well, that's good news…I think. So, what do you want to do today?"

"What are you talking about?"

"Well, I thought we could do something today. Maybe take a drive up north or check out the horse show out at Benson's arena."

"No, I can't. I have a son, remember? He's been with his father for the weekend and he comes home this morning. I can't go anywhere today." I held my breath as I waited for the excuses to begin. Seemed like things always went smoothly until I mentioned my son, and then they would begin to back-pedal. They'd stammer and say it was fine, but pretty soon they stopped calling or avoided me altogether.

Without missing a beat, he simply said, "The zoo it is, then. What time should we pick you two up?"

He never flinched.

Huh? He's offering to take my kid along on a date?

I stammered a bit as I searched for words. "Hey, you don't have to try to impress me by offering to take my son along. We'll be fine hanging out here with a board game or something."

Again, he didn't miss a beat. "Okay, we like board games. What time should we be over?"

We? Who's we?

"What are you talking about? Who is 'we'?"

"We is me and my son, Tyler. Willy says he's a little younger than yours, but I think they'll get along. What time?"

"You have a son? I didn't know." My brain whirled like a windmill in a tornado.

Who is this guy and what does he want from me?

The last guy I'd dated who had a son turned out to have four sons and five wives—one of them still a <u>current</u> wife—so I asked, "You aren't married are you?"

"Yes, I have a son and no, I'm not...uh...not married. We'll be over about two. I'll bring the stuff to make hamburgers for dinner. You got a barbecue grill?"

"Yeah, I've got one but you'll have to bring some charcoal. It's the bargain basement model."

"Okay, you have the board games ready to go…and be prepared to lose your ass."

All I could think to say was, "Wait, don't you want to know where I live?"

"I already know where you live. I had to promise MJ I'd take the bullet for her too in order to get that tidbit of information." I could hear the smile in his voice as he said, "See you at two," and hung up.

Traitors! They're all traitors! My friends have sold me down the river without a second thought.

I hung up and glanced up at the clock. Two o'clock.

Eeek! Less than four hours away! I better get a move on if I'm going to look anywhere near presentable by two o'clock. Oh man, I don't have a clue what to wear. What does one wear to a board games date, anyway?

I quickly picked up the phone and dialed my ex-husband's number. Dustin answered. "Hello."

"Hi, honey. It's mommy. How ya doin'?"

"Hi, mommy," he said, "I'm doin' great! Daddy an' me went fishin' last night. I caught three crawdads an' a whole bag o' night-crawlers." I could just see him with his white-blond hair and his brown eyes sparkling as he smiled from ear to ear. His smile and laughter were always contagious.

"Ooooh, sounds like a good night of fishing. Is your daddy there?" I wasn't sure exactly what night crawlers were, but I was pretty sure they weren't something I'd be fishing for intentionally. What did they do, anyway, crawl onto your hook and ride it in to shore? I'd have to remember to ask.

He turned away from the phone and yelled, "Daddy. It's mommy."

My ex got on the phone. "Yeah." I always did like the strong, silent type.

"What time are you bringing Dustin home?"

"We'll be there in about an hour."

"Okay. See you then. Bye." I hung up the phone and sprinted for the shower, peeling off clothes and dropping them as I went, making a mental note to pick up my underwear before Jake arrived.

The facial repair wasn't as bad as I expected and an hour later, hair styled and makeup perfect, I stood back to survey my handiwork.

Not half bad.

I reached for my bathrobe just as the doorbell rang.

When I opened the door, Dustin was bouncing on his toes as he looked up at his dad adoringly and babbled on about the fishing trip. I wanted him to enjoy time with his dad, but I still couldn't help but be jealous that he always had fun when he was with Mark.

At home, we were always concerned with meals, school, babysitters, clothes, brushing teeth, doctors and dentists. I had been relegated to the role of disciplinarian, the practical one. Dad's house was fun. I gave him underwear for Christmas. Dad gave him motorized cars. A sharp twinge of jealousy slithered through me.

How could I compete?

Sometimes I'd lay awake at night and worry about screwing him up. Could I raise a kid alone?

Didn't matter, I had no option. Many other women had done it. Why not me? Even if I found a man to love us both, could I risk depending on him? Even a biological tie to your own child wasn't enough to keep a man from leaving. Like it or not, we were in this together, he and I—the dynamic duo.

I bent over, scooped him up in my arms, and squeezed him. "Ooooh, I missed you sooo much!"

He hugged me back, choking off my air supply for a moment, and then wiggled out of my arms and ran from the living room yammering on about missing the dog.

I looked at my ex and said, "Sounds like he had fun."

"Yeah, we didn't catch anything, but a good time was had by all." He stood there a moment and then handed me Dustin's suitcase. "Well, guess I'll see ya later. You look good. Got a date?"

"No, just got out of the shower and decided to clean up a bit," I lied, as I tugged at my bathrobe. Mark wasn't a particularly handsome man, but the way he carried himself made him much more attractive to women. He was fairly short, about 5'8", with dark hair and ice blue eyes. He had a good sense of humor and could be a lot of fun to be around when he was in a good mood. As we made small talk about the way I looked, I thought to myself we might still be married if he'd paid a little more attention to how I looked and a lot less attention to all those other women. The pain of being dumped for someone else had faded long ago and had been replaced with what I thought of as a healthy dose of anger and resentment, but he still had the ability to make my heart skip a beat. I hoped that, too, would fade with time.

Mark waved over his shoulder as he nodded and turned to leave. I watched him pull out of the driveway.

How did my life reach this point and where will it take me next? Will I ever love again as much as I loved Mark? Will I ever find someone who deserves my love more than Mark, someone who values me enough to stay and not jump into bed with the first hottie that comes along?

It was almost eleven thirty when I closed the door. I'd better get a move on if I was going to pick out some clothes and get dressed before Jake arrived at two o'clock. So I headed to the bedroom, rolled up the sleeves on my bathrobe, and stepped into my closet, ready to do battle with the fashion police.

I rummaged through everything in my closet, eyeing a cute blue evening dress with sequins that had been a hand-me-down from my neighbor when she'd gained thirty pounds last year. I'd never worn it and didn't have any shoes to go with it, but the dress was to die for and I looked really hot in it—even without shoes.

No, too dressy. It's board games and hamburgers on the grill.

I rummaged some more and came up with a cute pink top and some white slacks, threw them on and stood in front of the mirror to see how I looked.

Terrific. Perfect for board games.

So I threw on some white flip-flops and headed out to the kitchen to wash the pile of dirty dishes stacked in the sink. Thank God for dishwashers!

As I entered the kitchen, the back door opened and Dustin and the dog, Obleo, barreled into the kitchen, both of them covered with mud from head to toe.

Obleo was a blond Cocker Spaniel who hadn't been clipped in some time and wasn't overly bright. Actually, we weren't even sure his bulb was lit at all, but he was awfully cute and very, very sweet. There was a song on the radio when I was younger, about a kid named Oblio—the only kid with a round head in the land of point, where everyone else had a pointed head. So we changed the spelling to Obleo and he became the only dog with a round head in the land of point. He was different—very, very different.

Well, like I said, Obleo hadn't been clipped in quite a while and his feet looked like oversized dust mops, dipped in a mud bath, and headed straight for me. It was like watching a train wreck in slow motion and there was absolutely nothing I could do to stop it. Stumbling backward, I yelled at him to stay down, but it was too late. He was moving fast and I'd long suspected the long, floppy ears and all the hair had left him a bit hard of hearing. Before I could move away or jump on the counter, he'd lunged across the room and planted both front feet on my belly. In the commotion, I tripped over my feet and fell to the floor where I groaned and fought off the dog as I wondered what else was in my closet. Obleo absolutely couldn't believe his luck. I was a captive audience and he could reach every square inch of me. Before I could make a move to get up, he had done just that—jumped all over me and licked my face, neck, arms, and legs in a frenzied attempt to show me how much he loved me.

Kiss that bath and makeup job goodbye.

When the dog calmed down enough to be captured and I recovered enough to get up, I hauled him outside and told him to stay. I then turned to Dustin with a scowl, pointed to the bathroom and said, "March, Mister."

He shrugged his shoulders and began to plead his case. "I tried to keep him out, but he was excited to see you and I couldn't hold him. He loves you so much, Mom!"

A con if I'd ever I heard one. I narrowed my eyes and pointed at the bathroom. "Go get cleaned up. We have company coming over and I want you clean. I have to change my clothes and fix my make-up, so you're on your own to get ready. You better be squeaky clean and your clothes better match. You got it?"

He smiled and stuck his thumb in the air. "Got it."

I made a feeble attempt to clean up the mud on the floor and walls, and sprinted to the bathroom to survey the damage done to body and person. I was covered in drying mud from the top of my head to my feet and my mascara was smeared. I desperately needed another shower and a change of clothes. I would even have to wash my hair again. I'd never make it, but I had to try.

After another shower, another round of wash-dry-style, and another round of makeup, it was going on two o'clock. I ran to the closet, rummaged desperately through the stack of clothes I'd tried on earlier, and pulled out a red tee and a pair of jeans. Perfect for board games! I threw the clothes on, stuffed my feet into a pair of leather sandals, and headed for the mirror to see if I'd made it.

Just as I decided I liked the new look better than the first, I heard the dog bark and the sound of a car door out front. Dustin rushed down the hall and as I rounded the corner into the living room, all I could see were his feet sticking out from behind the front curtains as I heard him say, "They're here! They're here and there's a kid and he looks real nice. He's got brown hair and he's shorter than me."

My head hurt, I was about to hyperventilate, and I thought my heart would probably stop.

Slow down and take a deep breath. Walk to the door and open it. Be cool. Don't panic. It's not your first date. Act like it's no big deal. He'll be hung over anyway, so he'll be at a disadvantage.

As I stood there with my eyes shut, breathing and talking to myself, Dustin rushed to open the door. As it started to swing open, I opened my eyes and saw my red thong underwear lying on the floor where I'd left them earlier. I snatched them up and had just rolled them into a ball when I heard Dustin say, "Hi."

I looked up and quickly hid the thong behind my back as I stopped breathing completely. There stood Jake with his son in his arms, grinning like a damn Cheshire cat and looking better than a man had any right to look, especially a man who was supposed to be hung over.

Hell, my date looks better than I do. I should have gone for the evening dress, especially if I want to be the pretty one!

I stood with my hands behind my back and stupidly stared as he shot me a heart-wrenching grin and said, "Hi."

The spell broken, I sucked in a lung full of air and began to choke. Jake quickly put Tyler down and reached for me. "You okay? Is there anything I can do?"

"No!" I managed to sputter out as I doubled over, wheezing and choking. *God, don't let me wet my pants!* After a minute or two, I gained the upper hand and was pretty sure I had been spared the humiliation of wet underwear. At that point, I dared to look at him again and waived my hands in the air as I croaked out, "Sorry. Don't know what happened. Musta breathed wrong." As I waved my hands, the thong dropped to the floor between us, like a red flag on a football field.

Jake smiled and bent to retrieve the thong. "Oh, so it wasn't my overwhelming presence." He held the thong up in the air with one finger as he raised a brow and smiled.

I snatched the thong from his hands and stuffed it behind my back again as I scowled, refusing to let him know how dangerously close he had come to the truth, and silently daring him to mention the thong. He didn't.

There was a twinkle in his eye as he flashed me another incredible smile and took a step toward me, pulling Tyler with him. Purely from reflex, I stepped back.

"Tyler, this is Miss Katie. Miss Katie, this is my son, Tyler." In that instant, the look on his face melted my heart. This man beamed with pride. He clearly adored his son.

I looked at Tyler and smiled. What a beautiful child—about four years old with his father's dark hair and warm brown eyes.

"Hi, Tyler, it's very nice to meet you. This is my son, Dustin. Dustin, this is Tyler and his father, Mr. Jake." As I introduced Dustin, I turned to look at him and froze as I got my first really good look since I'd sent him off to clean up and dress for the occasion. There he stood in his favorite ratty old plaid shirt and frayed jeans that were about three sizes too short. His hair had been combed into something closely resembling a Mohawk and he apparently thought it would be cool to spray the Mohawk fire-engine red, like we had last Halloween. I gaped like a yawning toad. Jake had put a fist to his mouth and tried desperately not to laugh.

Dustin grinned and waved at Tyler. “Hi”.

Tyler returned the wave and said, “Hey, cool hair,” and off they went to Dustin’s room, without as much as a backward glance.

I looked up at Jake and smiled. “You have a beautiful child,” I said through clenched teeth, “unlike mine, who appears to be early for Halloween”.

He flashed me that heart-piercing lopsided grin of his. “Thanks. Dustin’s a good-looking kid too. He looks exactly like you, and he’s polite.” There was a short pause before he added, “Seems to have his mother’s sense of humor too.”

“Thanks,” I said as I rolled my eyes. “Honestly, he doesn’t always look like that. Guess I shouldn’t have let him dress himself. Next time, we’ll do an inspection before we open the door.”

He chuckled. “Well, you had your hands full.” As I narrowed my eyes, he cleared his throat. “Actually, I’m kinda glad you didn’t. We might have missed all the excitement.”

There were a few awkward seconds before I asked, “How do you feel today?”

He blushed and dropped his gaze to the floor. “I feel good, but I really owe you an apology for last night—another apology. Seems that’s all I do around you. You make me so nervous, I can’t seem to get anything right.”

Kayce Lassiter

My mouth dropped open and I blurted, "I make you nervous? Are you kidding me? I feel like some big, lumbering idiot who can't put a whole sentence together when I'm ar…"

He cut off the rest of what I was about to say as he reached out, pulled me to him, and kissed me squarely on the lips. Stunned, I stared at his eyelids as he kissed me. He pulled back and raised a brow in question. I shifted from the right foot to the left and chewed on my lower lip as I said, "Uhmm…uh, why don't we try it again. I think I can do better."

He smiled and wrapped his arms around me as he pulled me close and kissed me again. This time, I helped.

Chapter Five

The burgers were on the grill, the boys were playing with toy cars in the sandbox, the dog was locked away in the dog run, the mud had been cleaned off the dining room floor and walls, and I was parked in a lawn chair sipping iced tea. The lettuce and tomatoes were cut up on a plate on the kitchen counter next to the buns and condiments. Everything was ready and Jake and the boys and I were just waiting for the burgers to cook.

While we waited, we did the initial "stats swap"—you know, the part where you tell how old you are, where you were born, what you do for a living—all the little details. Jake and I discovered we were both native Arizonans. He was a few months younger than me. I was thirty and he was pushing it real close. Jake reiterated some of what David had told me the night before about their cattle ranch in Northern Arizona.

He slipped his hand over mine as it rested on the arm of my chair and sent a wave of goose bumps up my arm as he asked, "So, where are you originally from?"

With my free hand, I rubbed my arm hoping he hadn't noticed the electrifying effect he had on me. "I'm from here. I grew up on a dairy farm on the outskirts of Phoenix."

He grinned. "Ah, a farm girl. That's good. You know your way around cattle, then."

Kayce Lassiter

Checking to see if I can cut the mustard on a ranch?

I nodded. “Yep. Been there, done that. But ours were just plain old milk cows, nothing real expensive or registered, pretty much just mutts.”

He smiled. “A cow is a cow. They don’t know if they’ve got registration papers or not, they all behave the same. Did you like living on the farm?”

I hesitated a moment as the memories flooded in and a heaviness settled over my heart. It always happened when I thought back to life on the farm.

Guess you really can’t take the farm outta the girl.

”You know, that’s a complicated thing. I spent the first seventeen years of my life desperate to get off the farm and into the lights of the big city. But after a failed marriage and a few years in the city struggling to make it as a single mother and protect my son from unsavory influences, the city doesn’t glitter nearly as bright as it once did. Now I wish I’d never left.”

Jake’s eyes softened as he nodded. “That happens more than you might believe. It’s a pretty common ailment among farm kids. There were a few times when I thought I hated it too. Lots of work and kids and spouses don’t always understand.” He stood and held his glass up. “I’m going to get a refill. How’s yours?”

I held up my glass. “I’m good, thanks.”

With a nod, he headed into the house for more iced tea.

I snuggled deeper into my chair as I wondered about his comment that kids and spouses don’t always understand.

Did I detect a note of bitterness? Is that what happened in his marriage?

He seemed to be comfortable talking about personal things, so I'd probably find out in time. And for now, it just didn't get any better than this, engaged in conversation with a man that could make Mother Theresa give up sainthood. So I tucked the questions away for future reference.

What I hadn't told him was I'd often fantasized about finding a man who would move my son and I back to the country—a loving and honorable man who could provide a good, solid role model for my son, a faithful man who needed and wanted me enough to never leave.

In my wildest fantasies, the man of my dreams was a rich rancher and we married and had three or four more kids. When our children grew up and got married, we'd build each of them a big house somewhere on the ranch, and we'd be surrounded by our children and grandchildren as we grew old together.

In reality, it didn't matter if the man didn't have a penny to his name, as long as he had plenty of love to give and a faithful soul. Which was a good thing, because every man I tried to view through the filter of my fantasy came up short.

Maybe for once, the fantasy won't crack and crumble. Is this the man of my dreams? How much love does he have to give? How faithful is his soul? Could he be my prince or just another toad in disguise?

With a deep breath, I swallowed the lump of fear in my throat. I'd been hurt enough times to know all that glitters is not gold...sometimes it's just a spray-painted egg. As soon as you test its strength, you have one hell of a mess.

When Jake returned from the kitchen with his ice tea, I heard him walk up behind me and set his drink on the table. He put his hands on my shoulders and he began to massage my neck as he leaned down and nuzzled my ear. A shiver shot through me like a bolt of lightning.

He chuckled as he pulled away and I turned and shot him my most steely-eyed glare just to make sure he didn't get all full of himself. He raised both hands in the air and backed up a step. "Whoa, not looking for any trouble here, just trying to be friendly."

"Huh! I think it's about time you checked those burgers."

Yeah, he definitely knows the effect he has on me. Talk about being transparent as country air!

As he grinned and headed for the grill, I drank in the sight of him. He was heartbreakingly handsome. Where I had ever gotten the impression he had a hard look about him? The man in front of my grill right now was a warm, funny man who loved his son, had great hands and an ass to die for.

Whoa there, girl—rein those horses in a titch! There's kids around. Get too carried away and you're liable to forget where you're at.

While his back was to me, I fanned my face real quick and tried not to think about his hands or the way his jeans snugged over his butt.

Flipping the burgers off the grill and onto the platter, Jake yelled out to the boys, "Burgers are done. You boys go help Miss Katie carry out the plates. Let's eat!"

I jumped up and ran into the house with the boys close on my heels. I handed them each some plates and utensils, stacked up the buns and condiments and headed for the door. Jake met me halfway and relieved me of some of the condiments, giving me a quick kiss on the cheek as he moved in behind to usher me out the door.

As we all sat at the patio table, the boys chatted excitedly and bounced up and down with their forks in their hands, clamoring for catsup on their burgers.

Jake flipped hamburgers in the air and caught them on plates as the boys squealed in delight at this marvelous trick they acted like they'd never ever seen before. Everything was going great until the third burger hit the ground. We all went quiet at the same time, stunned Jake had missed the plate.

I laughed. "That's taking 'ground beef' a little too seriously, isn't it? Good thing there are extras or you might be having cereal for dinner."

He shrugged and grinned. "Oh well, guess the dog eats too."

We all munched our way through the burgers and chips in no time flat. There was a lot of table conversation and laughter in between chews, but I was so overwhelmed by the presence of the man next to me, I couldn't have told you later what was said. I was keenly aware of his leg pressed up against mine and every so often, he would wrap his arm around my waist and pull me close or rest his hand on my knee as he leaned over to whisper in my ear. Nothing he said was suggestive or secret, simply an excuse to be close and I ate it up. This man had every cell in my body tuned into his frequency and doing a mambo.

After dinner, we cleared the table and everything except the condiment bottles and the spatula went into the garbage. Jake grabbed up each of the boys, turned to me and asked, "Well, what is it? Board games or a movie? I brought a great old cowboy movie."

Yay!

I hadn't seen an old cowboy movie since my dad died. We used to watch one every Saturday night when I was a kid. That was our special time, just me and my dad on the couch with a shoot-'em-up western and popcorn.

The boys looked at each other and began to wave their arms and chant, "Movie! Movie! Movie!

"Okay, okay," said Jake. "A movie it is." Then he smiled at me. "I hope you like Clint Eastwood westerns. I'm an old cowboy movie freak, but if you don't like them, we don't have to watch it."

"Are you kidding? I love them." I led the way to the living room.

Clint Eastwood looks damn hot in his jeans too!

Jake went out to his truck and returned with the movie and two packages of microwave popcorn while the boys flopped down on a blanket I spread on the floor.

They spied the bags of popcorn and squealed, "Popcorn!"

I turned to Jake. "You get the movie started and keep the natives from getting restless, while I go rustle up some popcorn."

"You got it, ma'am," he said in his best Texas drawl, as he turned toward the DVD player.

I had just started the second bag of popcorn and was emptying the first bag into a bowl when Jake walked up behind me. I straightened as his arm snaked around my waist and he pulled my hair back as he softly kissed my neck. My stomach did a loop-de-loop and I sucked in a breath and leaned into him. We stood that way for what seemed like a very long time as I listened to the pounding of our hearts. Then he slipped his hands onto my shoulders and turned me toward him. "You are the most remarkable woman and I am absolutely, hopelessly caught." He pulled me close and kissed me.

It had been a very long time since anyone had kissed me like that, warm lips brushing mine and his tongue gently tasting my lips like he savored a sweet fine wine. My knees went weak and my head got fuzzy, like the blood had pooled in my feet. I clung to him like a wet leaf. I was a woman on the edge of a precipice.

Should I jump or turn and run? What's at the bottom? Cool water or hard, jagged rocks? What is it about him that draws me forward, but holds me back at the same time? Is it past failures or is there something real to fear? My luck, it'd be a long drop into a burning pit of snakes.

When the kiss ended, I snuggled into his arms and held on for dear life. Did it really matter?

About the time the blood flow returned to my brain, Dustin asked, "Hey, where's our popcorn?" I looked over to find both boys in the doorway with their hands over their mouths, giggling.

Like kids who had been caught playing doctor, Jake and I jumped apart and stammered out excuses as to why the popcorn wasn't ready yet. Jake shooed the boys back into the living room as they both giggled and made obnoxious little kissing noises.

My face heated up like a fired pistol as I busied myself with the popcorn and tried not to think about the kiss, the man, or the burn in my belly.

Slow and steady, girl. Remember, you're not the only one who stands to get hurt if this doesn't work. You're a package deal, so this has to be more than just Fourth of July fireworks.

An hour and a half later, I was snuggled up against Jake on the couch and the credits rolled on the movie. "Do you think they're asleep?" His deep voice rumbled through me like slow summer thunder.

I looked down at their little backs and watched the heavy, slow, steady breathing for a moment. "Yeah, looks like it."

Jake stood and tugged at the corner of the blanket to pull it gently over the sleeping boys. With a smile, he straightened and turned to me with his hand extended to help me up.

"Wanna go out and sit on the patio for a spell?"

My heart leapt as I gulped and took a deep breath. "Yeah, I'd like that."

We walked hand-in-hand onto the patio and sat on the porch swing. A huge yellow moon filled the night sky. When a cool breeze wafted over us, Jake put his arm around me and pulled me close as he rubbed my bare arm to smooth the chill bumps. With my head on his shoulder, I listened to the gentle squeak of the swing as we sat in silence.

This is what everyone seeks—the company of another soul, the warmth and companionship of someone you care about. Is he beginning to care for me as much as I am for him?

After a few minutes, I sensed his eyes on me and turned to find him smiling. I smiled back and said, "This has been a wonderful evening. I'm so glad you and Tyler came over."

"Me too." He reached over and stroked my arm. "How long have you been divorced?"

"Almost three years. How about you?"

He hesitated for a second before he replied, "Not long."

When he didn't offer anything more right away, I asked, "What happened?"

I could hear his teeth grind as he answered, "My wife cheated on me." A moment of silence passed. "We'd only been dating for a few months when she turned up pregnant. So I asked her to marry me. I'm still not sure why she accepted. Maybe she just needed help financially."

"Did you love her?"

Jake gave me a surprised look. "No, I don't guess I did at first. It seemed like the right thing to do. She had a daughter from her first marriage, and then Tyler was born and we had a family. I loved it and tried to make it work, and things were good until I found out she was cheating on me."

Reaching for his hand, I gently rubbed the top of it, surprised to find it softer than I'd expected. "Sorry. I know how painful it can be."

His gaze met mine and held as he shrugged. "It's over now. I tried, but nothing ever worked. Everything was always about her, always about what she wanted or didn't want. She was a terrible housekeeper, a moderately good mother, and eventually proved to be a lousy wife. When I found out she was cheating, she even tried to blame it on me. Said it was my fault she'd cheated because she was miserable living in the country, said she never wanted to see another cow as long as she lived."

My gut churned at his description of a cheating wife. It was eerily close to what I'd experienced and I wondered if the pain of rejection ever went away. I nodded. "Yeah, I remember saying the same thing once. Funny, how the grass always looks greener on the other side. Never imagined I'd ever miss cows as much as I do."

"Really?" A note of skepticism crept into his voice.

"Yeah." I looked down at my hands in my lap. "Strangely, I do miss farm life. It was a lot of hard work and it seemed lonely as a kid, but now that I've lived in the city for a while, I realize what I've lost. There's something about a farm you can't find in the city, honesty and a peace that resonates within your soul."

As I looked up, I caught a strange and haunted look in his eyes that I didn't know how to interpret.

He nodded. "I know what you mean." He leaned in and kissed me, a slow, tender kiss that made my heart ache to be held by this man forever.

I laid my head on his shoulder. "So, was Tyler the only child the two of you had?"

"Yeah, the only one we had together. I adopted Nikki, my wife's daughter from her first marriage. She's ten now and that's the toughest part. Because I'm the adoptive parent, Brenda will…well, she has custody of her. I get to see her sometimes on weekends."

"That must be very hard for both of you. What about Tyler?"

"Tyler lives with me. Brenda's living with her boyfriend now and I don't think he wanted either of the kids, but Brenda wouldn't let me have Nikki. Guess she felt it wouldn't look right, and she's all about appearances. Anyway, she agreed to let Tyler live with me without a fight. I'm hopeful that in time, the boyfriend will talk her into letting Nikki come live with me too."

"What about Nikki's birth father? Is he still around?"

"No, he abandoned Brenda before Nikki was born and didn't want any part of fatherhood. He gave up his parental rights and walked to avoid child support. We never heard from him again after the adoption."

"Wow. Poor kid. How are the kids handling the split?"

Jake shrugged. "Tyler does okay with it most of the time. Sometimes he misses Nikki and cries at night. But Nikki's not dealing well at all. She hates the new boyfriend. I told Brenda it was a mistake to move in with the guy, but she wouldn't listen. Everything's still all about what she wants."

He was quiet for a minute or two before he continued. "Brenda even had the gall when I first caught her cheating to tell me I needed to hire someone to take over my responsibilities at the ranch, move into town full-time, and get a job. My whole life has been the ranch, marketing, and cows, and she wants me to give it up for a cheating wife who can't be trusted. I love my kids, but it's too much to ask of a man."

Something about his last statement struck a wrong chord in my gut, but I could see the hurt in his eyes and chalked it up to anger oozing from an open wound. This man was still in pain and hadn't fully resolved the issues with his ex-wife. I could hear in his voice how desperate he'd been to hold his family together and how much it hurt him to see the kids separated. Beyond the desperation and pain, I could also hear the anger over a cheating wife.

Dangerous territory. I better move carefully with this guy or that pit of burning snakes will look like a walk in the park.

"Well, enough of my depressing situation. What about you? You still see Dustin's dad?"

"Yeah, I do. We had a lousy marriage. He cheated on me and he's living with his girlfriend now, too. She's pregnant, but they're not sure if they're gonna get married or not. We've had a couple of years to work on the divorce, though, and it's actually pretty successful—if you can call any divorce a success. He takes Dustin every other weekend and for about a month in the summer. We make the critical decisions together and I bite my tongue when he tells me how he thinks I should run my life. Fortunately, he's not a bad guy, so it gets easier with time."

"Does Dustin miss having his dad in the house?"

I shook my head. "No, not really. He was only eighteen months old when we divorced, too young to really understand. He doesn't remember having his dad in the house, so he doesn't seem to miss it. At least, I hope he doesn't." Dustin was the best thing going in my life and if I only ever did one thing right, I wanted to be a good mother. Of course, the good mother medal was a hard one to come by, and there was no instruction manual.

Jake nodded and reached to brush a stray lock of hair back from my face. We sat for a few minutes, quietly gazing into each other's eyes. Neither of us seemed willing to break the spell. Finally, he broke it. "Well, this was fun. I had a great time." With a wink, he added, "If you'll invite me back again soon, I promise not to drop any hamburgers next time."

Soon? How about…like now! I almost laughed out loud when I heard granny's voice in my head say, "this man makes me happier than a tick on a fat dog."

Covering my mouth, I coughed to stave off laughter and said, "Yeah, I had a good time, too. And I think I can speak for everyone, including the dog, when I say you and Tyler can come back any time. Thanks for bringing dinner and being so great with the boys."

Jake pulled me close and nuzzled my ear. "You're an incredible woman and if I'd come alone, you'd have a tough time getting rid of me tonight."

Holy freaking cow! My nether-parts were absolutely twitching with joy. *Calm down, girls, the man said 'if'.*

As I looked up at him, pulling back hard on my mental reins, he took a deep breath and smiled gently as he added, "But I didn't come alone and I'd best go while I still can."

I smiled and nodded.

Yep, because if you wait any longer than a minute and a half, I'm liable to throw and hog tie you on the living room floor.

For the space of a few seconds, my brain was high centered on the hog tying concept and I totally spaced out that Jake was speaking to me. When he snapped his fingers in front of my face, I lurched awkwardly back to the present. "Huh? Did you say something?"

His eyebrows rose halfway to his hairline as he nodded. "Yes. I asked if you would like me to carry Dustin to bed for you."

"Oh, yeah. That would be great. Thanks. He's getting so heavy these days that I'd probably be tempted to just put a pillow under his head and leave him here for the night."

Jake scooped Dustin up and followed me down the hall where we put him to bed and tucked him in. Then we returned to the living room where Jake gathered up Tyler and headed for the door. As I let them out, he leaned over and touched his soft lips to mine, gently tasting my tongue with his as he gave me a quick kiss . "Are you working tomorrow night?"

I shook my head. "No. I'm filling in for the day bartender a couple of hours in the afternoon while she takes her kid to the doctor."

"Then I'll call you tomorrow night. What time do you get home?"

My heart soared at knowing I'd see him again. "About six thirty."

He winked and walked down the sidewalk with Tyler in his arms. I watched him put Tyler in the truck and waved as they backed out of the driveway, surprised to find a sense of loss washing through me. I hadn't felt that way since Mark walked out on me and it scared me a bit to realize how fast I was falling for this man. An old quote from Gilda Radner buzzed in my brain as goose bumps skittered up my arms. "Dreams are like paper, they tear so easily."

Chapter Six

It was Monday and the day was almost over. I'd had such a wonderful time the evening before that I couldn't wait to get home and talk to Jake when he called. He'd been on my mind all day and it had been impossible to concentrate on anything else.

I picked Dustin up from his friend's house, where he'd stayed while I worked, and we headed home. He was in a chatty mood, totally impressed with both Jake and Tyler, so we talked about the previous evening the entire way to the house. Dustin made me promise to let him talk to Tyler when Jake called. I couldn't blame the kid, I was excited too.

Duh! About as excited as a kitten alone in a house with three balls of yarn.

We got home and I fixed dinner while Dustin went out in the backyard to play. By eight o'clock, we'd finished dinner and Dustin was ready for bed. He begged to stay up and talk to Jake and Tyler when they called, but I explained Tyler was probably already in bed and promised if Jake called, I'd ask him to call earlier next time.

Dustin reluctantly agreed to go to bed, but it took him almost an hour to fall asleep. By ten, I was showered and ready for bed, and pretty sure Jake wasn't going to call.

It figures! Why do men do that?

We'd had such a wonderful evening and we'd shared some pretty special moments. How could he be so callous? If he didn't want to see me again, why didn't he just say so, or say nothing at all? It was disappointing and painful to wait for the call that never came, and now my kid was disappointed too.

Well, he wouldn't get away with it. I'd see him again and when I did, he'd get an earful, that's for sure.

I've had enough lies and rejection to last me three lifetimes. I don't need him adding to the pile. And no one messes with my kid and gets away with it, not with all his body parts in tact!

The heavy blanket of rejection that settled over me puddled like lead in my shoes as I dragged myself off to bed. I tossed and turned for over an hour as I grew angrier and angrier. Finally, about eleven thirty, I drifted off to sleep.

About midnight, I awoke to a tremendous clamor as someone pounded on the front door. Obleo was raising such a ruckus in the backyard, I was sure he'd wake the entire neighborhood.

Who the hell can that be at this time of night?

My heart pounded in my chest as I jumped up, threw on my robe, and started for the door. I stopped midway to check on Dustin and he was safe and sound, sleeping like a baby.

Amazing. Wish I could do that.

I ran to the front door and peeked out the window. It was Jake. Now I was good 'n mad! I threw the door open and snapped, "Come in and sit down while I go shut the dog up." Then I spun toward the back door to calm the dog and assure him we were not being butchered in our sleep. When he finally calmed down, I returned to the living room.

As I entered the room, I stopped and stood in the doorway with my hands on my hips. Jake sat on the couch looking very sheepish as I said, "Well?"

He shook his head and shrugged. "I'm sorry. I know it's late, but I promised to call and…well, I was afraid if I called this late, you wouldn't answer the phone. And if you did, you'd hang up on me. It didn't dawn on me I'd practically have to knock your door down to get you to answer it.

"I was asleep," I replied. "You should try it sometime. It's the mainstream thing to do. You realize you probably woke up half the neighborhood, don't you?" Anger surged through me like a freight train—anger at the chaos he'd created and anger at the rejection I'd felt by not getting the promised call.

He got up and walked toward me. "I'm sorry. I know it's late, but I didn't want you to think I was a heel because I didn't call." He reached for me, but I stepped back quickly and he dropped his hands to his side. "Katie, please. Don't be mad. It's been a very difficult day and all I wanted was to talk to you, or just be with you. I couldn't get you out of my head all day."

"Oh, you thought about me so much you forgot to call? Yeah, that happens to me all the time. What kind of fool do you think I am?" I looked him over and stabbed my fists on my hips. "Well, you're not dead or bleeding, so it had better be divine intervention that kept you from calling."

Men always think they can plunge a dagger into your heart and then say they're sorry and you're supposed to just drop it and be all sweetness and love. Hell no!

Jake ducked his head, looked at the front door, and deflated like an old balloon. "If you want me to leave, I will, but not before you promise I can call tomorrow." He rubbed his forehead and sighed, "I promise I <u>will</u> call."

"And you think I'm gonna believe that? You son-of-a-bitch! I waited all evening for you to call. Why? Because I trusted you and I said I'd be here and my word means something to me. Dustin waited on the edge of his seat all night. He trusted you too. I was raised to believe a man is only as good as his word. What does that say about you?"

Jake took a deep, slow breath as his gaze held mine. I could see him pull his shoulders back as he seemed to screw up some courage. "Katie, I'm sorry. I'm really sorry. Look, I like you. I really like you a lot. Please let me call again. I promise I will call this time. It won't happen again. I am so sorry. When I dropped Tyler off at Brenda's, she started an argument and I couldn't leave or call until it was worked out."

I crossed my arms in front of me and stared as my heart leapt and I struggled to sort out my feeling. I was pissed he hadn't called and pissed he'd hurt Dustin's feelings too, but there was also a little niggle of relief in there too and I almost hated myself for that. I knew all too well that sometimes things came up that you had to deal with right away. But what I didn't know was if it was a pattern with Jake.

He seems truly sorry, but I've been to that rodeo before. Just because he says he really likes me and has a decent excuse, it doesn't mean it's the truth or that he won't turn out to be a Grade-A jackass.

His eyes, so filled with pain and remorse, softened my heart a little bit more. "Okay, but you'd better not let us down again. You won't get away with it twice."

He swallowed and shook his head. "I'm so sorry. I just didn't think. I promise it won't happen again." He reached out and took me in his arms. "Let me make it up to you. Why don't you and Dustin come up to the ranch with me for a week? It'll be like a vacation. We can ride horses and swim in the creek. The boys will have a great time. It'll be fun."

I didn't relax into his arms right away. I was still leery of what he might not be telling me…something in my gut resisted and I didn't know why. "I don't know. It's one thing if I get hurt, but I'm not sure it's a good idea to bring Dustin into this relationship before we know where it's going. I don't want him hurt again."

Jake lifted my chin as he gave me a soft peck on the lips. "I understand how you feel, but if we cut him out now, he will be hurt. We'll all be hurt. Our children are part of who we are. How can we develop a full relationship if we don't include them?"

He does have a good point and he keeps saying all the right things but so far, his follow-thru sucks. Is he for real?

"Okay, we'll come, but you let us down again and we're done."

"Fair enough," he said as he stroked the side of my face. "Sorry I woke you up. It just took a long time to get Brenda calmed down and get things smoothed over. And by the time we'd worked through it enough that I could leave, it was late. I came straight here to apologize. I really am sorry."

Smoothed over, not resolved. Wonder if this is an on-going feud or if it has anything to do with the fact that they were over here yesterday. I wouldn't be the first woman to run into a jealous ex.

I nodded. “Those things happen. We can talk about it tomorrow night.”

“Okay. I’ll call early enough for Dustin and Tyler to talk before bedtime.” He turned and led me to the door. “Lock up after me,” he said as he stepped out and motioned for me to lock the door. I locked the door and went to the window to watch him walk to the truck and drive away.

As I headed for bed, I wondered again how long this guy had been divorced. If he was still fighting with his ex-wife, it probably hadn’t been too long. Did he have too much baggage to start a new relationship? Once again, I cautioned myself not to move too fast. My father’s words rang in my mind—“Make sure the water’s deep enough before you dive in”.

Last time I took a plunge into the deep end, it turned out to be a bucket of concrete. Maybe I should throw a few rocks first.

Chapter Seven

The huge dark brown horse snorted and pawed the ground as the saddle was thrown on its back. I eyed the pawing beast.

Is it too late to back out?

I'd ridden horses a lot as a kid and was beginning to wish I hadn't made such a point of it when the ranch hand had asked if I needed a "beginner" horse. This one didn't look like it wanted to be ridden, and I suddenly wanted to ride this horse about as much as a chicken wants to swim. Considering how self-conscious and uncoordinated I seemed to be around Jake, maybe this wasn't such a hot idea.

'Maybe I should stay here and keep an eye on the boys. I wouldn't want them to get into any trouble." I took my best shot.

Jake kept a straight face as he said, "Don't worry about the boys. We gave them a chance to go and they both said they'd rather hang here with the ranch hands. They'll be fine. The boys'll keep an eye on them."

I snuck a quick peek at Jake standing next to his horse. He watched me from the corner of his eye with about a half a grin on his face.

His look rubbed the wrong way up against something inside me and I was suddenly Jackie Chan taking on a biker gang. I stood up straight and said, "Well, he looks like he'll do nicely."

Jake still had a half-grin on his face. "Are you sure you want this horse? He seems a bit high-strung today."

"That's the way I like 'em. Besides, he doesn't look so high-strung to me, just energetic." The lie slid off my tongue just like I knew what I was doing. Then, in a moment of clarity and inspiration, I added, "Unless you'd rather I rode something slower, maybe easier to keep up with?"

Jake grinned and shrugged. "No, it's up to you. If you're happy with this horse, I'm good."

I scowled. What now? Riding this horse ranked right up there with getting a root canal.

The ranch hand who had been holding the reins took Jake's horse too as Jake stepped over to help me up on the huge, pawing creature.

Pussycat? Who's he kidding?

The horse turned his head toward me and I'd swear his eyes glowed red and fire shot out his nostrils.

"I think I'll take a minute to introduce myself," I said as I screwed up my courage and walked over to the horse's head. Reaching out to touch the huge head, I used my smoothest voice. "Hi there, big fella. How ya doin'? Oh, you and I are gonna be great friends. Wanna go for a ride?"

Wanna set my hair on fire and crush me like a bug?

From the corner of my eye, I caught a look and a snicker pass between Roy and Jake. Okay, it was now or never. Another minute and I'd become a quivering pile of goo on the ground. I stepped over to where Roy waited and put my left foot in the stirrup. As I tried to lift myself into the saddle, the horse sidestepped and I felt myself start to slip. Just then, I felt Jake's hand on my butt as he pushed me up onto the horse.

Startled, I almost overshot and fell off the other side. After regaining my balance, I settled my butt in the saddle and turned to scowl at Jake. "Was that really necessary?"

He smiled. "Well, we had to get you up there before the horse stepped out from under ya. Just seemed like the quickest way to get it done."

I frowned as Jake looked the other way, but I could see his shoulders shake as I asked, "What's so funny?"

He covered his mouth with his hand and coughed. "Nothing. I've got a bit of an itch in my throat, is all." He cleared his throat a couple of times, just for effect, and shot me a toothy white smile. "You ready to go?"

I raised one brow at him. "Yeah, sure." I looked down at Roy. "I guess you can let go now."

"You sure you're ready?" Roy grinned as Jake mounted his own horse.

I gulped to swallow past the lump in my throat. "Yeah." I sounded almost casual, even though a painful and humiliating death was only seconds away.

When old Roy turned loose of the horse, it lunged forward like it had been let out of a starting gate. I grabbed the saddle horn as I was thrown about a foot up in the air. Well, it felt like a foot. Maybe it was only two or three inches, but air's hard to measure. Proud I'd managed to stay in the saddle, I held tight to the saddle horn and prayed.

As we rode away, Roy hollered at Jake to "be on the lookout for those damned mountain lions that been poachin' calves from all the ranches hereabouts."

Mountain lions? What the hell did I get myself into?

I didn't know whether to hope for the painful and humiliating death or the one where I became a crunchy snack.

After going a few hundred feet, Cody settled into a quick walk that wasn't too bad. After about five minutes, my hands began to ache from wringing the saddle horn like the cowardly lion with his tail. *Stupid girl.* Roy had been right. Cody really was a pussycat once you were on him and moving. He didn't yet respond eagerly to all my requests, but he had a fairly smooth gait, which I knew from experience, would make it a much more pleasant day.

Jake stayed close by my side, which was good since he was clearly an experienced rider. When I looked at him and smiled, he visibly relaxed. I liked that he was concerned for me.

About a half hour out, I realized I'd been so nervous about going riding that I'd left without my cell phone. "Darn it. I left my phone back at the ranch." When Jake just looked at me but didn't say anything, I continued. "We have to go back. I need my cell phone in case something happens to Dustin."

"Don't worry about it," Jake advised. "I have mine. If anything happens to one of the boys, they'd call me anyway. They don't have your number."

"Okay, I guess you're right." Well, of course he was right. But as a single mother, I almost never went anywhere without my phone.

I feel naked without it.

We continued our ride for the better part of another hour at a nice, easy pace and it all came back.

I found my "seat" again and actually began to gain some control over Cody, who was warming up to me and responding to my instructions.

Several times, I caught Jake watching me with an emotion in his eyes I couldn't interpret, so I stole glances at him whenever he wasn't looking. He was so handsome and seemed so full of strength and "in control"—the kind of man who made a woman feel safe, like nothing bad could happen to you as long as you were with him.

After we'd ridden for a couple of hours, Jake turned in his saddle. "I had Roy load up our saddlebags with some lunch. Would you like to find a spot to take a break? I've got a blanket tied to my saddle. We could roll it out and have ourselves a picnic."

"Are you sure we should stay gone so long?" I asked. "The boys might miss us."

"Don't worry about them. Mom said she'd make her special mouse-face pancakes for lunch, Roy's all set to teach them how to train a horse or braid a halter, and if they get bored, there's a whole library full of books, board games, and movies to entertain them. They'll be too busy to miss us. Besides, it's only lunch." He grinned and winked at me.

My stomach did a little loop-de-loop. Food sounded good and my backside was ready for a break too, so I agreed. Jake said he knew where there was a small spring-fed creek about a mile away, across the meadow and back in the trees. So off we headed in the direction of the creek.

We hadn't gone far when we heard hoof beats coming up behind us. Reining the horses in, we turned to find David riding at a pretty good clip. As he pulled to a stop, a frown passed quickly over Jake's face. "What are you doing here?"

David smiled and rocked back in his saddle as he pushed up the front of his hat with his forefinger. "Heard you and Katie were out for a ride and thought I'd join ya, is all. You don't look real happy to see me, big brother."

The statement hung in the air as David turned and flashed me a dazzling smile. "Hello, Katie. Good to see you again."

I flinched slightly as goose bumps skittered up my spine. "Hello, David. Good to see you too."

Must be something about that family smile. Stupid girl.

"Met your son, Dustin, back at the ranch. Handsome young man…polite, too." David held out his fist, knuckles down. "He said to give you this."

I held my hand out, palm up, and he dropped a red rock into my hand.

When I looked up, he was still smiling. "He said he found it out behind the barn this morning and Roy told him red rocks were always good luck. He wanted you to have it so you didn't fall off the horse and get hurt."

I laughed as I looked from David back to the red rock in the palm of my hand.

"He said to bring it back, though, because he'll need it later."

"Oh, of course." Feeling playful, I looked from David to Jake as I asked, "But what are you two going to do for luck? Shouldn't you have red rocks too?"

Jake didn't seem amused, but David dug in his pocket and pulled out another rock. "Well, he only had two of these special red rocks, but he did send the other one along. He suggested Jake and I share it." Grinning, he tossed the second rock to Jake. "Here, big brother. I'm feeling lucky today."

Jake caught the rock, but sent David a scathing look. "Katie and I were about to find a quiet spot for a picnic lunch."

David acted like he hadn't heard the warning note in Jake's voice making it clear he wasn't invited. "Hey, a picnic sounds like a great idea. Count me in!"

I almost laughed as David tried his best to look innocent while Jake shot him a murderously dark look.

For some reason, David seemed bent on tagging along and it didn't look like he'd be easily dissuaded. I was okay with it, as long as things didn't turn ugly. David was fun and it would keep things with Jake from getting too intimate. There was still something niggling at the back of my brain that all was not as it appeared, so slow was good.

"Okay, boys, let's go." Hoping to head off an ugly confrontation, I turned Cody back in the direction we'd been headed and touched my heels to his ribs. Anxious to be on the move again, he stepped forward quickly, leaving the two men no choice but to put away the testosterone and follow.

About half way across the meadow, I thought I heard music. When I looked around to see where it came from, Jake cursed as he reined in his horse and flipped open one of his saddle bags to retrieve his cell phone.

"Hello," he growled as he held it to his ear.

David came alongside and put himself between Jake's horse and mine, so I had no choice but to look at him.

He smiled and shrugged. "Duty calls. I'm glad marketing is Jake's responsibility. I couldn't handle all the calls. It'd drive me crazy to have to carry a damn phone everywhere I went."

I glanced at Jake.

He does seem a bit tethered to it. He probably brought it for security, just in case something happens out here. I can't fault him for that.

Jake scowled as he talked. "Dammit, Mike, I'm trying to take some time off here. Can't you handle it?"

Uh-oh, looks like lunch might be a drive-thru...or maybe a ride-thru in this case. Probably not many golden arches in this neighborhood.

Jake listened for a minute before he cursed again and slapped his fingers against the screen to shut the phone down.

"I have to go." He shot me a look of apology. "I'm sorry. We've got twenty head of prize stock on their way down from up north. But there's an issue with the health papers and they're stuck in Wyoming. I've got to make some calls to see if I can get 'em cut loose."

Before I could say anything, David piped up. "Well, I'll tell ya what, why don't Katie and I finish our ride while you take care of business. No need to make her go back and sit at the house while you're on the phone. We'll have some lunch and then come on back and maybe you'll be freed up by the time we get there."

Jake shot him another dark look and I could almost see the sparks fly as their eyes held for a moment.

"No, it's probably better if I go back with Jake," I offered, disappointed the ride would be cut short, but not at all anxious to have these two explode here in the middle of nowhere.

My momma didn't raise no fool. Besides, I probably didn't need to give David any encouragement.

Jake looked at me and took a deep breath as he visibly willed himself to remain calm. "No, Katie, David's right. It'll probably take most of the afternoon to get this straightened out. You go ahead and finish your ride."

He glanced at David and continued, "He can show you the creek and you can eat lunch." A growl crept back into his voice and he added for David's benefit, "He'll get you back to the ranch before dark and I should have this mess straightened out by then."

Jake's expression softened as his gaze returned to me. "Then you and I'll go into town for dinner tonight. We'll do it up special, get dressed up and maybe go dancing, if you'd like."

I was like a treed cat. Was it safer to climb down or stay in the tree? "Uh…I…uh…maybe I should go back with you, Jake. The boys are probably wondering where we are by now anyway."

He shook his head, "No, I won't hear of it. The boys are having a ball. I'm sure of it. You finish your ride."

He touched his heels to his horse and moved to position himself on my other side, where he leaned forward and cupped his hand around the back of my neck and gently pulled me forward to kiss me on the lips as he whispered. "You go. Have a good time. I'll see you when you get back to the ranch."

Then he turned his horse and rode over to David. "Here," he said as he turned in the saddle, unclipped the saddle bags and picnic blanket, and handed them to David. "Take these. There's a blanket and food and whatever else you'll need. You be sure she gets back to the ranch okay, and don't forget she's my girl. Keep your hands off!"

I was torn over Jake's statement. Part of me was surprised and annoyed at the vehemence in Jake's voice and the tone that almost implied ownership, while another part of me was relieved he cared. And yet a third part of me was pissed about the underlying thread of mistrust, as if I would allow his brother to put his hands on me.

David never responded. He took the saddle bags and just sat stock still as he watched his brother ride away. After a minute or two, he dismounted and fastened the bags to his saddle. When he finally remounted and turned his horse to face me, there was a smile on his face. "You ready?"

"David, I'm not sure this is a good idea. Maybe I should go back."

Not sure it's a good idea? Really? This is probably the worst idea ever in the history of bad ideas! Boarding the Titanic was a better idea than this.

He smiled. "Darlin', this is the best idea my brother has had in a month of Sundays. Come on, Buck", he said to his horse, "let's go."

When I hesitated, he looked back over his shoulder. "I promise to behave." With a wink, he turned his horse toward the tree line.

I stared after him for a moment. David had always been the perfect gentleman. I was more concerned about Jake. When it came to David, my granny would've said Jake could get "hotter than a goat's butt in a pepper patch." He'd zoom straight to mad. Was there a history here?

David liked to yank Jake's chain by flirting, but I didn't think he'd follow through, especially now that I was officially "dating" Jake. He was just teasing. But there was an undercurrent I couldn't decipher—almost a protectiveness, big brother making sure little sis didn't get hurt. Did he feel the need to protect me? Why? Was there a valid reason for Jake's anger? Maybe some time alone with David would give me some insight into the dynamics between these two brothers. Or maybe it would just leave me stranded on an iceberg. I gave Cody his head and urged him to follow David and Buck.

Chapter Eight

The meadow was wider than it looked and it took us almost an hour to get across it. I relaxed as David told me the names and legends attached to the various mountains and landmarks that surrounded us. He was more talkative than Jake and I enjoyed the ride more and more as we made our way across the meadow.

Once again, I couldn't help but wonder why this younger brother seemed so bent on protecting me. He didn't seem the type to steal his brother's girlfriend and there were times when Jake seemed to be as puzzled as I about David's behavior. Yet, Jake still trusted him enough to send me off into the wilderness with him, so he couldn't really see him as a true threat.

"David, can I ask you something?" He might not answer me, but I had to ask.

"Sure."

"Why do you get such a kick out of teasing Jake by flirting with me?"

His shoulders tensed as he sat straighter in the saddle and turned to look at me. He reined his horse to a stop as Cody stepped close and stopped next to Buck.

He didn't answer right away, but seemed to debate something in his mind as he stared into my eyes. "Katie, I'd love to see both you and my brother happy, but I know my brother. Right now, he truly believes you might be the one to make him happy, but you're not."

Stunned at his blunt answer, anger flared as my stomach churned.

What the hell gives him the right?!

David held up his hand. "Now, before you get pissed off, let me make something clear. Yes, I'm attracted to you. I'm seriously attracted to you and I'd love to take you in my arms right now. But it has nothing to do with why I think you're all wrong for Jake, and it isn't a case of wanting what big brother has. You don't belong together and he isn't thinking straight right now. I don't want to see either of you hurt."

Before he could finish, I exploded. "Who the hell do you think you are to play God with our lives? Whether we're right or wrong for each other isn't your choice to make. We're adults and that's for us to decide." Taking a breath, I collected my thoughts. "I think that's exactly what this is...big brother's got a new toy and you're jealous. This isn't about your feelings for me or protecting your brother from me. This is about winning, isn't it?"

Without a thought for where I was going, I kicked Cody hard in the sides and he shot forward, almost unseating me as he bolted across the meadow. I heard David shout my name and then I heard another set of hooves pound behind me.

Just before we reached the trees, Buck screamed from behind me and I turned my head in time to see Buck hit the ground as David pitched forward over the top of his head and hit the ground hard.

I reined Cody to a stop and turned back to see if David and Buck were okay. My stomach pulled into a hard knot. David was on the ground, not moving. Buck tried to stand, but stepped on his reins before he could get his footing, jerking his head hard to one side and causing him to fall again. This time, he didn't try to get up right away. He laid there, sides heaving.

I pulled Cody to a stop and jumped off, pulling him after as I ran to David. Buck finally got to his feet and as he bolted by me, I snagged the reins to keep him from running off. David was lying on the ground dead still. Something about the angle of his left leg wasn't right.

The horses tried to pull away from me. I had to calm them before I could tend to David or we'd be on foot in the middle of nowhere. After walking them in a circle and talking softly, they finally calmed enough that I could safely tie them to the nearest tree.

When I got to David, I could see right away how severely the leg was broken. He was out like a light, so I checked for vitals and any sign of blood. His pulse was strong. David was alive, but I didn't know how badly he was injured or why he was unconscious. I called his name and lightly patted his cheeks to see if I could get any kind of response. Nothing!

Damn, it always works in the movies.

Scared, I searched desperately for some sign of a building or a house, anything to indicate help was close. Again, nothing! "Oh, God, don't let him be hurt bad!"

I looked around again and tried to assess the situation. I needed to either get him to help or bring help to him.

Dammit, I left my cell phone at the ranch.

I eyed the saddle bags Jake had moved from his horse to David's. Probably no chance there was an extra phone in those and Jake had taken his with him. My only hope was that David might have one on him, so I began to check his pockets.

Nothing. No cell phone. No way to call for help.

There had to be something I could do.

Think!

Could I get him up on his horse by myself? Was it safe? Would it do more damage and injure him further? Tears began to well up and I gritted my teeth as I moved toward the horses to see if there was a rope tied anywhere on one of those saddles or anywhere in one of those bags.

There was no rope to tie him onto the horse, even if I could get him up there. I did find a gun in one of the saddlebags, but no rope.

Typical man—got a gun, but no rope! And no cell phone.

I turned to look at David again. He was a big man, well over six foot and maybe a hundred ninety pounds. I was no delicate little flower, but I couldn't get all that dead weight up on a horse by myself, let alone keep him there for the ride home. No, I would have to bring the help to him.

As I racked my brain, panic set in and the tears began to fall. David was the better rider and he was the strong one. I was the one who couldn't ride as well and if I had been injured, he could easily have gotten me up on the horse and back to the barn. It wasn't supposed to happen this way!

My heart ached at the sight of David lying there in an impossible position, every bit of color drained from his face.

I took a deep breath, wiped my eyes and said out loud, "Okay, you've got to get a grip. You're the only conscious person here. David needs help. You can't stand around crying like a girl. Do something!" The self-talk steadied my nerves.

I grabbed the blanket tied to David's saddle and went back to check him out. The leg was broken, but I wanted to make sure there weren't any hidden injuries that might be worse. After a bit of gentle rolling and groping, which might have been embarrassing if he'd been awake, I determined there were no cuts or external signs of any further injuries. I was surprised I couldn't find any sign of a head wound—no goose eggs, nothing to indicate he'd been knocked unconscious. I wondered if the pain in the leg could be severe enough to cause him to pass out. Not being a doctor or a nurse, I didn't know for sure.

Carefully, I rolled him onto the blanket, wrapped it over him, and straightened his leg the best I could. He moaned as I handled his leg and sweat beaded up on his forehead. That couldn't be good.

I stood and looked toward the west. Plenty of daylight left. I had time on the clock, but I wasn't sure how much time David had. I needed a plan, and I needed it fast.

David still hadn't moved and it worried me. I would think he should have come around by now if he'd just passed out. Maybe it was a blessing—for him, at least. But I worried it might mean he was badly injured, maybe internal injuries or a head injury I couldn't find.

"Think…think," I said to myself as I rubbed my forehead and took a steadying breath. "I can't get him up on the horse. Can I leave him alone and ride for help?" Chewing on my lip, I answered my own question, "Not with mountain lions around. Alone and unconscious, he'd be nothing more than bait."

Oh man, how can this be happening? Am I over-reacting? This is something straight out of a scary movie. Where the hell is Batman when you need him? Probably out promoting his next movie or marketing a new line of Batman underwear.

Was David injured badly enough to go into shock? It would get cold when the sun went down. I had to find a way to keep him warm. We'd need a fire if help didn't come soon. I prayed there were matches somewhere in those saddlebags. Maybe I'd get lucky and there would be a can of gasoline too. My dad had always called it Boy Scout juice whenever we went camping. It made fire starting a whole lot easier. I eyed the saddlebags. Fat chance. I'd have to settle for matches.

We were a long ways from the barn. No one would see a fire from there, but it might help them find us if they came looking. If we weren't back at the barn by dark, they'd come looking. Jake would know the general route we took. But the dark would make it harder to find us, even if we weren't that far off the expected route.

I'd either have to get a message to them or I'd have to find a way to signal them. Would they hear a gunshot? Probably wasn't a good idea unless I knew someone was in the area. The gun was in the saddlebags for a reason. Maybe there was something to fear out here. What if those mountain lions showed up? I briefly wondered if Roy had been serious or if it was some private joke between the two men. Better save the bullets just in case.

My mind raced as I glanced over at the horses. "Think…think. If they don't find us by morning, I might be able to leave him and ride for help. But I can't leave him injured and unconscious, alone in the dark. Besides, I probably couldn't find my way back to the ranch in the dark."

I froze as a thought formed in my panic-stricken brain. "I've got two horses, but I can only ride one. Even if I could find a way to get David up on his horse, I have no way to keep him there."

Thinking back to when I was a kid, I remembered an untethered horse always goes back to the barn. "If I turned one loose, he'd head straight to the barn and they'd know we were in trouble." My heart pounded as my brain spun faster. Just as I saw a ray of hope, a blood-curdling scream somewhere off to the west sent goose-bumps straight up my spine and made my breath come in quick bursts.

The blood pounded in my ears and my head felt like it might explode. Roy said mountain lions were poaching calves. My throat slammed shut.

Do they eat people too? Probably.

I'd heard mountain lions scream before on those nature shows on television, and that scream sure sounded like one.

I have to move fast. Think!

The ranch was to the east and that was the direction the horse would head. He would probably be safe from the mountain lion, but would we? I stiffened my spine and resolved to find a way to keep us safe until help arrived.

God, I wish David was conscious. How dare he leave me to figure everything out alone. He'll pay for this!

The tears began to flow again and I stopped for a minute as I sent up a prayer asking God to protect us and to help me think straight. With a deep breath, I got a grip on my emotions.

What to do first?

I ticked off tasks on my fingers as I talked to myself. "First, I need to send Buck off to the ranch. Then I need to gather wood and start a fire."

Okay, the first thing was to send for help. I sprinted toward Buck. He tossed his head and snorted as I ran up to him, but didn't try to bolt. I untied his reins from the tree and tied them to the saddle so he wouldn't step on them again or get his legs tangled up.

If I sent Buck home alone, they'd know we were in trouble, but not where to look. I searched the saddlebags for something to write with. Nothing. I found a book of matches and crammed them into my shirt pocket, but no pencil or pen, no paper, and no gas can.

Think...think!

My mind screamed like a banshee.

Go back through the bags again. Something has to work.

As I got to the food bag, I found mustard packets. "That might work. I can write on a napkin or paper towel, if there are any." I prayed Roy had thought to pack napkins as I tore back into the saddle bags. It appeared all those episodes of MacGyver would actually pay off. Finding a wad of paper towels and a plastic knife, I broke open the mustard packet and squeezed some out onto the seat of the saddle. Dipping the end of the plastic knife into it, I wrote a message in mustard. It took a few minutes, but I was able to say David was hurt and to describe where I thought we were.

As I fanned the note in the air to dry the mustard, I tried to decide where to leave it. Would they think to look for a note? How long would it be before the note was found in the saddlebags? How could I tell them to look in the saddlebags?

As I looked over all the equipment, the mustard on the saddle gave me an idea. I groped around in the food bag again and came up with another packet of mustard. I broke it open and squeezed some mustard out on my finger. Using my finger, I drew an arrow on the saddle, pointing to the saddlebag with the note in it. Then I went around to the other side of the horse and drew another arrow on that side of the saddle, pointing over the top of the horse to the other side, toward the saddlebag.

Will it work? What happens when the mustard dries?

It would change colors and they might not see it as easily. It couldn't be helped. I had to try. My ex always said professionals were very particular about the care of their tools and cowboys were the same about their saddles. Maybe they would spot the smear of mustard right away.

Hope sprung in my heart as I turned Buck toward home. I put my arms around his neck and whispered a prayer for his safe return. Before I turned him loose, I took everything off of the saddle except the one saddlebag with the note and I checked the tie to make sure it wouldn't come loose. Then I gave him a hug, told him to go safe and fast. I stood back as he looked at me, wondering what I was up to. I stepped behind him and hollered as I smacked him on the butt. He bolted for home like the devil himself was on his heels.

Go, Buck!

Chapter Nine

David was so pale it broke my heart and the tears started to well up again. I kneeled next to him and tucked the blanket in to keep him warm while I went in search of firewood. A tear fell on the front of my shirt as I took a deep breath and reminded myself this still wasn't the time to cry. Our lives depended on me keeping a clear head.

I made my way through the trees, gathering wood. When I had enough for a decent fire, I piled it close to where David was wrapped in the blanket. It took a couple of tries to get the kindling to catch. As soon as I had a small fire going, I returned to gathering wood and made another dozen trips back to the fire to drop it off and check on David. No change. Was that good or bad?

Twice more, the same chilling scream came from the west and sent goose bumps skittering up my arms. It seemed to be getting closer. If there was something dangerous out there, it might be a good idea to have more than one fire to discourage anything from coming too close. It would also keep us warmer and might make it easier for a rescue party to find us.

So I collected wood until there were several large piles at intervals around the central fire. It was getting too dark to see, so it would have to be enough. I moved Cody to a tree inside the perimeter and piled everything I'd taken off of Buck next to

David. Cody snorted and stomped a bit when I moved him close to the fire, but I stroked him and talked softly until he got used to the idea.

I built an outer ring of four perimeter fires close enough together to discourage a wary cat from walking between them, but far enough away to keep Cody from freaking out. Four fires would help me see anything trying to sneak up on us.

As I lit the perimeter fires, Cody snorted and rolled his eyes but settled down once I was back at his side. If he got spooked, I didn't want him to run off with all our stuff on his back, so I removed the saddlebags and added them to our growing pile. Then I unsaddled Cody, dragged a good size log close to David, and set the saddle on top so I could lean back against it. I placed the thicker saddle pad on the ground in front of the saddle and sat on it, with the lighter saddle blanket over my legs. Then I dug the gun out of the saddlebag and sat back to wait.

How long before we were rescued? By the time Buck got to the ranch, it could take half the night to organize a search party. The terrain was fairly level, so they could probably get to us by four-wheel drive. I dearly hoped it wouldn't be something out of an old Western movie, where they came in by buckboard—that would take forever!

Somewhere out to my left, the cat screamed again. Definitely the same scream I'd heard on the nature show, and definitely closer. When Cody shifted and snorted again, I got up and went to calm him.

As I returned to my spot, I wondered if I could actually shoot the cat if it came into camp. Not that I had any hang-ups about shooting animals out to make a Scooby-snack of me. I simply wondered if I was a good enough shot to actually hit it. The last time I tried to shoot anything, Grampa was teaching me how to shoot. I aimed at a pop can on top of a fence rail. The bullet missed the pop can, ricocheted off a boulder, and blew a hole in the crotch of Gramma's panties hanging on the line to dry. When I said I was sure glad Gramma hadn't been in them, Grampa mumbled something about unused body parts that wouldn't be missed.

Would the bullets in this gun actually stop a mountain lion?

That was most likely the purpose for which it had been packed, but I might have to hit it exactly right. I chuckled as I looked at Cody. "Maybe it'll be wearing panties." Cody rolled his eyes in my direction as his ears swiveled forward and then back again. The memory of Gramma's panties lightened my mood a bit and calmed the panic as I giggled over the image of a mountain lion in Gramma's panties.

My stomach rumbled. I hadn't eaten since breakfast. I looked at David, feeling a bit guilty he wouldn't be able to share in the meal. Oh well, he'd want me to keep up my strength.

So I rummaged through the packs, grabbed a plastic spoon, and proceeded to eat potato salad right out of the container, wishing it was Rocky Road ice cream. About four bites into my meal, David croaked, "Not gonna share?" I jumped and almost bobbled the container of potato salad into the fire before I realized he was awake and his eyes were open.

I thumped the food container on the ground, gulped down what I had in my mouth, and frantically crab-crawled over to hug him. When he saw how fast

I was coming at him, he held up a hand. "Whoa, take it easy."

I stopped and exclaimed, "Oh, my God. I can't believe it. You're awake. You're okay. Oh, my God, you're alive. Oh my God, oh my God!

David gave me a half smile and tried to move—clearly a bad choice. He moaned, his eyes rolled back in his head, and he passed out again.

I stared at him, willing him to open his eyes. Nothing. "I can't believe it! He finally comes around and now he's out again and I have to deal with all this alone. Jerk. Creep!" I took a deep breath and exhaled slowly as the lump returned to my throat. It wasn't his fault. He couldn't help me in his condition anyway, but I would have liked some company. I almost collapsed to the ground under the weight of the depression that suddenly rolled over me like a tidal wave. I returned to my saddle blanket and swallowed against the boulder lodged in my windpipe. It would take more than potato salad to make me feel better.

This calls for chocolate—lots and lots of chocolate. Maybe I should check those saddlebags again.

As I was about to rummage through the saddlebags, Cody pulled back and started to dance at the end of his tether. I grabbed the gun and ran to calm him. The fires were all burning low and I searched the darkness beyond the perimeter fires. Something flashed off to my right, like eyes reflecting light in the dark. The hair stood up on the back of my neck and my heart thundered in my ears like Thor's hammer. I frantically searched the inky blackness beyond the ring of firelight.

With my hand shaking, I held the gun out in front of me and scanned the night as I tossed another log onto the central fire. It only took a minute for the log to catch and the flames jumped higher as the fire crackled with new life. There was a faint scraping sound out beyond the perimeter, like something sharp against a rock.

I stood frozen as I searched the direction the sound had come from. Cody slowly stilled. His sides heaved and his eyes rolled wildly as his ears swiveled to catch any sound. Eventually, he calmed a bit, but he continued to snort and stare into the darkness with me.

Would it be safe to move around and put more wood on the outer fires? It had to be safer than letting them go cold, so I moved toward the closest fire. After quickly putting on several new logs, I backed away, toward the main fire. When the logs caught, the area of visibility pushed out another twenty or thirty feet and there didn't appear to be anything out there. I did the same thing with the next fire and repeated these steps until all the perimeter fires were again burning brightly.

When I returned to my saddle pad, David was awake again, but lying quietly. As he watched me sit, he said, "I'm really sorry about all of this," and closed his eyes. I thought he might have passed out again, but he opened them after a few minutes and asked, "How long have we been here?"

I shrugged, "I don't know. A while. Sun's been down for an hour or two. Do you want something to eat or drink?"

"I'd really like a sip of water if it survived."

"Yeah, plenty of water." I reached behind the saddle and grabbed a canteen, removed the top, and put it to his lips, thinking to trickle a bit over them. He swallowed and croaked, “More.” So I turned the canteen up a bit until he indicated he’d had enough.

I brushed a lock of hair off his forehead. “I’m so glad you’re awake. Please don’t move. I don’t want you to pass out again. It’s so lonely with no one to talk to,” and then the tears began to flow. When I leaned over to lay my head gently against his shoulder, he slowly reached up and pulled me tighter against him. I cried into his shoulder until the tears dried up, while he stroked my hair and told me how sorry he was. When I finally moved away and looked at him again, my heart hurt. He was in so much pain and he’d comforted me. So I screwed up my courage and returned to my saddle pad.

“Would you like me to feed you?” I asked.

“No.” He slowly turned his head to look at Cody. “Where’s Buck?”

I explained what I’d done to leave a note in the saddlebags and send Buck back to the ranch. “Good thinking. How long since you turned him loose?”

“I don’t know. Three, maybe four hours. Maybe more.”

“It’s a little over an hour to the ranch and another hour back. By the time they find the note, organize themselves, and find us, it’s at least three or four hours. If they can find us.”

My spirits plummeted. “They’ve got to be able to find us. I’ve got five fires lit and we’re at the edge of the tree line, so it’s fairly open. They should be able to see the fires from quite a ways away.”

He smiled. “Why five fires?”

I was embarrassed to admit I’d been scared. In the light of his question, it seemed so silly. I shrugged and blushed. "I heard a mountain lion and I thought the fires might keep him away."

He closed his eyes and nodded. "Might." When he opened his eyes and looked at me again, he asked, "Where'd you get all the wood?"

"It was lying all over the place. I had enough time to collect quite a bit before the sun went down."

He kept his gaze on mine as I talked, and some emotion I didn't recognize flickered across his face. Then he closed his eyes again. "You did good. Now we wait." A few minutes passed before he spoke again. "Any sign of the mountain lion?"

"Yeah. I heard it a few more times and it seems to be coming closer. A little while ago, Cody acted like there was something out there, but I couldn't see anything. So I built the fires up a little bit."

"Could you shoot it if you had to?"

"Yeah," I replied. "Not sure I'm a good enough shot to hit it unless it's wearing panties, but I could shoot <u>at</u> it."

He cocked his head in my direction and raised one brow. "Not sure they wear panties out here, but it sounds like a story I wouldn't want to miss. You'll have to tell me about it when we get out of this mess."

For the first time, a laugh bubbled up from inside, but I wasn't sure if it was because of his humor or if it was hysteria setting in.

We sat quietly for a little while and David asked me about the extent of his injuries. I told him the leg was clearly and badly broken and he had a few scrapes, but no cuts and I hadn't found any sign of head injury. The color returned to his face and I was encouraged he was able to remain conscious for a period of time.

Twice more, Cody got what David referred to as “fussed up”, but we never saw anything. I stoked the perimeter fires twice more and was worried we might not have enough wood to keep all of the fires going through the night. David suggested we alternate and stoke two fires at a time and let the other two burn lower, then we reverse it the next time. We also agreed to keep the main fire lower since it hadn’t turned as cold as I’d expected.

Sometime in the very early morning hours, Cody got scared again. He reared up and pulled on his ties so hard, they almost broke. As I ran to Cody, I tried to stuff the gun into my waistband when David yelled, “No, don’t put it away. If there’s something out there, we may need the gun more than the horse.” So as I held onto the gun with one hand and struggled to hold the horse with the other, David added, “But for God’s sake, don’t shoot the horse!”

My heart pounded in my chest and my head hurt like it was in a giant vice. Suddenly, a loud noise came from everywhere at once. Cody panicked and lunged back, knocking me to the ground as the reins snapped. The gun went off and Cody spun away and bolted into the night.

“Nooo!”

I called to David, “Are you hurt? Did I hit you?” I couldn’t hear my own voice over that horrible thwacking noise. I ran to see if David was ok, tripped over a log, and sprawled face-down in the dirt. “What the hell is it? David, what is it?!”

As I scrabbled in circles and tried to stand, the entire area was bathed in bright light. A fierce wind shook the trees and twisted them in all directions.

Thoroughly panicked, I got to my feet and made it to David. I threw myself on the ground next to him, holding the gun in front of me and still screaming, "What is it? What is it?"

David grabbed the gun, gave me a half-grin filled with pain, and pointed up as he shouted, "Helicopter."

Comprehension was slow to come, but when it finally penetrated my terror-fogged brain, I looked up. He was right. They'd found us. But as my heart soared and I jumped to my feet to meet them, they pulled up and left. "No!" I screamed. "You can't leave! Where are you going?" I ran in the direction they headed and waved my arms over my head.

I'd gone about a hundred feet when I stopped and looked back at David and he yelled at me, "Get back here! They saw us. You don't know what else is out there. You have to stay close to the fire!"

Torn between running back to David and running after the Helicopter, I looked around. The original five fires had grown to eight or ten. The wind from the helicopter had whipped the flames and little fires sprung up everywhere.

By the time I got back to David, he'd opened the canteen and poured water all over the saddle pad and blanket. I grabbed the saddle pad and began to beat out the fires.

Within moments, there were other people coming out of the dark with blankets and jackets to help. I could hear Jake somewhere in the dark issuing commands as he organized everyone. We smothered flames for almost an hour. Fortunately, there were enough of us to keep things under control.

Suddenly, everything came to a standstill and there was a pregnant silence as we all looked around for more fires. Everyone breathed a sigh of relief. All of the uncontained fires were out.

A man I didn't know softly said, "I'm sorry. I never thought about the fires spreading. I was so happy to find you two, all I could think about was setting down. Man, that was close!" I was in a trance as he asked, "Are you okay? Are you injured?"

I shook my head and pointed to David. "His leg's badly broken." As he turned toward David, I crumpled to the ground, where I sat with my head in my hands and thanked God for rescuing us—from the night, from the mountain lion, from the fire, from everything. Adrenaline was pounding through my system so hard that I began to shake from head to toe and sobs clawed their way up my throat. As I sat there sobbing, Jake knelt next to me and took me in his arms. I leaned into his shoulder and cried as he stroked my hair and told me everything was okay.

Thank God! Thank God, we are okay.

But it could just as easily have ended horribly. Where was Jake when I needed him? Was his business more important than my safety?

Stop it! That's just crazy. How could he have known there would be an accident? That's not fair.

I was ashamed to find that there was a little tiny corner of my mind that didn't care that it wasn't fair. I'd needed Jake and he hadn't been there.

When the shock of the emergency wore off, I looked up to see what was happening. They'd moved David onto a large board and were carrying him toward the helicopter. Jake stood and pulled me up. As I looked up into his eyes, so full of concern, I forgot all about my anger. I'd never seen a more beautiful face. I smiled and he returned the smile.

"Good. You can smile. Everything's alright. They'll airlift David to the hospital and we'll follow in the truck. You hurt?"

I shook my head as I opened my hands and looked at them. There were burns on both palms. "No, just a few burns on my hands."

He took my hands and looked at the burns. "Doesn't look too bad. I've got ice in the truck. Come on, let's get you checked out at the hospital."

As we walked toward the truck, I noticed about a dozen people in the area. Most of them looked to be cowboys from the ranch. "Did you all come in the helicopter?"

Jake laughed. "Hell No! The helicopter got here right before we did. The rest of us came in those trucks over there," and as he pointed back toward the ranch, I could see the outline of three large pickup trucks parked beyond one of the perimeter fires. I nodded and let him lead me the rest of the way to the truck.

Thank God for technology. Four wheel drives and helicopters certainly beat the hell out of wagons.

Jake helped me into the truck from the driver's side as they loaded David into the helicopter. I looked up at Jake and he gave me a gentle smile. "Thank God, you're okay. You could've been killed. I never should've left."

I shook my head. "No, I'm okay. David was in the most danger. He'll be okay, won't he?"

Jake nodded. "The paramedic says he's stable. The leg looks like the only injury." I scooted across the seat as Jake slid in beside me.

When Jake was situated behind the wheel and we were on our way, I breathed a sigh of relief and snuggled against him as I slid off into oblivion.

Chapter Ten

I opened my eyes to find myself on a bed in an examining room with the curtains drawn. Disoriented at first, it took a moment to remember I was in the emergency room. I must've fallen asleep. There was a nurse at a desk filling out paperwork as I asked, "Is David okay?"

She turned and smiled. "Well, hello. Yes, he'll be fine. His leg was broken pretty badly and he's in surgery right now to fix it. He'll be just fine and so will you. Sounds like you had a rough time of it out there but you got lucky, just some minor burns on your hands. Doc wants to keep you overnight for observation and to make sure you get some good, sound sleep."

She hesitated a moment and then continued, "Jake's pacing like an expectant father in the waiting room. He'll probably take it apart before long if we don't let him in."

I smiled. "Let him come back. I'd hate to have to pay for damages."

She grinned and slipped past the curtain.

Within seconds, Jake bolted through the split in the curtain. He was wound tight as he sat on the side of the bed and put his arms around me. I snaked my arms around his waist and leaned into him.

He cleared his throat. "You two scared the hell out of us."

"Scared me too."

Nothing more was said for a few minutes. When I pulled away and leaned back on the bed, Jake looked down at me but said nothing. His eyes filled with warmth and caring as he held my gaze.

"The nurse said David will be okay. Have you seen him?"

Jake ground his teeth together and stood as he stuffed his hands in the pockets of his jacket. "No. They took him up to surgery right away. The doctor said he'd come talk to me as soon as they were done."

There was silence for a few minutes as our eyes met and held. There was an intensity that made me uncomfortable. I couldn't help but look away.

I sensed Jake stand up straighter. "Well, I'd better call out to the ranch and let everyone know you're okay. Mom made me promise I'd call as soon as there was anything definite on either of you. I'll be right back."

As he turned to leave, I realized how much he and David looked alike from the back. They were so much alike, yet different in so many ways. David had an underlying calmness, where Jake felt more like a wound spring.

It was then that I remembered the argument David and I had right before the accident, when he'd said I was wrong for Jake.

Why would he say that? Was it sour grapes talking? How far would he go to keep me from Jake? Was he trying to tell me something or just trying to keep us apart? Maybe I should have held my temper and listened. Maybe if I'd held my temper, he wouldn't be lying on the operating table right now.

Exhausted, I let my mind wander until I found myself in very dangerous territory. I had to admit I was very attracted to both men.

Am I really wrong for Jake? Is David right? Would he would be a better choice? He seems calmer and more comfortable with his life. Would David make a better husband and father? Why am I so torn? Jake seems to be adrift and confused about his family. Maybe I can help him, maybe he needs me. David doesn't seem to need anyone. He seems to have it all under control. Where would I fit into a life like that?

I had more questions than answers. I was in big trouble. There was a very real danger here if I didn't make a clear and firm choice. If I hesitated or wavered, I could make an enemy and damage the life-long relationship between two brothers. I couldn't jeopardize their relationship. Jake was my first choice and I had to stand firm.

A few minutes later, Jake returned to say his mom wanted me to know how grateful she was for everything I'd done. She'd told Jake to tell me not to worry, the boys were fine. Roy was watching them and they were having a ball, and looking forward to a big adventure story when we got home.

I smiled. "Thank you."

He brushed a stray lock of hair off my face as he leaned in and kissed me tenderly. "I'm so glad you're okay. I don't know what I'd do if something happened to you. I'm sorry I wasn't there, but sometimes the business has to come first."

I took a deep breath as I rolled his statement around in my head—sometimes the business has to come first.

Really? Even when safety is involved? Maybe I'm not being fair.

Just as I thought he was about to say more, the curtain parted and the doctor entered.

"Well, our patient is awake." He smiled a big, toothy grin. "How are you feeling?"

"Tired."

He nodded and crossed his arms over his chest. "Well, you should be. But it doesn't look like there's anything wrong that a good night's sleep and a little TLC won't cure. And that's exactly what I intend for you to have. We'll keep you overnight for observation. You've got some wheezing in your chest and I want to make sure you didn't inhale too much smoke. When we get you into a room, we'll set you up with a chest x-ray and a breathing treatment, just to be sure."

He turned his attention to Jake. "Now, about your brother, he's got some badly bruised ribs in addition to the broken leg. The surgeon says he was damn lucky. The breaks were clean. They'll put in a couple of pins and he'll have a cast for a while. We'll keep him a couple of days and run some more tests, just to make sure there's no internal damage. You'll need to make sure he's set up at home so he doesn't have any stairs to navigate, but it looks like he'll be fine. The ribs won't be so sore in a few days and the leg should be good as new in a couple months' time."

Jake nodded and shook the doctor's hand. "Good. Thanks, Doc. Appreciate the help."

The doctor nodded and patted my leg as he turned to leave. Halfway through the curtain, he turned and looked at Jake. "You look tired too. You'd better go home and get some sleep. Let this girl rest—she's had a big day." With that, he left us alone with an uncomfortable silence.

"Well," Jake said as he cleared his throat, "guess I'd better go and let you get to sleep." He smiled and winked as he gathered me into his arms for a goodnight kiss.

"Okay," I whispered as our lips met.

He gently skimmed his lips over mine and with very little pressure, slipped his tongue inside. I slid my arms around his neck and leaned into the kiss, pushing my tongue as far into his mouth as I could, desperate for a connection, desperate to feel him around me.

When the kiss ended, he smiled down at me. "I'll come by for you early in the morning," he promised as his eyes held mine for a moment. Then he turned and was gone.

I stared at the curtain, suddenly alone and abandoned. I felt like a little kid lost in the big bad world and wished he'd come back and stay with me tonight. With a sigh, I reminded myself he wasn't a mind reader. If that's what I wanted, I should have asked. He would have given it to me.

Wouldn't he?

Before I could formulate an answer, the nurse whisked into the room. "Well, sweetie, would you like a bite to eat before they take you up to your room and tuck you in for the night?"

I nodded. "Absolutely. I'm so hungry, my stomach thinks my throat's been cut."

She laughed and hustled off to see what she could find in the kitchen.

Well, we survived it. I'm okay and David will be fine. All's well that ends well, so they say. Of course, Granny woulda said just because the cow didn't kick over the bucket, that don't mean the milk's any good. But then granny wasn't always an optimist.

I thought of Cody and sent up a little prayer he'd make it back to the ranch okay. I hated to think he might have run into a mountain lion and been hurt—or worse.

When the nurse returned, she had a ham and cheese sandwich that looked good enough to kill for. As she set it in front of me, I tore into it and, with my mouth full, tried to ask her how long David would be in surgery.

She laughed and shook her head. "Another hour or so."

When I finished the sandwich, she brought me another, along with some pudding, a bag of chips, and a soda from the machine, which I polished off also.

As she turned to make a note on my chart, she laughed again. "Well, your appetite's good. I think you're gonna live."

I chuckled. "What time is it?"

She looked at her watch. "It's a little after four in the morning, honey. Doctor said I should get you into a room so you can get some sleep." She looked over the top of her glasses and added, "But if you want, I can let you wait here until David gets out of surgery."

Nodding, I thanked her as I closed my eyes. The sound of a door opening woke me a short time later as an attendant wheeled someone into the recovery room. I heard the nurse say, "Ah, there's our boy now." She drew the curtain open and told the attendant to put David in the spot next to mine.

As they wheeled him into place, I drank in the sight of him. He was still out from the anesthesia, but his color was good and I'd never seen him look better. Well, maybe my perception was a bit colored by what we'd been through, but he did look mighty fine to me.

I watched as the nurse went about her business, taking vitals, making notes in his chart, and checking his IV's. Finally, he opened his eyes and turned his head to look over at me.

I smiled. "Hey."

He half smiled and closed his eyes. A minute later, he opened his eyes again. "I'm real proud of you, Katie. Killed that mountain lion. Good shot."

Huh? What's he talking about? Must be the drugs.

I watched as he regained consciousness and opened his eyes several more times. Each time the story continued to grow. By the time David was fully awake, the nurse and I were laughing hysterically, and neither of us knew how to break it to him the mountain lion had lived—panties and all!

* * *

Shortly before ten the next morning, Jake stuck his head in my door. "Anybody here need a ride?"

I smiled and waved. "Pick me, pick me!" We both laughed.

He walked in and sat in a chair. "So, you all released and ready to go?"

"The doc's been and gone, but they told me to wait a bit for the paperwork." As we waited, I remembered Cody. "Hey, did Cody make it back to the ranch okay?"

Jake's face fell and my heart dropped. "We haven't found him yet. Some of the guys went out on horseback early this morning to see if they could pick up his trail."

The nurse walked in and handed me my release papers. "Well, honey, you're sprung. You take care of yourself, and I'm glad it all worked out okay. You come back right away if you have any problems."

On the way out, we stopped to see David before we left the hospital. We walked into his room to find him scowling at the nurse. When he saw me, his face brightened and then the scowl returned when he spotted Jake close behind. The nurse turned and saw us then turned back to David and said, "See, there she is. Now, are you happy?" She turned and walked out of the room, and David stuck his tongue out behind her back.

"Oh, now you're acting like a big boy," I teased.

"Well, she ticked me off," he whined. "I asked her last night to put me in the bed next to yours so I could keep an eye on you and the old biddy refused. I told her I'd be good and stay in my own bed, but she acted like I intended to ravish everyone in that wing of the hospital. She intentionally moved me to another floor."

It was cute David was pitching such a fit, so I bent to kiss him lightly on the cheek. Caught totally off-guard, he blushed right down to the roots of his hair.

As I straightened and turned toward Jake, the anger on his face startled me and I immediately looked away, hoping David hadn't noticed. I was always in the middle with these two and always doing something stupid.

"Well, I suppose you're going home today, huh?" David winked when I met his gaze, and I knew he'd noticed. "Tell mom I'll be home tomorrow. The nurse said they'll release me in the morning." As Jake and David looked at each other and their eyes held, he added, "Send Roy in to get me early."

Jake nodded and continued to stare for a long moment. "Doc said they'd send some equipment out to the house this afternoon to help with your rehabilitation." Then he took my elbow to usher me from the room.

As we headed for the door, David called out behind us, "Katie, you rest up and take it easy. Don't do anything crazy without me, okay?"

I felt Jake tense up and he squeezed my elbow tighter, so I replied, "Alright. No nurse pinching."

As I followed Jake to the parking lot, anger began to build. He stole glances my way when he thought I wasn't looking, but I held my tongue and didn't say anything, afraid if I opened my mouth, I'd pick a fight.

Why is he being such a jackass? Is he really that insecure about David? Doesn't say a lot for how much he trusts me. I honestly like David and would like to be able to treat him like any other friend, but this jealousy of Jake's just won't allow me to relax and just be me.

With my face turned to the window, I laid my head on the back of the seat and thought about how to handle the situation. I still wasn't sure if David's feelings were really serious, or if it was simply a matter of wanting what he couldn't have, and I didn't have a clue what to do about Jake's jealousy. I'd have to play it cool with David until I could sort it all out. None of us needed this to blow up in our faces.

"Why do you do that?"

Jake's question startled me.

"Do what?"

"Flirt with my brother. Is there something between you two?"

"What! I can't believe you asked that. I'm not flirting. He's a nice guy and I genuinely like him. But we're just friends. I'm <u>with</u> you. And while we're on the subject, why do you always overreact when your brother's around? I feel like you'd put a leash around my neck if you could do it."

That seemed to take him by surprise. He looked at me and blinked twice before he turned his eyes back to the road ahead. Silence sat on the seat between us and festered like a pile of vomit the rest of the way home.

I didn't want to cause a rift between these brothers and I certainly didn't want to hurt Jake or embarrass David. My choice had been made. I'd fallen for Jake. But I couldn't handle his jealousy, and I didn't want to go through life on pins and needles. Why didn't he trust me? Was it because his ex-wife cheated on him? By the time we were within a couple miles of the ranch, the anger had cooled and I'd stuffed the hurt and frustration deep.

Poor Cody. I hated to think of what he might have faced out there alone. I turned to look out the window as a cramp began in my chest and a tear slid down my face. I sent up a silent prayer he would be okay.

Chapter Eleven

When we pulled into the driveway, the boys were there to meet us, jumping up and down and waving frantically with big smiles on their faces. My chest tightened and tears filled my eyes when I saw Dustin. The thought of what might have happened if things had gone badly, or I had been the one injured, rolled over me like a diesel truck. I was riding on a thin crust over a teeming pit of emotion and I needed rest.

We parked the truck and each of us scooped up a boy and hugged tight.

"Are you okay, Mommy?"

"Yep, I sure am." My voice cracked a bit and I cleared my throat to help hold the tears in check. "Just a little tired right now, buddy. Did you and Tyler have fun?"

"Yeah, we've had lots of fun. We slept in the bunkhouse with the cowboys last night and we're gonna do it again tonight if we're good."

"Ooooh," I crooned as I put him down, "and have you been good so far?"

"Yep. We been real good." His head bobbled up and down like it was on a spring.

"Terrific!" I was a little woozy and as I stood still for a minute to let it pass, I noticed my head felt stuffed up. Probably getting one of those ear infections I always got when my allergies flared up.

Great! Just what I need.

"Mommy, is Uncle David okay?"

Taken back by Dustin's use of the familial title, I took a minute to answer. "Yes, honey, David is fine. He'll be home tomorrow, but he will have to use crutches for a while."

Dustin turned to Tyler. "See, I told you he needed his own rock!"

Tyler nodded. "Yeah, we better go find another one, huh?"

They were discussing the red rocks they'd sent out to us the day before.

Hmmm...could there be something to the legend?

I looked at Jake.

He tried not to laugh until the boys were out of sight. I raised a brow in question and he shook his head. "Don't go there," he whispered. "Roy made it up for the benefit of the boys."

"You sure?"

"Positive."

Before we could discuss it further, Jake's mother, Nell, came out on the porch. She was this wonderful, short, round woman with thick salt and pepper hair pulled back in a single braid that reached almost to her waist. As David had said, she lived on the ranch full time and was chief cook and bottle washer, as well as nurse and ranch counselor. She had a ready smile and a hug for everyone as she sat us shooed us toward the house.

"Now, Jake," she scolded, "you get Katie settled into her room. She needs to rest up after her ordeal. She doesn't need to stand around in the driveway lifting boys as big as those two."

I smiled and said, "Thanks," as I followed Nell into the house.

"Jake, you go up and get Katie's things out of the upstairs bedroom and bring them down here. We'll put her in the first floor bedroom so she doesn't have to go up and down those stairs."

Jake started for the stairs and I stopped him. "No, don't move me. I'm okay with the stairs." When Nell objected, I added, "Besides, when David gets home tomorrow, he'll have a cast on his leg and he'll need the downstairs bedroom. Really, I'm fine. I can stay upstairs."

At the mention of David, Jake ground his teeth, but said nothing as he planted his feet and waited for the final decision.

"Oh. Well, you're right, of course" said Nell, "I hadn't thought about that. Katie, are you sure you're okay to do those stairs? We could move you down for tonight and see how you are tomorrow."

"I'm sure. I'll be fine. I've got a bit of a headache and a sniffle. I think it might be an ear infection, but the stairs won't be a problem."

"Well, okay, if you're sure. Come on. Let's get you upstairs. You're probably dying for a nice hot bath."

"Ooooh, a bath does sound heavenly."

Laughing, she waved her apron in my direction and followed me up the stairs, leaving Jake in the living room.

As she ran the hot water for a bath, Nell said, "Tomorrow we'll get some of Jake's old stuff moved out of this room and make it more accommodating for a woman."

"Nell, that's so sweet. But it's not necessary."

"Oh yes it is. Now, I won't have any argument over it. I want you to feel welcome and comfortable here."

What a generous and loving woman.

"You've made me feel very welcome and I don't want to be a bother."

"Don't be silly. It's no trouble at all. Now, let's get you clean so you can relax and take a nice long nap."

It was a nice room, large and comfortable. It had been Jake's old room before he moved into his own house, and it felt like him. Nell continued to fuss over me as I bathed, changed into a t-shirt, and climbed into bed for the nap she insisted I take. Snuggling into the soft, clean sheets and surrounded by the familiar smell of soap, I decided it wasn't a half-bad idea.

Satisfied I was where I should be, Nell headed for the door but stopped and turned with tears in her eyes. "Thank you for taking care of my son. The boys told me what you did out there yesterday and I will never be able to thank you enough."

"He would've done the same for me."

She nodded. "Yes, he would have. But it takes a special kind of woman to step up to the plate when the going gets tough. If it'd been any other woman, he'd probably be dead now." She hesitated a moment before she added, "I think I'm going to like you a lot."

I smiled. "Me too."

She nodded and closed the door behind her. I was asleep before she got to the bottom of the stairs and, tired as I was, I slept straight thru the night.

* * *

I woke to the sound of the blinds being gently opened. Bright light flooded the room and sent me back under the covers.

Nell chuckled. "Well, you slept good last night. How do you feel this morning?"

I peeked out. "Sore, but alive…I think. Any idea where I can find a cup of coffee?"

She smiled and winked. "Coffee's ready, and so's breakfast. Come on down and get it while it's hot."

Slowly peeling back the covers, I swung my legs off the bed and tried to stand, but the room started to spin and I quickly dropped back onto the bed.

"What's wrong?" Nell scowled as she watched me closely.

I shook my head. "Nothing. I was a bit dizzy, is all. Guess I got up too fast." I sniffled. "My head's still stuffed up, probably just a cold or allergies."

Nell hurried to the bed and put her hand on my forehead. "Well, land sakes, girl, you've got a fever." She gently pushed me back into bed, pulled the covers up, and tucked them in around my shoulders. "You're not going anywhere, missy! You're sick. I'm going downstairs to call the doctor. You stay right here."

I felt a bit silly at first but after a few more minutes in bed, it really didn't feel wrong. My head hurt and I felt kinda "sicky"—where you want to climb into bed and pull the covers over your head. Well, here I was, under the covers, and it felt pretty darn good.

After a few minutes, Nell returned with a food tray. "I called the doctor and he said you probably caught something being out there in the cold, what with the stress and smoke and all. He wants you to come into town with Roy when he goes to get David so he can take a look at you and make sure it isn't something serious. Until then, you're to stay in bed, keep warm, and drink plenty of fluids. So I heated you up some of my homemade chicken soup. It should help get you right in no time."

I thanked her as I sat up in bed and she set up the tray. I tasted the soup and it was to die for. She sat on the foot of the bed and we talked until I'd finished the soup. She had a great sense of humor and I liked her a lot. She saw me as her son's savior and she liked me too…a match made in heaven.

At ten o'clock, I dressed and went downstairs to find Roy waiting in the kitchen. He loaded me up in the truck and we headed in to town.

"I didn't see Jake around," I said when we were well on our way. "Did he go somewhere?"

Roy peeked over at me quickly. "Yeah, he had to go into Flagstaff on business. He said he'd be back some time this evening."

"Oh. Gee, I guess vacation has a different meaning for Jake than it does for me."

Roy smiled. "Vacation has always meant something different for Jake than it does for most people. He's a perfectionist. Drives himself hard. Always working, that boy."

I stared straight ahead at the road as I digested what he'd said. A perfectionist? It hadn't registered before, but it did fit. Maybe it explained the fact that there didn't seem to be any gray areas with Jake, it was all or nothing.

It could also explain some of his trust issues. Hard to trust someone when you're expecting them to be perfect. No one can live up to that.

I quietly mulled it over on the way to the hospital. Could I live up to the expectations of a perfectionist? Or would it set the bar so high I would always fall short? Did that happen to his ex-wife?

When we arrived, the same nurse who'd treated me was on duty and she already knew I was coming in sick. She ushered me into a treatment room and sent Roy upstairs to fetch David while the doctor checked me out.

The verdict was exactly as we had expected. I'd caught a cold and my ears were infected, which affected my equilibrium. The doctor sent me home with a bottle of pills and told me to take it easy, keep warm, and drink plenty of fluids.

When I got back to the lobby, David and Roy were there. David looked great. His color had returned to normal and he was complaining about having to use the crutches. Apparently, they'd refused to give him a walking cast.

Roy turned to me and winked. "Well, I guess our boy's gonna be okay. In fact, I'm thinkin' I shoulda brought him a horse to ride home 'cuz if he can bitch this much, he can darn sure ride."

David scowled and we laughed.

With that, we all headed for the truck with me holding onto Roy's arm to keep me steady as David hobbled along behind on his much-maligned crutches.

When we pulled in at the ranch, there were riders and horses everywhere. A truck pulled in behind us and one look told me it was the local vet. I jumped out of the truck as one of the riders told

David they'd found Cody "tore up pretty bad" about three miles from the ranch. Another group of riders had come back in to report they'd come upon a dead mountain lion another mile out. From the tracks and his injuries, they guessed Cody had tangled with the mountain lion and managed to kill him, but not before he sustained some serious injuries to himself. Then, amazingly, he'd made it another mile closer before they found him limping slowly toward home. So they loaded him up in the horse trailer and called the vet to meet them back at the ranch.

David and I rushed to the barn and my first sight of Cody broke my heart. I turned away as the tears rushed up and David stood there on his crutches, staring. When he turned back, I could see him grind his teeth and there were tears in his eyes too as he rolled up his sleeves and prepared to help the vet. No one said a word as the vet walked in with a bucket in his hand, looked at Cody, and shook his head.

I dried my eyes, took a deep breath, swallowed, and exhaled slowly as I asked the vet if I could help.

He looked up and nodded. "Yeah, I'll need a couple of you to help me. This old boy's gonna need a whole boatload of stitches. Looks like he's lost a lot of blood, too, so I'm going to put him on an IV. I can't put him completely to sleep and there's a lot of wounds to close, so I'll give him a little something to take the edge off and we'll handle the bigger ones with a local." With a glance in my direction, he asked, "Think you can hold his head and talk to him, help us keep him calm?"

Unable to speak past the lump in my throat, I nodded and took hold of the lead rope. Cody had a huge gash down one side of his face that had laid open the bottom eyelid on his left eye, exposing more of the white of the eye and giving him a crazed look. My stomach rolled and I swallowed hard to keep the bile down as I laid my cheek against his and talked softly to him. I could feel him relax against my cheek as the pain meds began to take effect.

David and the vet started an IV and began to clean and stitch wounds. David had thrown off his crutches and sat on an overturned bucket with his leg out to the side as he stitched away. Two of the riders had stayed to help by keeping the buckets of water changed and doing whatever else needed to be done. Every once in a while, one of them would help David move his bucket and re-situate himself to stitch up another wound. The rest of the riders all moved off to unsaddle their horses and put them away. Then they set about cleaning out the blood-smeared trailer.

There were so many wounds to be closed and Cody stood so quietly under sedation that I left his head after a few minutes and began to help clean wounds. He had a number of major cuts and tears like the one on his face, along with countless smaller cuts and scratches everywhere. There was a lot of dried blood and some of the larger wounds were still oozing.

David and Roy worked to stitch up some of the smaller, cleaner wounds while the vet worked on the more complicated ones requiring more skill to close properly. Three hours later, we had cleaned, stitched and bandaged everything needing attention. The rest were minor enough that they would heal on their own. The vet had given Cody several injections of antibiotics and pain medication. The boys had cleaned out a stall inside the barn and put down fresh bedding. When the anesthesia the vet had administered wore off enough for Cody to walk, we moved him into the stall and Roy gave him fresh water and a warm mash, which he ate slowly.

Exhausted, we collapsed on feed buckets and benches in the barn while Cody ate. For a few minutes, no one said anything.

As I sat there on my bucket, my mind flipped through the events of the day as I'd worked side-by-side with David, Roy, and Mac to treat Cody's wounds. It felt good, felt like I belonged. This was the first time since my folks died that I'd felt like I belonged anywhere. What made me feel that way? Was it the place or the people? The people. These were people I respected, people I could love. I smiled as it dawned on me I was falling in love with this entire family. But where was Jake?

David broke the spell of silence when he turned to the vet and said, "Thanks, Mac. I know it's your daughter's birthday today and I appreciate you coming all the way out here to take care of us."

"No problem. We decided we're gonna go out and get pizza tomorrow night for Annie's birthday. You know how crazy she is about Cody. She was adamant I had to fix him. If you guys are hungry about seven tomorrow night, you oughta stop by the Pizza Emporium and join us for the celebration. My treat. We're even gonna have a band."

"Well, tell her I said thanks for loaning you to us. We'll come by if we can, but the birthday party's gonna be our treat," David informed him.

"Oh, don't worry," Mac replied with a smile, "you're gonna owe me a fortune for this farm visit and all those stitches. I can afford to be generous and feed you a few slices of pizza."

David laughed and shook his head as Mac filled a couple of syringes with pain medicine. When he was done, Mac picked up his bucket and handed the syringes to David. "Here's some extra shots for the pain, just in case I can't get back first thing in the morning or he has trouble through the night. Tell Roy to keep an eye out for excessive bleeding and don't hesitate to give me a call if you need me."

David thanked him and we all followed Mac out to his truck. As he pulled down the driveway, we headed to the house, where we all sat around the table for a quick dinner. No one had much of an appetite, but we hadn't eaten since early that morning and it was a little after four o'clock. So Nell insisted we all sit down and have some soup. When we finished the soup, we all felt a bit better and thanked her as she shooed the ranch hands out the door and insisted the rest of us go rest.

Dustin and Tyler were busy out in the barn with Roy and the other cowboys, so they were in hog heaven and I was free to do as I pleased, and a nap sounded pretty darn good right now. When I turned to follow Nell out of the kitchen, I heard David clear his throat behind me and I turned to face him. He smiled a tired and grateful smile. "You were a real trooper today, Slick. Well, yesterday and today, actually. My brother's a very lucky man."

Too tired to really say much, I smiled. "Thanks."

David moved close and put his hands on my shoulders. "You know, Katie, whenever I'm around you, there's a constant battle raging inside. Half of me wants to do the honorable thing and back down, and the other half wants to challenge my brother for you." There was a long moment of silence as he looked into my eyes and softly added, "We could be so good together."

I took a deep breath as our eyes held. "The last thing I want is to come between you and your brother." I hesitated for a moment and then continued, "You're a wonderful, attractive man. Any woman would be thrilled to have a guy like you. We have fun together and I care a lot for you, but your brother worked his way into my heart first." I waited a moment to gauge his reaction before I finished, "David, there is no 'we'. You've got to turn loose."

His face fell as the truth of my words struck him. He looked down at the floor and closed his eyes as he took a deep breath. When he opened his eyes and looked up, the emotion was gone as he smiled and stepped back. He removed his hands from my shoulders and nodded. "You're absolutely right. It wasn't fair to put you in the middle."

As I left the kitchen, my gut twisted into a knot. Had I just made a huge mistake? David was a wonderful and loving man, a strong but gentle man, a trusting man—a man who could be trusted. He so deserved a woman who would love and care for him. A small part of me was sad it wouldn't be me. It broke my heart to have to hurt him, but I was with Jake and I couldn't drive a wedge between these two brothers. I had to stay the course.

At the top of the stairs, goose bumps skittered up the back of my neck and I turned to look over my shoulder. David stood in the doorway to the kitchen. When I looked back, he turned and ducked into the kitchen without another word.

Early that evening, I heard Jake's truck pull into the driveway. I'd only been up from my nap about an hour, but was still tired and dragging. As I headed out the front door to meet him in the driveway, I saw the boys had beaten me to it. They waved and grinned from ear to ear as they swarmed the truck.

After lots of high-fiving, the boys began to chatter all at once about how Cody had come home and needed stitches everywhere.

Jake looked at me. “Is it true? He made it home?”

I nodded. “Yeah, he did, but he’s in really rough shape. Took us three hours to get all the wounds cleaned and stitched.”

“Damn! We’ll never be able to use him for competition again with scars.”

That threw me for a loop. The poor horse had battled a mountain lion and struggled for two days to get home and Jake’s first concern was scars. All I could do was stare and he must’ve realized how it sounded.

“Sorry. I didn’t mean to sound like I don’t care about the horse. Of course, I’m glad he’s home. But he won’t be any good to us if he’s all scarred up. We’ll have to get rid of him.”

The tears welled up in my eyes as the callousness of his statement hit me. Before I could reply, the screen door slammed and I turned to find David behind me on his crutches.

“He’s not going anywhere. The scars won’t affect his usefulness as a workin’ horse.”

I could feel the tension flare like a hot match as David and Jake squared off over the fate of the damaged horse. Finally, Jake looked at me and back to David as he started up the steps. “Well, little brother, I think we have enough cow horses, but that would be your area of expertise. It’s up to you to decide if you can make your budget work with an extra horse, but he's no good to me any more."

As Jake moved past me, he took my arm and propelled me ahead of him into the house, leaving David alone on the front porch.

Chapter Twelve

The next morning, Roy took the boys out riding while I stayed in bed with an earache and Jake did some work on the books. The boys returned about lunch time and announced they were "starved to death". As we washed our hands and took our places at the table, Roy announced he would take charge of the two boys again after lunch, and would do it down at the swimming hole, which drew squeals of delight from both boys.

Jake entered the kitchen from the living room and began to wash his hands as he asked Nell where David went. I caught the hesitation in her voice as she said David had decided to run into Phoenix to pick up some supplies and wouldn't be back probably until the end of the week. Jake frowned slightly. "What supplies?"

Nell's gaze quickly darted in my direction and then shifted away. "He didn't say. Just said he'd be back toward the end of the week."

Jake's frown deepened. "Well, I need to talk to him. Did he take his cell phone with him this time?"

"I don't know," Nell answered. "It's not a vacation this time, so I assume he did."

Jake didn't say any more, but he looked like he intended to stay in a bad mood, so everyone around him ate in silence. Even the two boys were quieter than usual.

After lunch, Nell ran us all out of the kitchen so she could clean it up.

I offered to stay and help, but she wouldn't hear of it. So I suggested to Jake we should find a spot on the front porch swing where we could sit in the shade for a few minutes and talk.

He looked almost annoyed. "What do you want to talk about?"

A little surprised by his curtness, I replied, "Nothing in particular. I thought we might spend a few minutes together. We haven't had a lot of time since the issue with the health papers came up the other day." Truth was, I'd seen almost nothing of him since I got home from the hospital. He was locked up in the office on the phone all day and when he came out for meals, he was so distracted that it was impossible to carry on a conversation.

He stared at me for a moment before relenting. "Oh. Okay. Sorry, guess I got distracted. The transport issues snowballed on me and I'm still trying to clean up the mess." He took my hand and we walked out to the porch where we sat on a swing in the shade.

When Jake finally spoke, it was clear he was still frustrated. "I can't believe David went off to Phoenix and didn't tell me, right in the middle of this mess. First, he manages to get himself hurt, which means we'll have to pay overtime to some of the hands to pick up what he can't handle on crutches. Now we'll be even further behind because he can't send one of the hands to pick up the parts. I don't know what he's thinking."

"Maybe he was thinking he'd do it himself since there isn't a whole lot he can do here on crutches."

Jake just looked at me.

Before I could find a way to change the subject, the boys trotted across the drive in the direction of the swimming hole. They had on swimsuits and picked their way carefully between the rocks with bare feet.

Jake laughed as he swung his arm around my shoulders. “Those boys are two peas in a pod, aren’t they? What one doesn’t think of, the other will.”

I laughed. “Yeah, Dustin’s really having a great time up here. He’s not gonna to want to go home.”

“He’s a good kid. I like him. Not too many kids are so nice and well mannered.”

“Thanks. He’s got his moments, but he really is a good kid.”

“Well, I’ve never seen him be anything less than perfect.” He touched his forehead to mine and added, “That’s because he’s got the perfect mom.”

There was that word again. Why did it make me so uncomfortable? It was silly. Jake was a businessman. He was organized and “in control”, but it didn’t mean he was a perfectionist. And what if he was? Lots of people were. So far, he hadn’t expected perfection from me or from Dustin.

I looked at my watch. Time for my medication. “You know what, I’m tired. I think I’m gonna go lay down for a bit.”

Jake gave me a funny look. “In the middle of the day?”

“Yeah, they call it a nap.” I laughed. “You oughta try it some time. They’re delicious.”

He followed me as I got off the swing and headed for the house. When we walked into the kitchen, he grabbed me around the waist from behind and whispered in my ear, "Which side of the bed do you want?"

Unfortunately, Nell was where she could hear and she reached out and swatted him on the back of the head. "I'm watching you, mister, if it means I have to personally guard her door with a shotgun."

The image of Nell in a chair outside my door with a shotgun was too much for either of us to bear and we burst out laughing, which drew another swat from Nell as she chased us from the kitchen.

As I stepped onto the second floor landing, I was really tired and my ears had started to ache again. Bed was definitely a good idea.

Nell had re-decorated Jake's room somewhat with some mirrors and flowers to make it feel more like a woman's room. I decided I kind of missed the strong, masculine feel I'd originally noticed the first time I walked into the room, but the flowers were a nice touch. I opened the French doors which lead to a second-floor porch completely shaded by a big Cottonwood. A cool breeze wafted through as I pulled back the covers and climbed into bed.

I was about to drop off when there was a light tap on the door. I mentally rolled my eyes at Jake trying to sneak into my room. "Come in."

It was Nell. She stuck her head in and asked, "You need anything, honey? Did you remember to take your medicine?"

I waved her in as I sat up and reached for the pill bottle on the night stand. "No, I almost forgot. Thanks for the reminder."

With the pill swallowed, I lay back against the pillow again, but Nell still stood at the foot of the bed and didn't offer to leave.

"What's up?"

"Well, I wanted to say something, and I hope you don't mind."

"Oh, Nell, don't be silly. Go ahead. You can say anything to me."

"Well, I wanted to say I like the way Jake lights up when you're around. It's been a long time since I've seen him like that. You're good for him and it warms my heart to see it. I think he's in love with you."

I stared at her, absorbing what she'd said and wondering why I hadn't noticed it. Why was I the last to see something like that?

She watched me for a moment and smiled as she added, "Don't worry about David. He'll get over it in time and things will be right as rain again." Then she turned and walked out, shutting the door behind her.

Boy, that woman's as sharp as a barn owl on food patrol. She doesn't miss a thing!

I lay there for a few minutes as my mind whirled about what she'd said.

Is Jake really in love with me? Am I in love with him?

He seemed to be everything I'd ever dreamed of, and then some. Yes, this was a man I could love. He was a man I might already be in love with, and he came complete with something I missed terribly—a loving family.

When the medication kicked in and my eyelids were too heavy to hold open, I rolled onto my side and sighed as I drifted off to sleep to dream about Jake, weddings, and happily ever afters.

I slept the sleep of the dead until about six in the evening, when I woke to find Jake in a chair next to the bed with a big grin on his face. I smiled and stretched my arms above my head. "How long have you been there?"

"Just a few minutes." He smiled and reached over to stroke the side of my face.

"Was I drooling?" I asked as I tried to determine exactly how unattractive I might have been.

"Nope. You were a perfect angel."

I raised both eyebrows. *Aw, crud.* If he had to take it that far over the top, I must've drooled.

Jake hitched his thumb toward the door. "A bunch of us are going into town celebrate Annie's birthday. You up for it?"

"Yeah, it sounds like fun. What time?"

"Well, we probably oughta leave any time now. Mom said the party starts at seven."

I looked over at the clock on the wall. We should have been on the road about five minutes earlier if we were going to make seven o'clock.

"Okay, get out and give me four minutes to throw myself together."

He gave me a curious look. "Why four minutes? Why not five?"

"Out!" I ordered as I swung my legs out from under the covers. "I don't have time to mince words with you…out, out, out!"

He laughed as he headed for the door. I jumped out of bed and headed for the closet, shucking the t-shirt I'd slept in. As I got to the closet, the room slowly began to spin. I grabbed the doorframe to steady myself and breathed deep until the spinning stopped and my head cleared. I'd have to take it easy until the infection cleared up.

I grabbed a clean pair of jeans from the shelf in the closet, pulled my new green sweater off the hanger and sat on the side of the bed to dress. I'd purchased the sweater specifically for this trip and hoped the emerald green color would knocks Jake's socks off. I tugged on the jeans, pulled the sweater over my head, stuffed my feet into some socks and a pair of boots, ran a brush through my hair, put on some lipstick, grabbed my purse and was on my way.

When I opened the door, I found Jake right outside my door, leaned back against the railing. He looked up and whistled—exactly the reaction I'd hoped for.

Man, I love this sweater!

I smiled. "Were you waiting patiently out here or should I check the railing for signs of gnawing?"

He grinned and shrugged. "I was trying to decide if I wanted to face my mother alone or with protection."

"Oh, and you thought I was going to protect your sorry butt?"

Before he could answer, Nell came through the kitchen door with an armload of birthday presents and scowled when she saw Jake outside my room. Then she shrugged and said, "Well, are we going? We'd better get a move-on if we are."

Jake jumped as if he'd been hit with a cattle prod, and I laughed all the way down the stairs. We grabbed our jackets, headed out the front door, and hopped into Jake's truck.

When I asked where the boys were, Jake laughed. "They said they didn't want to go to 'no girl's party'. So Roy offered to take them into town to a movie and let 'em sleep out in the bunkhouse again tonight."

I made a face. "Man, Roy sure is a tough old buzzard!" Everyone agreed and laughed as we headed out the drive. With Nell behind the wheel, we pulled up in front of the Pizza Emporium about five minutes before seven o'clock. I sure liked her style!

We walked in and the place was packed. It looked like everyone from the ranch had come into town for Annie's birthday, and half the townsfolk too. Mac met us about three steps inside the door, shaking hands with Jake and hugging both Nell and me. As he broke out of our hug, Mac winked and whistled as he held me at arms length. He shook his head and looked at Jake. "You'd better keep a close eye on her. Every cowboy within ten miles of town is gonna be here tonight and you're gonna have your hands full making sure she leaves with the guy who brung her to the dance."

Nell and I laughed. Jake didn't. He scowled and looked around the room, as if he dared anyone to talk to me. I punched him in the arm. "Relax, Bucko, I promise I'll save the last dance for you."

Jake put his arm around me and growled, "You gotta be kidding! You think I'm gonna let you get more than two feet away from me in that sweater? You're gonna save me ALL the dances, sweetheart!"

What a sweater!

We found an empty table and Nell grabbed a pitcher of soda as Jake got us some mugs. We were getting situated at a table when a man I'd not met before came up to us. "Hi, Nell, how you been?"

Nell nodded and rather coolly replied, "Hello, Chance, I'm fine. How have you been?"

The guy she called Chance turned his attention to me and smiled as he stepped in close and reached for my hand. "I've been fine, Nell. Aren't you going to introduce me to this enchanting young lady?"

Nell scowled. "Chance, this is Jake's girlfriend. Katie, this is Chance. He chases anything in skirts and is particularly fond of the women Jake dates."

This guy was gorgeous, but it was obvious he thought he was God's gift to women. He came off like a real slime ball and I didn't like the way he looked at me or the way he invaded my space and took possession of my hand. So I pulled my hand back quickly. "Hello." Before I could say any more, Jake was at my side with a scowl plastered on his face.

"Hello, Chance. Couldn't find a date of your own again, huh? Well, this one's taken, so you can put your eyes back in your head and keep your hands off." Jake positioned the right side of his body in front of me as he set two mugs on the table, but he kept hold of one mug as he stood his ground, clearly daring Chance to do something stupid.

I didn't like the way Jake acted, but I liked Chance even less. So I kept quiet and moved closer to Jake's back.

Chance shot me a blinding smile and almost leered as he said, "Well, Katie, if you decide you'd like to dance later, you let me know. I'm the best dancer in the county and I'd love to move you around the floor."

I felt Jake flinch in front of me and as he started forward, I wrapped my arms around his waist and pulled him close as I peeked around him and smiled. "Thanks for the invitation, Chance, but I'll stay with the guy who brought me to the dance. I don't switch horses in the middle of a race, and certainly not when I've got the winner."

Chance was a man used to having his way with women and he was clearly surprised at my blunt reply, but he rallied quickly and shrugged as he said, "Let me know if you come to your senses," and he turned and walked away.

The anger radiated off Jake in waves as I held onto him and laid my head against his back and whispered, "Relax. He's a jerk. It's not worth your time."

Jake set the mug on the table and pulled me close. "You're a real treasure, you know it?" I smiled as we looked into each other's eyes for a moment before he leaned over and kissed me softly and sweetly.

There were no more incidents that evening and we had a great time. Annie was a beautiful little girl and she got loads of great presents. Everyone was in a good mood and there were lots of stories swapped and lots of beer and soda consumed. Jake stayed at my side and we saw very little of Chance—always from across the room.

About eleven o'clock, I found myself fading and leaned on Jake. He had one arm wrapped around me and my head was laid against his chest as he talked with Mac. Annie plopped down next to me and leaned her head on my shoulder. "I'm tired. Do you think it's enough birthday?"

She was a real precocious kid and I liked her a lot. I chuckled and put my arm around her. "Never, never can a girl have too much birthday! But the rest of us are pretty old and if some of us poop out, you're gonna have to bear up and be brave." She looked up to see if I was serious and we both laughed as I winked at her.

We looked up and caught Mac smiling. He looked over at Jake and said, "Well, Jake, it looks like our ladies are a bit worn out. Maybe we need to get them home and put them to bed."

Jake bent to nuzzle my neck as he whispered into my ear, "Sounds like a good idea to me. Time for bed?"

I blushed as I ducked my head and put my face next to his and whispered, "You wish!"

Jake threw his head back and laughed as he looked over at Mac. "Guess you're right. Worn out and a bit cranky, I think." Mac laughed and got to his feet, reaching out to give Jake a pull up.

With that, it seemed like everyone in the place finished their drinks and got to their feet. They all shook hands, waved and hugged, and reached for coats. It seemed like the whole place cleared out all at once and suddenly we were all in the parking lot, headed for our trucks.

Nell got behind the wheel again and Jake and I snuggled in next to her on the front seat. Before we were even out of the parking lot, I was asleep on Jake's shoulder.

At one point during the drive home, my consciousness surfaced and I could hear Jake and Nell talking. At first, I didn't move or open my eyes because they were in a serious conversation and I didn't want to interrupt. After a few minutes, I realized I was eavesdropping and I didn't want them to know I'd heard what they'd said. So I remained quiet and let them think I was asleep as I listened to what they said, mostly about me.

Nell told Jake she really liked me and she'd almost split a gut when she heard my exchange with Chance. Jake swore, made a disparaging remark about Chance's ancestry, and said he liked me too.

It got quiet for a minute or two and then Nell said, "Jake, you're a damn fool if you don't marry this girl. She's perfect for you. You need to forget about Brenda and move on, and I'm gonna stay on you until you do."

Jake sighed. "Mom, you know how I feel about Brenda. I don't want her back, but I can't stand to see the kids ripped apart. I know you like Katie, and I like her too, but this is a choice I've got to make. There's a lot to consider here. Besides, you know I couldn't get married right now anyway."

A choice? Between whom? Me and Brenda? What the hell?

"You love her, don't you?" Nell wouldn't give up.

"I think I might," Jake replied as my heart leapt in my chest. Then it plunged as he added, "But it's not so easy. I'm not sure I can live with having my family ripped apart. I worked so hard for so long to hold my family together and I'm not sure I can walk away from it, even for love. I've got to think of the kids and what's best for them. They're miserable being separated and it breaks my heart. I'm not sure I can live like this."

I could hear my blood pound in my ears and I was afraid they would discover I wasn't asleep. I tried to relax and steady my breathing as I attempted to make sense of what had been said.

Jake might be in love with me and Nell wants me in the family. But it might not be enough? What's he talking about? Is Jake afraid of the commitment? Are there still unresolved issues with his ex-wife?

My stomach clenched as my mind raced to still darker thoughts.

Is he still in love with Brenda? What does he mean about what's best for the kids?

I held my breath as the worst thought of all struck me.

Is there some chance he and Brenda might get back together?

By the time we arrived back at the ranch, I had uncovered more questions than answers.

Did I love him? Was there a future for us? Would I fight for him if I had to? What would I do if I fought and lost?

My chest hurt like a thousand pounds pressed down on it and my windpipe was caught in a vice.

We pulled into the driveway and parked. Jake shook me and I pretended to wake and followed him into the house. Jake and I sat on the couch in the living room and I leaned against him quietly with my head on his shoulder as I tried to put my scattered thoughts in order. Nell came into the room from the kitchen, threw us a quick wave and said goodnight as she headed for her room with a glass of water.

Jake and I quietly held hands and hugged for some time. When I could no longer stand the pain of silence, I said, "Well, I guess I'd better hit the sack. I'm pooped and those boys will be up here early in the morning."

Jake put a finger under my chin, tipped my head back, and looked into my eyes. "Thanks for going with me tonight. Having you at my side made me the proudest man there. You were the prettiest, sweetest, sexiest, bestest girl at the party and I'm so glad you were there with me."

I reached up and stroked the side of his face. "I was proud to be your date. You're a good man." I was quiet for a moment before I got up the nerve to continue, "Jake, I'm falling for you in a big way. If you're not up for long-term, you'd better tell me now because...well, I'm falling pretty hard and I've had enough hurt in my life. I don't need any more, and neither does Dustin."

Jake hugged me to him. "You're incredible. How could any man not want you...and your son? You're both almost perfect."

There was that word again. But this time, we were only <u>almost</u> perfect. Did I read too much into it?

Jake continued, "I've never developed such strong feelings for anyone so fast in my entire life. I...well, I have some issues I have to clear up." Then he leaned in and kissed me passionately and possessively.

There was definitely nothing short-term about his kiss as his lips took possession of mine and his tongue moved against mine like it was storming the keep. But the heavy feeling in the pit of my stomach wouldn't go away. Something wasn't right, something I couldn't put my finger on. But it felt real, and it felt scary.

* * *

The week had gone by quickly. This time tomorrow, I'd be back behind the bar pouring drinks and listening to sad tales. It had been a glorious six days and we had bonded the way a real family might.

We'd laughed and cried together and I was sad to see the week come to an end.

After lunch, we helped Nell clear the table and Jake said it was time to go. I nodded and headed out through the living room to pick up my purse and the boys' backpacks.

Nell followed us from the kitchen. "It'll be so quiet around here without those boys. Don't know what I'm gonna do with myself. Those crusty old ranch hands make a woman old. Those boys keep me young, and it's surely nice to have a woman's company now and again."

She reached out and ruffled the heads of both boys. "You boys come back soon." When it came my turn to say goodbye, Nell and I both had tears in our eyes. "Be patient with him," she whispered as I hugged her. "Give him time to get things straight in his head."

I smiled. "I'll try. I really will."

But will it be enough?

She patted my cheek. "Good. I love you. Next time you come up, let me know and we'll have the whole town over for a barbecue. You can meet everyone you didn't meet this time around. Okay?"

I nodded and discreetly swiped at the tears threatening to fall. Dustin and Tyler bolted out the door, waving and hollering bye to Nell. She waved and hollered after them that she couldn't wait to see "both" her grandsons soon. I don't think Dustin caught the reference, but I did and I peeked to see what Jake's response was. His brows pulled together as he looked quickly at Nell with a troubled expression. A split second later, he waved us into the truck. I didn't know what to make of it, but the solid lump was back in the pit of my stomach.

The boys slept in the back seat the whole way home while Jake and I talked about our dreams, what we wanted out of life, the goals we had set for ourselves. We were both careful not to go too near the spot where commitments are expected. There seemed to be an unspoken agreement to carefully avoid any emotional snares for the moment and I couldn't shake the uneasy feeling I'd picked up at the ranch. It rode right between my shoulder blades like a backpack full of rocks.

We arrived at my house about two in the afternoon and the boys bounded out of the truck like they'd been shot out of a cannon.

I wrapped my arms around Jake's waist. "I can't believe the week's over. It's going to be lonely around here without you and Tyler."

"Yeah, I know. I wish we could take you both home with us. If you didn't own your own home..." The thought hovered in the air between us, unclear and unfinished.

I looked at him, surprised. Was he hinting at marriage? No, this didn't feel like it was about marriage so much as location. Is he talking about us moving in with him? My mind recognized the truth as it screamed the answer.

That isn't the kind of limited commitment I want from this man!

I wanted nothing short of marriage and forever. I could sense he was even more confused than I, so I didn't push him. Part of me didn't want to hear the answer right now. So I smiled and shrugged as we headed into the house, a coward to the bone.

The boy met us at the door and Dustin pleaded, "Can Tyler stay here tonight?"

Jake and I both said, “No,” at the same time.

Then I said, “Honey, you both have school tomorrow and we all need to get our things unpacked. Maybe Jake and Tyler will come over for dinner tomorrow night.”

Dustin looked hopefully at Jake. “Will you?”

Jake smiled and reached out to ruffle Dustin’s hair. “Wild horses couldn’t keep us away! Huh, Tyler?”

Tyler nodded like a little bobble head doll. We all laughed and walked the boys to the truck. Jake got Tyler buckled in and turned to kiss me goodnight. Then he hopped into the driver’s seat and waved.

As I watched my two newest boys head down the street, emptiness wrapped itself around my heart like a smothering blanket and I dragged in a hard breath. I had to find a way to help this man see what a wonderful future we could have as a family. We wouldn’t be perfect, but we’d be awfully good.

I bent over to pick Dustin up and he wrapped his legs around my waist and his arms around my neck. “I’m sad, mommy. I don’t want them to go home.”

I hugged him back hard. “Me too, honey, me too.” My heart twisted in my chest like a knife.

Me too.

Chapter Thirteen

We'd been back from the ranch a couple of weeks and settled into a routine of alternating dinner at Jake's house and mine. Each night, we went to our respective homes and slept alone. The next night, we talked about how lonely it had been and then we repeated the cycle.

It was Saturday afternoon. Dustin was with his dad for the weekend and I was getting ready to pull the night shift at the bar, along with MJ. Jake had called earlier to say Tyler was at Brenda's for the night and he and Willy would be in later to take MJ and me to breakfast after we got off.

I put the finishing touches on my makeup, grabbed my purse, turned off the lights, and headed out the door.

The bar was almost empty when I arrived. We had a new band tonight and I wasn't sure how well they'd go over. I dearly hoped they would sound better tonight than they did at rehearsal earlier in the week.

I was a little early and Kendall, who had covered the daytime shift, was still on for another forty-five minutes, so she asked if I wanted to sit and have a drink first.

"Yeah, I'll have a tall Coke." I pulled up a stool next to Mad Harry and handed her my purse to put behind the bar.

Harry looked up and nodded when I said, "Hey, Harry, how ya doin'?"

"Good," he replied and turned back to his beer. Like I said earlier, Harry was a man of few words.

The band was warming up and so far, I didn't see any improvement. When I mentioned it to Kendall, she rolled her eyes. "Oh, man, I cocktailed last night and they're awful. I expect word's traveled by now. You'll probably have a slow night."

I made a face and took a sip of my drink as I sensed someone taking the stool on the other side of me. I looked over and MJ smiled. "Hi, Kat."

"Hey, how's it goin'?" I asked as she settled herself and ordered a soda water.

"Good. How you been?" She didn't wait for my response. "Willy says we're all going out to breakfast after we get off tonight, right?"

"That's what Jake said. Unfortunately, the band sucks, so one of us may be going to breakfast early.

"Oh, man, that sucks." MJ scrunched up her face and looked over at the band. "It's gonna be a real long night. Well, I get dibs on early breakfast."

I laughed and shrugged. "Doesn't matter to me. If it's slow, I can visit with Jake here or at the coffee shop. Did Willy say what time they'd be in?"

"Nope, no clue." A funny look came over MJ's face as she said, "Willy just said they were going to sit somewhere and have a quiet beer before coming here. Said Jake had something he wanted to talk about." As I looked over and raised a brow, she focused on her drink and didn't make eye contact.

"What's goin' on?" I asked her.

"Dunno."

Still no eye contact. MJ was a bad liar.

"MJ, you're lying. What's going on?"

She looked at me and smiled apologetically. "Kat, I can't tell you. I promised. Please. I can tell you, it's really good. You'll like it, I promise."

I scowled at her.

"Please," she begged.

"Okay," I replied as I turned away and took a drink. "I won't beat it out of you, but you'd better be right. It had better be good. And if anyone gets off early tonight, it's gonna be me. I don't want this to hang over my head any longer than it has to."

Her face brightened as she decided it was a good deal. "Okay, you got it. Tell you what, I'll go on first. You sit here and relax. You can come on when it starts to get busy."

I nodded as she slid her drink across the bar and got up off her stool. As she passed behind me, she put her arm around my shoulders and said, "I promise it's good."

As MJ switched places with Kendall and the band began to play in earnest, I nursed my drink and racked my brain to figure out what Jake might have to say. I tried to remember exactly how MJ had phrased it. Had she said he would "tell" me something or "ask" me something? As the word "ask" came into my mind, my heart soared.

Will he ask me to marry him? Am I ready for that? Is he?

Replaying our conversation in my head, I realized she hadn't said "ask". She had said "tell". What did she mean? What could he tell me that was good? Well, he hadn't yet told me he loved me. I sensed he did, but he always held back. Not wanting to push him or scare him off, I hadn't said it either.

More than once, I'd wrestled with the idea of saying it first, thinking it might open the door to a deeper commitment. But something always stopped me short. No, it was better to wait. Let him take the lead in this I told myself each time and, still, the words remained unsaid—a hot lump in the back of my throat.

Will he tell me tonight? Is he working up the courage?

We had talked about marriage and commitment and how we felt about the fact that both our spouses had cheated on us. He knew how passionate I was about commitment and faithfulness in a marriage and how I believed if you loved a person enough to make the commitment to live with them, you should be prepared to marry them. Half-commitments weren't my style and, by now, he knew it.

He'd been desperate to hold his family together, willing to live in a loveless marriage if that was what it took. The split hadn't been his choice, but was forced on him when his wife left him for another man. He didn't give up and new commitments wouldn't come easily to him. I wasn't even sure his old commitments were dead yet.

Where did that leave us? Willy and MJ made jokes and teased us about being the perfect couple. MJ and Willy believed Jake was in love with me and it was only a matter of time before he proposed.

But would love be enough to make him marry me? Jake was all about commitment and responsibility and keeping his family together. Did he have room in his life for another wife? What if she wants him back? Would he go? I didn't think he loved her, but he'd made a commitment to take care of her forever. How much did that commitment mean to him? Jake was passionate about commitment and crazy as it sounded, part of me worried he might take her back if it meant his family could be together again. I hoped it was my run-away imagination, but it was like a grain of sand stuck under my saddle and I couldn't seem to ignore it.

As I surfaced briefly from my deep thoughts, I looked up and found MJ looking at me from down the bar. I smiled and she nodded and turned to serve a customer. I looked over and saw Mad Harry still scratching at the label on his bottle.

When he noticed me looking, he said, "Heard you got yourself a new boyfriend."

I wondered if I had heard him right. "What?"

He half-smiled and looked at me out of the corner of his eye. "Heard you got yourself a new boyfriend."

"Yeah, I guess I did." Where was he was going with this?

He nodded. "You let me know if he doesn't treat you right. Woman like you deserves to be treated like a queen." That was it. He didn't say anything more.

Stunned, I nodded. "Okay, Harry. Thanks." I took another drink.

A full minute of silence must have gone by before Mad Harry again spoke, "I thought a couple of times I might ask you out myself, but decided you deserved better. You let me know if he doesn't treat you right. I'll make sure he does."

These were more words than I had heard Harry speak in the last six months and, somehow, they moved me deeply. They were horribly scary when taken in context, but the gesture was sweet.

Impulsively, I reached over and put my arm across his back and hugged him as I quickly touched my head to his shoulder. He reached across his chest and cupped my face with his hand, lightly squeezing my face to his shoulder, never making eye contact.

As I pulled away and sat up on my stool, my heart thrashed. I'd hugged a murderer. What was I thinking? I looked down the bar and saw MJ staring at me, horrified. Her eyes were wide, mouth open, and she looked like she was about to come over the bar to rescue me. Maybe she should. Maybe I needed rescuing—from myself.

"Think Martha Jean's gonna bean me with a pool cue?" Harry continued to peel his label.

"No, she's just jealous." I held my breath and looked over to see his reaction. Harry's grin broke the tension and I couldn't help but laugh. Once I began to laugh, I couldn't seem to stop the flow. Every time I looked over at Mad Harry, his grin made me laugh harder and eventually I lost my breath and began to choke. This brought MJ down the bar to my rescue—Mad Harry or no.

After much coughing, crying, and backslapping, I recovered and eventually caught my breath. Having recovered before I wet my pants, I counted myself very lucky as I made a quick trip to the bathroom to empty my bladder and check my makeup.

When I returned, Jake was perched on the stool next to where I had been, talking with MJ. They both snapped shut like a couple of clams when I walked up. I smiled at Jake and climbed back onto my stool. Glancing over at Mad Harry, I saw a muscle working in his jaw. Had they said something to set him off? Was he jealous Jake had shown up while we were having fun? I made a mental note to watch him carefully. I didn't want this time bomb to explode in my face, or in the face of anyone I cared about.

Jake put his arm around me and pulled my stool closer, kissing me lightly on the lips. He smelled like soap and I couldn't resist the urge to nuzzle my face into his shoulder and drink in the smell of him. I hoped MJ was right and what he had to say would be good.

I looked up at the clock. It was a little after ten. As predicted, business had slowed after the band started and I couldn't blame the customers. The band was awful. I asked MJ, "You want me to come back there?"

She looked around and glanced at the clock as she answered, "You know what, why don't you spell me for a half hour. Then I'll take over and you two can head out. Willy and I'll catch up to you after I close."

"You got it." I slid off the stool and let myself behind the bar. Holding the gate open for MJ, I asked, "You want a drink?"

"Yeah, make me a Long Island Iced Tea. That should get me through the rest of the night." She took my spot between Jake and Mad Harry. As she got herself situated on the stool, she peeked over at Mad Harry, who silently concentrated on his beer.

I set a drink in front of MJ, smiled at Jake and headed down the bar to make sure everyone had full drinks…and the band played on. The next half-hour seemed to drag by. I felt sorry for MJ having to work in this. The crowd was sparse and the band was awful. Those last two hours would be pure hell for MJ. Poor thing!

Shortly before eleven, MJ slid back behind the bar and slapped me on the butt like a football player. "Okay, coach, send me in."

I laughed and handed her the bar towel from my back pocket. "It's all yours. Hey, you might want to tell the band to knock off early and switch back to non-band prices. Might liven the crowd and, if nothing else, you wouldn't have to finish out the night with a headache."

She brightened and threw her arms up in the air. "Great idea! We save money on the band. We give the customers a break. I give my headache a break. We warm up the pool tables. Everybody wins. Kat, you're a genius. Now, you go find out what your man has to say."

I nodded and returned to my stool. Jake asked if I wanted another drink and when I shook my head, he threw a five on the bar and stood to leave. We waved at MJ and as I turned, Mad Harry looked at me out of the corner of his eye. I reached out and patted him on the back as I went by and said, "Goodnight, Harry. Be careful going home." Harry nodded and lifted one hand to wave goodbye.

As Jake and I pulled out of the parking lot in Jake's truck, Mad Harry came out the back door. Jake saw it too. "That guy's creepy and I'm worried he likes you."

I looked over at Jake and chuckled as I put my arms around his neck. "I think I'd rather have him like me than not."

Jake harrumphed. "I'm not so sure it's good news either way. You be careful of him. Don't encourage him or flirt with him. He's weird and could get the wrong idea."

"I won't." I laid my head on his shoulder. "Where we going?"

Jake thought for a minute and said, "Let's find a quiet bar, somewhere we can talk without a band or any eavesdroppers."

"Uh-oh," I said, "this sounds ominous."

"No, not ominous. Good news. At least, I hope you're gonna see it that way. I don't know. We'll see."

I didn't like the sound of that, but I was determined not to make trouble where trouble didn't exist. So I nodded and snuggled in against his shoulder as he searched for a quiet place to talk.

We found a quiet neighborhood bar down the street and the waitress, whom neither of us knew, set us up in a corner booth with a couple of beers. We sat quietly for a few minutes and when I could stand the suspense no longer, I said, "Jake, what was it you wanted to talk about?"

He looked up at me like he was surprised, like it was the first he'd heard of it. "What?"

"You wanted to talk to me," I reminded him. "What did you want to talk about?"

The look of surprise quickly turned to that of a deer in headlights. "Well, I'm not sure where to start. I don't know how you're gonna take it."

I watched him for a minute as he stared at his drink and doodled on the tabletop with his finger. Then I took a deep breath and plunged in, "Well, we'll never know how I'm gonna take it if you never tell me. Why don't you just start at the beginning?" When he flinched, I added, "Or you can start at the end and work your way backwards, if you'd prefer."

He continued to stare at the table in silence for a few minutes and then looked up into my eyes and stared for a moment before he finally said, “I lied to you.”

My heart dropped to my stomach as I caught my breath to steady myself and said in a careful, measured tone, “About what?” Then I held my breath as I waited for the answer I didn’t think I wanted to hear.

“About being divorced,” he answered as he stared at the tabletop.

My heart dropped the rest of the way to my feet and my throat constricted as my eyes began to sting and my breath caught in my lungs. “What do you mean?” I whispered, desperately hoping I’d heard him wrong, wanting to hear the answer, and terrified of what he might say next.

“I lied about being divorced when I met you.” I could hardly hear him over the pounding of my heart. “I wasn’t divorced. I’ve been married the whole time we’ve dated. I know how you feel about honesty and I’m terrified you won’t forgive me. Willy told me you’d never date me if you knew I was married, so I lied. I’m sorry. I’m really sorry.”

I struggled to catch my breath and half gasped as the blood pounded in my ears. Tears streamed down my face, and a lump the size of Texas lodged in my throat. I couldn’t speak. All I could do was stare as he looked into my eyes. Apparently seeing the hurt there, he flinched and reached to take me in his arms.

Instinctively, I pulled back. He dropped his hands onto the table and waited for me to say something. I couldn’t. All I could do was stare through a veil of tears. My mind wouldn’t work. I couldn’t think. All I could hear was him saying, “I’ve been married the whole time we’ve dated.” It played over and over again in my mind until I wanted to scream. Finally, I took a deep breath and whispered, "Why would you do that to me? How could you hurt me that way?"

I could see the pain in his face. "I'm sorry. I fell for you the first night we talked at the bar. I couldn't stay away and I knew you wouldn't date a married man, even if I was separated. I didn't think I had any other choice."

I stared at him, incredulous. Was this his excuse? Was it all about him? Was he making this my fault? Who was this man?

"But you're married," I blurted out as the tears began to flow harder. "What made you think you had the right to date anyone? You know how I feel about infidelity, even if you're separated. How could you? How could you put me in this position?" By the time I got all this out, I was sobbing and searching for a napkin.

Jake started to speak, but stopped as the waitress came to the table and asked if I was okay. I told her I was fine. She asked, "You sure? If this guy's giving you trouble, I could get the bouncer to take care of it."

I thought about it as I looked at Jake. He stared at the waitress. Finally, I told her, "No. We're okay, just some things to work through. I'll be alright. Thanks."

She patted me on the shoulder and said, "Okay. You need me, you let me know, honey." She laid a stack of napkins on the table and walked away to wait on her other customers.

I took a handful of napkins and began to dry my tears. As he watched me closely, Jake said, "Katie, please forgive me. It's not like Brenda and I were living together. The marriage was dead. We had split up and were getting a divorce. It was just a matter of time before I'd be a free man. She's been living with another guy for months. It wasn't like I was cheating. I was afraid if I waited, you'd find someone else. I wanted to tell you the truth, but Willy said…well, I was afraid you'd move on and I was so drawn to you. Please forgive me."

"Jake, you're married. I don't care if you're living together or not. You're a married man. I can't do this," I told him.

He blinked as he apparently realized what I'd said. "No, I'm not married anymore."

This time it was my turn to blink and stare at him as I hiccupped. "What?"

"My divorce was final yesterday. I was afraid to tell you last night, so I put it off until tonight. That's why Willy and I went out for a drink before you got off. I had to work up the courage to tell you I'd lied. Katie, I'm divorced now. I'm a free man. Please, forgive me for lying to you. I want you more than I can begin to tell you. You can't end this now, not when we've finally got a chance to put it all together. Please."

My brain was stalled in the center lane as traffic whipped by me on all sides. Nothing would compute. I took a deep breath and got up from the table. "I need some fresh air and a few minutes to think. You stay here. I'll be back as soon as I can clear my head and think straight."

I spun on my heel and left the bar, leaving Jake alone at the table. As I headed out of the bar and across the parking lot, I spied a planter box at the back near the alley. I crossed the lot and sat on the side of the planter with my head between my knees as

I sucked in one lungful of cool air after another. My entire body shook and sweat trickled down my back like a whore in church. It felt like my heart would jump out of my chest, my nose was running, and it was a toss-up whether I'd pass out or throw up first.

As I sat there, breathing, wiping my nose, and trying to clear my head, a light flashed across the parking lot as the back door opened and closed. I looked up to find Jake watching me, with my purse in his hand. He didn't make a move to come close, just watched and waited. I stood and walked around the planter to sit on the far side, putting my back to Jake so I didn't have to see him as I struggled to pull myself together.

It took probably ten or fifteen minutes of steady breathing to calm my heart and slow the sweating. My nose was still running, but the shaking began to subside and I no longer felt like I was going to throw up. As my head cleared and I could form coherent thoughts again, I began to sort through everything he'd said.

Jake's divorce was final and he was now free to pursue a relationship. But he had lied to me all along—the old good news, bad news story. Was I happy about the good news?

Yes.

Could I forgive him the bad news? I looked over at the bar as he held my purse and watched me. In that moment, I knew the answer.

Yes.

I could forgive him almost anything, and I would forgive him this. God help me, I would forgive him this.

I got up and crossed the parking lot to where Jake leaned against the building. As I approached, he moved away from the wall and fumbled with my purse, unsure what to do with it. I walked up to him, grabbed the shoulder strap on the purse and looped it over his shoulder. Then I opened the back door and walked into the bar. Jake followed me to the table, sheepishly, with my purse strapped over his shoulder and swinging at his side. If the situation hadn't been so fraught with emotion, I would have laughed.

I sat in the booth and he slid in as close as he could, as close as he dared. Then he waited. I looked up at him. "You're a son-of-a-bitch and it was an unspeakable thing to do. If you ever do anything like that again, it'll be the end of us." He nodded as I continued, "But I think this relationship could be really wonderful if we can get past this. So I'll give you another chance to prove you can be honest with me. But you've got to know, my faith has been shaken and you'll have to earn my trust all over again. I won't be lied to, no matter what the justification."

As I finished what I had to say, a single tear rolled down my cheek and he reached out to wipe it away as he took me in his arms. "Katie, I'm so sorry. I know you have no reason to ever trust me again, but I swear I'll do everything in my power to earn back your trust. I don't think I could bear to lose you."

We sat there in each other's arms for the longest time. The ice melted in our drinks, the bartender announced "last call", and the waitress came around to pick up the glasses before we finally broke apart. She winked at me. "Well, he's a cute one, honey. I can see why you forgave him." Then she shook her finger at me as she turned to leave. "But don't let him make a habit of asking you to forgive him." She looked over at Jake as she finished, "He ain't that cute."

I looked at Jake and he blushed as he ducked his head and stared at the tabletop. "Let's go." I scooted out of the booth and waited for him to slide out. As we headed for the door, I noticed my purse swinging on his shoulder and started to laugh. "Nice purse you got there, guy."

He blushed as he realized he still had my purse on his shoulder and, not missing a beat, said, "Thanks. I got it on sale." With that, the ice was broken and we laughed all the way to the truck. As he opened the truck door, I started forward and he stopped me, pulling me into his arms to kiss me lightly on the lips. I looked up into his eyes as he kissed me again, softly and sweetly at first and then passionately, deeply, possessively.

As I leaned into him and clung tight, desperate to have his kisses wipe my mind of the lies he'd told, a thought wriggled its way into my consciousness. Were his lies the result of a character flaw or were they simply born of desperation. Did it matter? Could a relationship survive if it was rooted in a foundation built on a lie? Fear gripped my heart and squeezed it like a tube of toothpaste with the lid on. I'd forgiven him, but could I survive it?

Chapter Fourteen

The next couple of months went by quickly as Jake and I moved past our rocky start. We continued to alternate dinner at his house and mine while we talked in-depth about our relationships—our failures and successes. We talked about how important family was to us. We talked about our children, our hopes, and our dreams. We talked about the past as we worked to put it behind us and we talked about the future as we each hinted at the possibilities.

We grew very close and I began to trust Jake again. We had put the lies behind us and I believed everything was on the table now. I was certain it was only a matter of time before he proposed marriage and I was ready to accept.

The physical side of the relationship was still stalled, though. There was plenty of chemistry and the desire was certainly there for both of us, but we always stopped short of a big commitment. It seemed like we had some strange sort of unspoken agreement that it wasn't yet time to take things to the next level physically. So each night, we kissed passionately, hinted at a trip down the hall, and one or the other of us would muster up the courage to douse the fire and we'd go back to our respective homes and sleep alone.

One night, things went so far that our shirts ended up on the living room floor and we were halfway down the hallway when one of the boys called out for a drink of water. Talk about dousing the fire! In the frantic rush to get dressed again, I ended up wearing Jake's shirt while he hid in the laundry room because he couldn't get mine off once he'd jammed it over his head and stuffed one arm into it. Luckily, the boys were groggy enough they didn't notice the wardrobe switch when I delivered the glasses of water. It took almost five minutes to get Jake out of my shirt without ripping it. We took it as a sign it wasn't time.

One weekend, about two months after Jake's emotional revelation, we took the kids and went up to the ranch early on Saturday morning. I had a few days off and Jake had some business to take care of at the ranch. So we were going to stay until Tuesday or Wednesday, a short break for me and the boys while Jake got caught up and did a quick check on a few business items.

We arrived about eleven o'clock and piled out of the truck as Nell came out on the porch, grinning and waving. Both boys waved and called out, "Hi, Gramma!" as they rushed her and smothered her with kisses while Jake and I climbed the steps.

She hugged Jake and gave him a kiss on the cheek and then grabbed me, planting a kiss on my cheek and hugging me tight. "Oh, it's so good to see you again!" Then she looked over at Jake and asked, "When are you finally going to marry this girl so Dustin can really be my grandson?"

What a gal!

Jake turned bright red and stumbled forward as he looked up at her, clearly stunned. I couldn't help but laugh at his discomfort. We'd talked circles around marriage for a few weeks now. Neither one of us had actually said it out loud, but we were both thinking it. Now Nell had put it right out there on the table for everyone to deal with. I loved this woman and really wanted her for my mother-in-law. I couldn't imagine any other family I would want more than this one. What was not to love?

Jake was so surprised and flustered by his mother's blunt question and so at a loss to respond that he looked at me to see my reaction and forgot to watch his step. He ran right smack dab into the doorframe and hit his nose so hard, blood began to drip everywhere. The boys both squealed in delight and Nell and I just stood, stunned, and then began to laugh. Jake moved to the edge of the porch and ordered someone to get him a towel.

Nell was the first to recover. She ducked inside to get a towel and handed it through the door to me. "Here. You get this on his nose while I throw together an ice pack."

I took the towel and tipped his head back as I laid it over his nose. He looked so annoyed I couldn't help but laugh again, which earned me another scowl and something indecipherable muttered under his breath. Nell came out with an ice pack and we walked Jake over to the porch swing and replaced the towel with the pack. He sat down on the swing and leaned his head back against the side of the house.

As he sat with the ice pack on his nose, I sat on the swing next to him. Nell headed into the house, determined to feed the boys a solid lunch before they ate up every potato chip in the house.

We sat there, quietly, for a few minutes—me breathing in the country air and enjoying the view of the trees and mountains, Jake holding the ice pack on his nose, scowling. I loved this place. Coming to the ranch was always like coming home. I had such a sense of belonging here.

When the bleeding stopped, I took the towel and spit on a clean corner to wipe the blood off of Jake's face.

He smiled. "I've never let anyone but my mother wipe my face with spit on a hankie."

"It's not a hankie. It's a towel and you'd best shut up or I might tell you where my mouth has been."

Jake never missed a beat. "Ooooh, I love it when you talk dirty to me."

My face heated up like a hot iron to have my smart remark turned on me. To cover my embarrassment, I popped him on the side of the head with the towel and fled into the house before he could retaliate.

In the kitchen, both boys sat at the table munching on ham and cheese sandwiches while Nell stood at the stove stirring a huge pot of something hot and steamy. There were fresh made pies on the counter across the room and the kitchen was filled with the smell of home cooking. It was a scene straight out of a Norman Rockwell picture and I soaked it up like a dry sponge, overwhelmed by the rightness of it all, wanting so badly to be part of this picture.

Nell turned and raised one brow as she saw me in the doorway. She looked around and must have recognized what it was I had seen because she quietly crossed the room and hugged me tight. "Give him time, honey. He loves you. We all do. He'll ask. He just has to work up to it."

I hugged her back and smiled as I took a deep breath and swallowed the lump in my throat. My brain knew she was right, but my heart seemed to be holding out to hear the actual words.

In an attempt to change the subject, I asked about Cody's injuries. "How's Cody? Is he healing up okay?"

She nodded her head as she moved across the room, wiping her hands on her apron out of habit. "Yes. Doc says he's healing up better than expected. Said he thinks he'll be rideable again in a couple of weeks, if we start him out slow."

I smiled. "Oh, good. That's so wonderful. The poor guy's had a rough time of it. How's his mind? Will there be any lasting psychological problems?"

"His mind is okay," she replied. "He's gonna be fine. Some horses don't handle severe trauma very well. They're never the same afterwards, but Doc says he thinks he's gonna be okay. Course, there's a good chance he'll always be afraid of the big cats, but Doc doesn't see any other problems with him right now. Roy's been ground-workin' him a bit in the round pen and says he's doin' real good."

"Good." I felt Jake come up behind me.

"What's for lunch?" Jake asked as he crossed to the sink to wash up his face and hands.

"Looks like ham and cheese sandwiches," I told him.

"Ooooh, it's my favorite," he replied as he tried to pinch a corner off Tyler's sandwich and got his hand slapped for it.

"Sit down and I'll bring you your own." Nell turned from the counter with two plates in her hand.

Jake and I sat at the table as she put a sandwich in front of each of us and grabbed another one for herself. She sat down next to me, across the table from Jake. The boys chattered excitedly and everyone seemed content to sit and listen as they laid out about two months worth of activities they planned to cram into the next two days.

Just as we finished our meal, Roy came in and hung his hat on the hook next to the back door. He smiled. "Howdy. How y'all doin?" Taking a cup from the cabinet, he poured himself a cup of coffee and pulled a chair up to the table.

"Great," we all responded in unison. He told us Mac was headed over to Seligman this morning and said he would try to stop by the ranch this afternoon on his way back into Williams. We finished up lunch and the boys headed out to play while the rest of us sat at the table and talked over coffee.

After a half-hour or so, Roy got up and headed back to his chores. As he got to the door, he announced Mac was coming up the driveway and we all followed him out onto the porch.

Mac saw us come out onto the porch and pulled up to the house, rather than going straight to the barn. He waved as he got out of the truck and climbed the steps to the porch as he extended his hand to Jake. "Hey, good to see you two. How ya doin'?"

"We're doing great." Jake shook Mac's hand.

Mac smiled and reached to hug me. "Hello there, Miss Katie."

I hugged him back. "Good to see you, Mac."

Jake stepped to my side. "I hear you been takin' good care of our boy, Cody, while we've been gone."

Mac nodded. "Cody's doing fine as frog hair. He's a tough little bugger. Give him another month or two and you'll never know it ever happened. I'm amazed at how well his scars are healing up. I thought we might have a problem with some proud flesh on those wounds, but they're healing up damn near perfect."

"That's really good news," replied Jake as we all nodded in agreement. "Have a seat," he pointed to one of the porch chairs.

"Don't mind if I do." Mac took a seat and looked over at me. "Well, Miss Katie, looks like you're still puttin' up with this crabby old cowboy." He cocked his head in Jake's direction.

"Yeah, he keeps followin' me around and it's easier to let him in the front door than to keep tryin' to run him off."

Everyone laughed except Jake. "I'll get even with you for that."

His response drew even more laughter than my smart remark.

As we all visited, we learned Annie had taken first place in a Gymkhana and won herself a new saddle. Mac said he'd be taking her down to the valley for another competition in Wickenburg the following weekend and suggested we should meet them there. Jake and I agreed it would be fun and the boys, who had snuck back up on the porch, hooted and hollered about a weekend together in Wickenburg.

Jake winked at me. "So much for a romantic weekend get-away." Everyone laughed.

Bummer. We've never had a romantic weekend together. The kids are always with us.

Hmmm. I'd never thought about it before but now that I did, I wondered why we never went anywhere, just the two of us. In fact, we hadn't even had an adult date since Jake's divorce had become final. A sliver of fear snaked through me, but I shoved it away.

No sense looking for trouble where there isn't any. Things have been good. Stop imagining trouble where there is none.

The afternoon passed slowly as we drank ice tea on the porch and visited. The boys went to the barn to check on Cody and returned to report he had some "gnarly scars" that made him look really tough.

About two o'clock, Mac got up and announced he'd better check on the horse and hit the road before his wife had a posse out looking for him. Jake and I followed him out to the barn and watched as he checked Cody over. "He's doing great. Tell Roy to keep doin' what he's doin'. I suspect he's treating him with more than what I left but, whatever it is, it's working. Tell him to keep it up and be prepared to share his secret with me later."

"Okay. I'll tell him," Jake agreed. "Thanks for coming by, Mac."

"No problem. I don't think I need to come by again, unless Roy sees some change I need to know about."

"Okay. I'll tell him."

As we left the barn, Mac told Jake, "We're going to stay Friday and Saturday night out at the Rockin-J Ranch on the north end of Wickenburg. If you decide to come out, leave a message at the desk and we'll get it when we check in." Jake nodded his head as Mac hesitated and then added, "Too bad Nikki isn't doing Gymkhana any more. Annie really misses her. We all do."

Jake's eyes turned cold as he shrugged and shook his head. "Well, Mac, we all know the story behind that."

Mac nodded. "No way she'll let you take her, huh?"

"No. I can't even get weekend visits. She's convinced the court it's too risky, with me not being her biological father."

"Strange. You'd think she'd want the child support for the extra kid."

"It's all about control, Mac. She sure as hell wants something, but I can't for the life of me figure out what it is right now. Ever since her boyfriend dumped her, she's acted really weird."

My gut clenched.

Her boyfriend dumped her?

The admission hit me right between the eyes. Jake hadn't told me his ex-wife's boyfriend had dumped her.

Why?

Of course, we weren't married, so he wasn't required to tell me every little detail, but this was a detail I wouldn't have expected him to omit.

What does she want?

I had a sneaking suspicion I knew, and the thought left me cold all over.

Mac shook his head and headed for his truck as Jake and I watched him leave. The boys were down at the end of the driveway and they both waved at Mac as he pulled out the gate.

When Mac was gone, I turned to Jake and said, "You didn't tell me Brenda's boyfriend left her. When did he leave?"

Jake looked at me and I could see the anger simmer behind his eyes. "He left a couple of weeks ago. Packed up his bags while she was at work and never came home or called. I told her he was a jerk, but she wouldn't listen." Then he shrugged and turned toward the house. "Her problem, not mine."

A cold chill ran up my spine as I watched him head for the house. About halfway, he turned and scowled. "You coming?" I nodded and blindly followed. My mind and stomach churned, and I wasn't sure if the chill I felt came from inside me or from him. Clearly he didn't want to talk about it now, but we'd have to eventually.

Tired from the drive and the change in altitude, we all went to our rooms to take a quick nap before dinner. Even the boys napped on the living room floor in front of the television.

I was grateful for the time alone to sift through my thoughts. I didn't like that Jake had kept something from me.

Why? Is he trying to spare me the concern or is there another reason?

Chapter Fifteen

I woke about an hour later, exhausted, and dragged myself out to the kitchen to see who was about. I found Nell at the sink, peeling potatoes for dinner and offered to help. She sat me down at the table with a bag of potatoes, a peeler, and a bucket for the skins as she informed me Jake had headed in to town about five minutes ago to pick up some parts for the tractor. As she watched me from the corner of her eye, she added. "He left in quite a hurry. Everything okay?"

I shrugged. "I don't know. He turned strange when Mac brought up Nikki and Brenda. Been quiet ever since." Nell didn't say anything and I was afraid to look up, so I concentrated on peeling potatoes and tried hard not to cry. I didn't understand what was going on either, but I'd be damned if I was going to be one of those clingy, helpless women who got desperate and clutching when her man got cranky. I tried to convince myself that's all it was. He was just a bit out of sorts and needed some time alone. I resolved to entertain myself and the boys this weekend and to give Jake the space he needed to sort it all out. He needed time to clear his head. After all, his divorce was still new and the scars hadn't had time to heal completely. I prayed I was right.

Halfway through dinner, we heard Jake's truck pull into the driveway. Nell scowled and snorted as she looked toward the door, but held her tongue.

Roy peeked at me out of the corner of his eye. "He musta had to go all the way into Phoenix for those parts."

Nell snorted again, but said nothing.

I stuffed my mouth full of potatoes and forced them down my painfully constricted throat.

Several minutes went by and still Jake didn't come into the house. We all finished dinner and helped Nell clear the table. The boys clamored to play a board game and I told them if they could get a bath and be ready for bed in twenty minutes, I'd play a game with them. Roy and Nell even offered to play too. Delighted, the boys raced down the hall for pajamas and towels.

Roy, Nell and I all pitched in and washed the dishes in silence, apparently all at a loss for what to say. When the dishes were done, Roy told us to start the game without him. He would check the animals and be right back. As he headed out the door and walked toward the barn, I went to the screen door and looked out. I knew there was a small efficiency apartment over the barn that no one ever used, but there was a light on up there now. Was it Jake? Had I made him angry? A moment later, a shadow moved across the window over the barn. It was Jake. I turned from the door to find Nell watching me.

Our eyes met and she said, "Don't worry, honey, it'll be okay. It takes some men longer than others to get their bearings."

I didn't respond. I wasn't sure I believed it would be okay. I prayed it would, but sometimes the answer to prayers is, "No."

When the boys returned, clean and damp from their baths, Nell and I set up the game and sat down to play. About a half-hour into the game, Roy returned and joined us at the table. There was heaviness in my heart and in the air when we first started the game, but the boys were oblivious to it and soon had lifted all our spirits. It was late and Nell and I had begun to hint this was the last round.

We were all laughing and cutting up when David came through the door. The boys immediately erupted in cheers for "Uncle David" and begged him to join us.

David laughed and pulled a chair up next to me. "I'll help Katie play her hand."

I blushed and looked down at the floor as he leaned over and kissed me on the cheek, whispering quietly, "You're still the prettiest girl around, you know that, Slick."

I laughed and tried to change the subject. "How's the leg?"

"Good as new." With a wink, he added, "Wanna see?"

I shook my head and rolled my eyes.

The boys were so excited and we were having so much fun that Nell and I relented and we played two more rounds. Finally, we packed up the game just as Jake came through the door. The whole room went silent for a moment before the boys yelled for Jake to carry them upstairs. Jake looked around and saw David next to me. His eyes turned hard and the muscle in his jaw jumped as he swung around and scooped up both boys, heading for the living room without a word.

As the door swung closed behind them, David put his hand on my shoulder and squeezed. We sat there in silence for a moment as the tears welled up in my eyes again.

Nell and Roy excused themselves and left the kitchen to say goodnight to the boys.

After a few more minutes, it was David who broke the silence. "Katie, I truly hope the two of you can make this work, for your sake and for the boys. But I want you to know I'm always here for you whether it does or doesn't." There was another moment of silence before he added, "I really mean it."

The painful lump in my throat prevented speech, but I reached out and laid my hand on his and squeezed as I nodded my head.

David stood and pushed his chair back from the table as he leaned forward and again kissed me gently on the cheek. He stood behind me quietly for a moment, with both hands on my shoulders, and then walked past me and out the door. I was glad he hadn't looked back because I really didn't want him to see me cry. I swallowed hard and took a deep breath. This was no time to fall apart. There were too many people around and I still had to tuck the boys in for the night. I promised myself that later, when I was alone in my bed, I'd open the faucets wide and let myself have a good, old-fashioned cry.

Just as I wiped my eyes on my sleeve and stood, Nell and Roy came back into the kitchen and she asked if anyone wanted more coffee. Roy and I both shook our heads. She turned the coffeepot off and said, "Well, then I'm off to bed."

Roy said he was too and as he passed in front of me, headed for the back door, he stopped and put his hand on my shoulder and squeezed. "Goodnight, princess. You let me know if our young prince needs a good thumping."

With that, the tears returned. I put my head down and reached up and patted his hand before he walked out the door and headed for the barn.

I looked up at Nell and saw tears in her eyes too. "You ever thought about going after Roy?"

She blinked and stared as if I'd grown a toe off the end of my nose. "Roy? No. Never thought about it."

"Well, you should." I took a deep breath. "He'd be a great catch."

She stared at me with her mouth open as I got up and headed out the kitchen door to the porch. It was a chilly, clear night and I sat out on the front porch for a few minutes and tried to clear my mind. When it wouldn't clear, I decided maybe a good night's sleep would help. As I got up off the porch swing to head back in the house, a shadow moved out by the barn. I turned my head to get a better look. It was David. He stood in the doorway of the barn, leaned against the doorframe, and watched me. The light was on behind him and his face was in shadow, so I couldn't see his expression, but I sensed he'd been there for some time. Somehow, it comforted me as I turned and went inside.

Jake was nowhere to be seen. I figured he'd gone straight to his room, so I went upstairs and gave each of the boys a goodnight kiss and a nuzzle as I tucked the blankets tight around them and headed back across the landing to my room. Nell had insisted Jake stay in the downstairs bedroom and I remain in Jake's room upstairs because she said I should have the quieter room closer to the boys.

The light was off when I entered the bedroom, but I knew where everything was by now and the dark was a comfort, so I left it off as I walked across the room. Just as I reached the bed, I sensed I wasn't alone. I stopped and listened, trying to see through the pitch-blackness in the room. I smelled soap. Jake. I waited for him to announce himself. When he didn't, I asked, "What's wrong?"

I felt him move in the dark and felt his arms go around me as he pulled me to him. I wrapped my arms around his waist and laid my head on his chest.

"Katie, I love you so much. I'm so afraid I'm going to do something stupid to screw this all up and then one day I'll wake up and wonder where you went."

I swallowed hard and filled my lungs with air to steady myself as I softly whispered, "I'm not going anywhere, Jake. I love you too." Regaining my composure, I found my voice again. "You'd have to beat me off with a stick to get rid of me."

I raised my head and his lips brushed mine. His kiss was soft and warm as his tongue slipped in briefly and then he ended it way before I was ready for it to end. I laid my head against his chest and simply listened to him breathe for a few moments. As I held him close, I heard his heart begin to beat faster and his breathing became ragged. My own heart matched the pace of his as I anticipated what was to come next. It was way past due.

Suddenly, he pulled me tight against him and as I lifted my face to his, warm lips came down hard on mine. This time, the kiss was passionate and demanding, his tongue dancing with mine as he delved deeper, his lips crushing, his hands pulling me tight. As he pressed his body forward into mine, the dresser pressed into my back. I leaned against it to steady myself and he pressed against me even harder. His hands roamed up and down my sides as if they searched for something they couldn't find. Goose bumps crawled across my body as he moved one hand up under my hair to circle the back of my neck and the other hand slowly up under my shirt in back.

The kiss deepened and became more frantic, until the urgency pounded in my head like a hammer. Then both of his hands were inside my shirt and my breath came in quick, ragged gasps as he worked at the hooks on my bra. Frustrated with hooks that refused to budge, Jake moved one hand to the front and gently began to plant kisses on my chest as he ran his fingers over my belly. I gasped and arched my back as a shiver shot through my body.

He moaned as his tongue slid slowly along the edge of my bra, dipping below the laced edges. His hands slid around my waist and again worked at the hooks in back. Just as the hooks released and his hands began to move forward, he froze. His body went rigid and I heard him suck in a lungful of air slowly as he dropped his hands to his sides and stepped away from me.

I was confused, but I didn't want this to end. I moaned an objection and reached to pull him close again, but he took another step back. There was nothing but air where he'd been just seconds before. I was stunned, and tried to get my bearings. "What's wrong? Why are you stopping?"

I sensed him move further away. "I'm sorry, Katie. I can't do this right now. I have to...well, it wouldn't be right, not now." I heard him drag in a ragged breath as he continued, "You'd better get some sleep. It's been a long day." With that, the door opened and closed. I couldn't hear him breathe anymore and when I reached out again, he wasn't there. I found the light switch and the light flooded the room. I was alone.

My heart constricted and I dragged in a heavy breath.

What the hell is happening?

I wanted to run after him and make him tell me what was going on, but I knew he wouldn't tell me anything until he was ready.

Numb and confused, I shivered as I mechanically changed into my sleep shirt. Then I crossed the room and killed the light, returned to the bed and climbed under the covers, where I cried until there were no tears left. When I finally fell asleep, I was plagued with the same dreams I'd had in the afternoon, dreams of passions crushed and unfulfilled promises, dreams of love lost.

The sun was up early the next morning and when I finally admitted defeat and dragged myself out of bed, it was all I could do to put one foot in front of the other. I dressed and attempted to fix the bags under my eyes with makeup, but to no avail. In another admission of total and utter defeat, I shrugged and stuffed my feet into my slippers and headed downstairs in search of coffee.

Maybe that'll help…something has to.

As I entered the kitchen, Nell was at the stove, humming. When she heard me shuffle in, she turned. "Good morning. Sleep well last night?" As I looked up, she froze, losing the grin and narrowing her eyes. "What the hell happened to you?" She fisted her hands on her hips.

I continued to shuffle toward the coffeepot. "It's that bad, huh?"

She sniffed. "Well, it don't look bad if you cried all night, but I thought..." She stopped for a minute, apparently considering what she was about to say. Then she scowled and turned back toward the stove. "No, I guess it don't look all that bad. You look fine, honey, pour yourself a cup of coffee and sit. I'll fix you up some breakfast and you'll be fit as a fiddle in no time."

"I don't want breakfast, thanks. My stomach couldn't handle it. Maybe just some toast, if you don't mind?" I poured a cup of coffee and dropped into a chair.

"You need to eat." When I looked at her pleadingly, she relented. "Okay, I'll fix you some toast."

As she set the toast on the table, she sat in a chair next to me. After a couple sips of coffee, she finally asked, "What happened last night?"

"Nothing. Absolutely nothing."

She looked at me hard, as if trying to decide if I was telling the truth or not. Then she patted my shoulder as she rose and turned back toward the stove again. "When I headed for bed last night, I thought I heard Jake's voice in your room. I thought...well, I hoped you two had made up and everything was okay now."

I shook my head and mindlessly stirred my coffee. "No. Everything's not okay. Jake <u>was</u> in my room when I headed for bed, but he just said he loved me but was afraid he'd screw everything up, kissed me goodnight, and left me alone in the dark." I looked up at her. "Something's wrong, Nell. Something's bad wrong and I don't know what it is. I don't know how to fix it."

Nell's face turned cold and hard. "It's that bitch he was married to, is what it is. She made everyone miserable the whole time she was married to him and now she's gonna make the rest of his life miserable."

I shrugged helplessly. "I don't know how to fight it. I love him. But if he won't let me in, I don't know how to help him. And I don't know how to hold on when he keeps me outside."

She got up and came around the table, leaned over and wrapped her arms around me. "Honey, you hang in there. He'll come to his senses. You're a good woman and he knows it. He's not a stupid man. No way he's gonna let you get away. You hold on, ya hear me?"

I started to cry and took a deep breath to plug the dam. Soggy toast wouldn't solve my problem. I had to buck up and clear my mind if I wanted to find a way to sort through this.

The boys and I busied ourselves around the house as Jake stayed gone most of the day. I tried to read a book but found myself reading the same sentence over and over again, with absolutely no comprehension. So I put the book down and took a glass of ice tea out to the porch to sit and think. Nell and Roy both joined me for a few minutes, but there wasn't anything to say so they eventually left me alone with my thoughts.

I went back to trying to read and after a few minutes, I had a prickly feeling on the back of my neck, like when someone's watching you. I looked around to find David on horseback off to the left of the barn. They told me he'd gone out early in the morning looking for strays. When he realized he'd been spotted, he took his hat off and waved it in the air. I smiled and waved back. He turned the horse and headed for the barn.

As I watched him ride toward the barn, I thought about him, about Jake, about Nell, Roy, Tyler, the ranch...everything. In the short time I'd known them, I'd fallen in love with the McAllisters and everything about them. On some level, they'd begun to fill the hole the loss of my parents had created. The thought of losing them was too painful to even consider.

The rest of the day passed uneventfully. Dinner was quiet, since Jake hadn't returned and no one really knew what to say. The boys didn't pick up on the mood at the table, so they chattered all through dinner, which was fine with everyone. It saved us the effort of trying to make small talk. We let the boys chatter, answering questions as they came up. After dinner, the boys settled in to watch a movie with Roy and Nell, while I went out to sit on the porch alone.

I wasn't alone long when David came out and sat in the chair next to me. Neither of us spoke. The moon was full and we sat in silence. Looking out across the ranch, I listened to frogs and crickets sing in the dark. The silence was comfortable and neither of us felt the need to talk. Somehow, it lent me strength just to sit quietly beside David. After about an hour, he stood and smiled. "Well, the sun comes up early around here. Guess I'd better hit the sack. You okay?"

I smiled up at him and nodded. "Yeah. I'm good. Thanks for the company...and for not needing conversation. It was nice to sit and not have to make small talk."

David smiled again and nodded as he turned away, waving at me as he headed down the road toward his house. I sat there for a few more minutes and watched him as he walked home. Again, I wondered what life would have been like if I'd chosen David instead of Jake. They were so much alike, yet so very different in so many ways. It seemed Jake always had secrets he held back from me. While David was always there with his hand out, ready to help me get back to my feet when life knocked me down.

No! Don't go there. David is only being nice. I love Jake and he loves me. He needs me. He just doesn't fully realize it yet. I just need to give him time, give him his space for a bit and he'll come around.

I just needed to get hold of myself and quiet the voices in my head, those stupid voices that kept questioning everything he did and whispering doubts in the back of my brain.

Chapter Sixteen

I awoke with the sun the next morning and, feeling a bit more energized than I had the day before, decided it would be a good day to ride.

Maybe the boys would like to go out.

I dressed quickly and headed out to the kitchen in the relentless pursuit of coffee.

The house was quiet and the kitchen was empty. Apparently, I was the first one up, so I set about making the coffee. Once I had the coffee started, I decided it would be fun to make breakfast too. Pancakes were my specialty, so pancakes it would be. First, I put some bacon on to fry while I rounded up all the fixin's I needed for pancakes. I'd never cooked for a group this big, so it took a few minutes to figure out how much batter I needed, but I decided to err on the conservative side. I could always make more if I ran short or if Jake had returned last night and decided to join us.

Just as the coffee was done and the bacon came out of the pan, I turned to find Nell in the doorway, chuckling. "You taking over my job?" She laughed and crossed the kitchen to pull a coffee cup out of the cupboard.

"Nope. It was my turn to contribute. I thought you could use a break." When she quirked a brow, I added, "Besides, I needed coffee and, I guess I've got some nervous energy to work off."

Nell smiled and hugged me before she grabbed a second cup for me and poured out two cups of coffee.

I had just started on the pancakes when David came in the back door and stopped dead in his tracks at seeing me at the stove and Nell at the kitchen table. His eyebrows wrinkled together. "What's wrong with this picture?"

Nell smiled. "Katie gave me the morning off. Nice, huh?"

David blinked slowly. "I don't know. Can she cook? I don't much fancy being poisoned on such a beautiful day."

I wheeled around and waived the pancake turner threateningly in the air. "You come over here and say it again, Mister, and I'll show you another way to die on a fine day like today."

He laughed and sat at the table with his hands in the air. "No, I think I'll sit quietly way over here, out of reach of any weapons, until Roy comes to get coffee for both of us."

It struck Nell so funny she snorted coffee out her nose, just as Roy came into the kitchen from the porch. Roy wasn't at his sharpest yet, so he shuffled over to the cupboard to get a cup, oblivious to what went on around him.

David spoke up. "Uh, Roy, would you get me a cup of coffee too?"

This brought Roy's head up and he looked around as he reached for another cup. When he saw everyone staring at him, he froze and looked around at each of us. Then he looked down. "What? Is my fly open?"

We all collapsed in laughter as Nell struggled not to snort coffee out her nose again. Figuring he'd been the brunt of a joke and not much caring, Roy simply shrugged, poured two cups of coffee, and sat next to David. After a minute, he looked at David and asked, "Anything I need to know?"

David smiled and sipped his coffee as he looked at me and shook his head. "No, not really. I think the girls are plotting to poison us."

Without missing a beat, old Roy nodded his head and took another sip of his coffee. "Okay. Just wondered."

I shook my head and laughed as I took the first two pancakes off the fire and set the plate down in front of David. "Okay, Mister, since you're so smart this morning, you get to be the official taster. If you survive, Roy gets the next plate." Then I wiggled my eyebrows up and down for effect.

David's brows shot up as he looked down at the pancakes on the plate in front of him. He leaned over to Roy and said, "Roy, you gonna help me out here?"

Roy smiled as he continued to drink his coffee. "Son, I think you're on your own. I don't mind waiting for the second batch to come off the grill."

David scowled. "Traitor."

Roy continued to drink his coffee.

By the time the second batch came off the stove, David was half way through his and was managing to "ooooh" and "aaaah" through a mouth full of pancakes. "Wow, these are really good. Didn't know you could cook, Katie. Might have to keep you around!"

We heard the back door close and turned to find Jake in the doorway, scowling at David. "That would be my job, little brother, not yours." Then he turned his scowl on me briefly as he stomped through the kitchen, headed for the living room.

Everyone in the room turned to see my reaction. Determined not to allow Jake's foul mood to spoil another day for everyone, I did the only appropriate thing I could do. I stuck my tongue out at his retreating back.

Apparently, it wasn't the reaction anybody expected, as they stared at me, stunned, until I set Roy's plate in front of him and mumbled, "Jackass!" As I turned back to the stove, David began to laugh, which brought everyone out of their stupor and we all had a good, quiet laugh at Jake's rude behavior.

After the boys had come down and everyone had eaten their fill, except Jake, we all sat around the table and talked about what we had planned for the day. I asked the boys if they wanted to go for a horseback ride and they were thrilled. They begged to take a picnic lunch and I agreed it sounded like fun. Nell insisted we should go ahead and get ready while she prepared the food. David hinted he would like to go with us and suggested he knew a great place down at the creek to wade and do some crawdaddin'. The boys literally erupted with delight at the thought of crawdaddin'. I wasn't sure it was a good idea for David to go with us, and I could tell Nell didn't like it much either, but the boys were so excited I couldn't refuse. "Okay," I said, "we'll all go. Then I looked over at Roy. "You wanna go with us?" Maybe he would rescue me.

He looked at Nell and she nodded discreetly, so he agreed. "Sure, I haven't been on a picnic in a long time. Don't reckon it'd hurt me any to go along." Then he smiled as he turned away, adding, "Never know when you might need a chaperone."

David scowled at Roy, but didn't say anything as he headed out to get the horses ready to go.

The boys and I headed for our rooms to change into riding clothes and we were all back out in the kitchen in about ten minutes. Nell packed the sandwiches and drinks into the saddlebags Roy had brought in from the barn. Roy and I grabbed up the saddlebags and began to shoo the chattering boys out the door. At the barn, we found David with five horses saddled and ready to go.

As we rode out away from the ranch, Roy took the lead. The boys rod next to him and pummeled him with questions about rabbits, lizards, mountain lions and all sorts of other creepy, crawly, and scary critters. David settled in next to me and we followed along behind Roy and the boys, quietly enjoying the scenery and the beautiful day. Occasionally, David would point out some landmark or tell a quick story about something that had happened when they were kids at some point along the trail but, for the most part, we rode quietly.

About two hours out, we found the creek and followed it until we came to the spot David had suggested. We dismounted and tethered the horses as the boys clamored for us to hurry up. The creek was beautiful and the spot David had selected was gorgeous. The water crashed over and around large rocks, creating the steady sound of rushing water. It was cool and shady and surrounded by a beautiful green meadow. Trees lined the edge of the creek and hung over the water. It was so inviting, my first thought was to wade out into the creek and find a dry rock to sit on.

As I stood on the bank and looked for a good rock, David came up beside me. "Well, what do you think?"

I smiled as I answered, "It's beautiful, David. Absolutely beautiful. Thank you." When I looked back toward the creek, I spied the perfect rock and headed for it as I called over my shoulder, "Now, I'm going to go find my rock and sit on it."

David threw back his head and laughed as he watched me pick my way across the creek to a large, flat rock in the middle of the stream. As I reached the rock and plopped myself down on it, I looked back and waved at everyone still on the bank.

The boys took it as permission to explore and they both hit the water feet first and were completely soaked within three seconds. Roy shook his head and laughed as he sat down on the creek bank, while David began to pick his way across the creek to join me on my rock.

Sitting next to me on the rock, David smiled. "Good choice. Nice rock."

"Yeah," I said as I smiled and looked around, patting the rock possessively as I continued, "it's a *great* rock. Look at the way it sits here in the middle of the stream. It doesn't rock or budge. It's big and tough. It's immovable and makes the water go around it. Yeah, this is a great rock." I nodded my head, threw my shoulders back, and stretched my arms wide as I continued to smile and look at David. "Yep, this is <u>my</u> rock."

David smiled until I thought his face might split and shook his head, but said nothing as he watched me wiggle my butt to find exactly the right spot on "<u>my</u> rock".

After a few minutes, the boys announced they were starved, so David jumped up and headed for the horses to get our lunch. He set the food out on a blanket and left Roy and the boys to fend for themselves, while he brought some sandwiches and juice out to the rock.

We sat and ate lunch quietly, neither of us eager to break the spell nature seemed to weave around our spot on my rock. We ate as we listened to the birds in the trees and the water crashing over the rocks. It was magical and the longer I sat on my rock, the more my spirits lifted.

When the sandwiches were gone and we were comfortably stuffed, David turned and looked at me. “Hey, Slick, thanks for sharing your rock with me.”

I looked up at him and shook my head. “Oh no, I did not share my rock with you. I allowed you to sit on it for a while, but don’t think for a minute that means I shared it. This is my rock and don’t you ever forget it.”

David laughed and shook his head as he put his hands up in the air. “Okay, I’ve got it. I can see we’re going to have to name this Katie’s Rock.”

As I looked at him and cocked one brow, he laughed again and nodded as he added, “And you don’t share the rock. You might graciously allow someone to sit on the rock beside you, but you don’t share it. Did I get it right?”

I stuck my chin in the air and tried to put on a regal air as I nodded. He shook his head and chuckled.

After about an hour of rock-sitting, lunch, and watching the boys explore and splash in the water, we all agreed it was time to head toward the house. David stood and offered me his hand. I knew if I stood up while he was still on the rock, I'd be forced to stand far too close for comfort. So I declined the offer and waived him off as I said, "I can manage this myself. You go round up those boys."

David grinned teasingly as he turned to pick his way back to shore. "Coward."

I stood and started down off the rock, but somehow I lost my footing on the first step and pitched forward, clutching for something to save myself from a good dunking. I grabbed the sleeve of David's shirt, spun him around, and pulled him off the rock he was about to step off of. That sent him backwards into the water, with me landing flat on top of him in the creek. Fortunately, we managed to miss any large rocks and landed in a slice of sand between the rocks where the water was only about six or eight inches deep. We lay there and sputtered, trying to get the water out of our eyes and mouths, as the boys whooped and hollered from shore.

When I caught my breath and opened my eyes, I found David's face only inches from mine. He grinned suggestively and moved one arm up to circle my waist and pull me closer as he whispered, "Hey, Slick, nice move, but you could have picked someplace more private."

I gasped.

OhmiGod!

I was pressed firmly against his body, breasts to chest and hips to hips. I tried to scramble off of him, but he held me tight. "Whoa. Hold on. Let's take this slow and easy so no one gets hurt, okay?"

I took a deep breath and nodded. As we untangled ourselves and David rolled out from under me, he stood and pulled me up after. We made it to shore without further incident, only to find the boys giggling with their hands over their mouths and Roy with his back to us, shoulders shaking.

I put my head down and walked around to the other side of my horse, in an attempt to hide my embarrassment, as I grabbed the blanket off the ground and set out to dry myself and the boys the best I could for the trip home.

OhmiGod, how embarrassing. Leave it to you to pull a stunt like that. Damn good thing Jake wasn't here. He wouldn't talk to you for a month.

That thought took me by surprise. It was an accident. Why should I be worried about Jake being pissed about an accident? But it was true. He was always pissed when David was around, no matter what was going on. This was bull.

Do I really want to live this way? Is this what it would be like with Jake? I keep thinking he'll settle down, but what if he doesn't?

My breath hitched in my chest and I twisted my head to relieve the kink that immediately settled in the back of my neck. I set that thought aside and continued drying the boys off. I couldn't think about that now. I'd pull it out again later, when I was back at the house alone.

David came around the horse and leaned against him as he watched me dry the boys. When I was done and turned toward him, he held his arms out as he grinned shamelessly. "I'm next." I felt my face go hot as I wadded up the blanket and threw it. He chuckled behind me as I stomped off to help the boys mount up.

The ride back went much faster than the ride out, since the boys were beginning to tire and didn't constantly clamor for side trips or stops to check out something they'd seen.

We arrived back at the ranch about three o'clock to find Jake waiting on the front porch and he looked madder than a rooster under a bucket. As we reined in, he scowled at David and then turned a dark look on me as he snapped, "It would have been nice if you'd checked with me before you decided to head out on an all-day jaunt. I've waited hours for you to return. We need to pack up and head home."

Stunned and angry that he was being so unreasonable, I dismounted and put my hands on my hips as I snapped, "How the hell was I supposed to know? You told me we'd stay until Tuesday or Wednesday. Besides, you've been in such a snit ever since we got here, it was impossible to talk to you."

As Jake shot me a hard look, a muscle jumped in his jaw. The boys whined for more time. Jake whirled and headed into the house as I informed the boys it was time to put the horses away and pack up.

David said he had something to check on and told us to get a couple of the boys in the barn to take care of the horses, as he mounted up and rode off down the road at a pretty good clip.

By the time we'd taken care of the horses and walked back to the house, Jake was already loading the boys' bags in silence. I went inside and gathered my bags together while the boys made the rounds in the barn to say their good-byes.

When we were all loaded up, we said our good-byes to Nell and Roy and got in the truck to head home. I waved as we pulled out the driveway, I wondered when I would see them again—wondered <u>if</u> I would see them again.

At the front gate, we spotted David on his horse just outside the gate. Jake pulled over and David rode up on his side of the truck.

Jake said, “I’ll confirm the price with the buyer and get back to you later in the week.”

David nodded and responded, “Okay. You drive careful.” He leaned over and looked in the window at me. “It was real nice to see you again, Slick, and thanks for the swim. If my brother gets out of line, you be sure to give me a call.” Then he grinned as he added, “I won’t be able to straighten him out, but I’ll sure be happy to help you forget all about his sorry ass.” Then he winked at me as Jake scowled and the boys giggled in the backseat.

I couldn’t help but chuckle. “Thanks for the offer. I’ll be sure to keep it in mind.” I was damn tired of tiptoeing around Jake’s feelings and apparently David was too.

The boys slept the whole way home and Jake didn’t talk at all, so it was a very quiet ride. I was angry and frustrated and the long, quiet drive did nothing to soften my anger. Jake drove us to the house, unloaded our bags and set them in the living room. He hugged Dustin goodbye and told him he’d see him in a couple of days. Then he turned to me and took me in his arms. I remained pretty stiff, not at all happy with him.

When I looked up into his face, I knew he could read the questions in my eyes, but all he told me was, “Katie, this isn’t about you and me. It isn’t anything you’ve done or haven’t done. I just need a couple of days to work through some things. Please be patient with me and allow me some space. I’ll call you in a couple of days. Okay?”

I swallowed my anger and nodded as he leaned over to kiss me. I expected a simple, warm peck on the lips, something very controlled, without commitment or passion. He surprised me. This kiss was raw, filled with passion and frustration as his lips crushed mine. It sent shivers all the way to my toes as I leaned into Jake and hung on for dear life. There was so much passion and hunger in his kiss that I thought my breath would be completely sucked from my body before it ended. When it did end, I couldn't move. My knees threatened to buckle under me as I clung to him. He did the same. We were like two drowning people clinging to the same life preserver, both too afraid to move.

I felt him take a deep breath as he pulled away and turned for the door. I said, "Jake, I love you." I hated the tremor in my voice.

He stopped, but didn't turn or look back. He simply said, "I love you too," and left.

Dammit! He didn't even look at me. What the hell is going on? He says it isn't anything I've done. Then what the hell is it? Is Nell right? Is it Brenda?

As I watched him back out of the driveway and pull away, I felt the distance between us grow wider with every spin of his tires and wondered what tomorrow would bring—and if we would survive it, if I would survive it.

Chapter Seventeen

Two days went by before I heard from Jake again—two very long days. Dustin and I amused ourselves with movies and board games, but we were both missing Jake and Tyler. I worried constantly about what was wrong but all I had were theories, and none of them was any good.

Finally, about nine o'clock Wednesday night, Jake called. When I answered, there was silence for a minute and then he said, "Hi. It's me. How are you?"

"Hi, me. I'm fine. How are you?" My heart was pounding.

"I'm okay. I miss you."

"Yeah? Well, I miss you too. What do you suppose we oughta do about it?" I held my breath, waiting for his answer.

He was silent for a minute before he replied, "I was thinking we could go out Friday night, just the two of us. Maybe get some dinner and have a drink somewhere. We need to talk."

"Friday?" Friday seemed an eternity away. "Okay, I'll get Mark to take Dustin."

"Okay. I'll pick you up at seven. See you then." He hung up. I was stunned at the abruptness with which the call ended, but consoled myself with the thought of seeing him Friday night.

I hung up the phone.

Where's he been the last few days? What happened?

My stomach was turning itself inside out and I could feel the vein in my forehead pounding.

What happens Friday? Good news or bad? What did he mean we needed to talk? Is that good talk or bad talk?

Weren't "we need to talk" the four worst words in the dating language? My mind whirled and my heart pounded in my chest.

Taking a deep breath, I called Mark. When he answered, I said, "Hi. It's me. You got plans for Friday night?"

"No, nothing special. Why?"

"I've got a date. Wondered if you wanted to take Dustin for the evening."

"Sure. Why don't you let him stay overnight? I've got a side job to do on the other side of town and I can bring him home early on Saturday morning."

"Okay. Thanks."

"Hey, you okay?" he asked.

"Yeah, I'm okay. Things are a bit...well, I don't know." I stammered as I tried to decide whether or not I really was okay.

"Got a problem with Jake?" he asked, like he had some sort of crystal ball.

"No, not really. Well, maybe." I sighed. "I don't know. He wants to talk."

"Uh-oh. Well, good luck. I hope everything turns out okay for you."

There was a moment of uncomfortable silence before I said, "Yeah, thanks. Can I drop Dustin off early so I can get ready without the interruptions?"

"Sure," Mark replied. "As a matter of fact, why don't I run by and pick him up on my way home from work. Then you'll have plenty of time to get ready."

"Okay. Thanks again." I hung up the phone and sat for a few minutes as my mind churned at super warp speed.

What does Jake want to talk about? Am I okay?

Unfortunately, I wouldn't know the answer to either question until Friday. After a few minutes, I took a deep breath and resolved to try and put it aside. Worry wouldn't make it any better. There was nothing to do but get on with my life…and wait.

Hurry up and freaking wait!

I picked up the phone and dialed MJ. "Hello."

"Hi, it's me," I said.

"Hey, Kat, how ya doin'?"

"Well, I guess I'm okay. You talked to Willy today?"

"Yeah, talked to him this morning. Why?"

"Jake called and said he wants to go out on Friday. Said we have to talk. He said he misses me, but he was very abrupt. I wondered if Willy said anything to you."

She hesitated for a minute. "No, he didn't. You okay?"

"Yeah, I'm okay. I hoped you might know what was up. He's been so strange and I'm half afraid he's going to break it off. And to be honest with you, I don't know how I feel about that. He's been such a jackass lately."

"You can't be serious. He's nuts about you. I'd be more inclined to think maybe he's gonna propose. Oh, honey, don't get yourself all worked up. It's probably nothing at all."

"No, I really don't think so. He hasn't called all week and then out of the blue, he says we need to talk and hangs up. MJ, I'm scared."

"Oh, wow, Kat. That can't be it. You must've read it wrong. You want me to come over tonight?"

"No. Thanks. I think I'll put Dustin to bed early and crash myself. Maybe things will look better in the morning."

"Maybe you should give Willy a call and see what he has to say," she suggested.

"No, I don't think so."

"Kat, you know how Willy feels about you—you're like a sister to him. You know he'll tell you the truth."

"Yeah, I know. But it wouldn't be fair to put him in the middle. It would be like making him choose between Jake and me. It wouldn't be right. I'll find a way to wait until Friday."

"All right, but you call me if you need to talk, okay?"

"Yeah, I will. Talk to ya later. Bye."

"Bye," she said as we disconnected.

Well, MJ clearly didn't know what was going on and now I had until Friday to worry myself to death.

How long does it take to worry yourself to death? Can I hold on that long?

It would be a long couple of days. Maybe I should entertain myself with a little shopping, maybe a new outfit for Friday night, something to knock Jake's socks off. The thought niggled at the back of my mind that a new outfit probably wouldn't help, but I pushed it aside and told myself it couldn't hurt either.

The rest of the week crawled by slower than molasses in January. I'd spent every spare minute shopping for the perfect outfit and finally settled on new designer jeans and a gorgeous red blouse. Friday finally arrived and I was petrified. Dustin was not happy that I had a date with Jake and he and Tyler were excluded. He fussed a bit, but gave up when I told him he'd be spending the night at his dad's. By the time Mark came by at four to get Dustin, I was chewing antacids every fifteen minutes to keep from throwing up.

I was dressed and ready by six o'clock, which gave me exactly one hour to work myself into a frenzy and chew another half a bottle of pills. I tried to call MJ, but there was no answer. She and Willy had been out every night this week and I hadn't had a chance to talk to her again since the night Jake called. I sat down on the couch to wait, but couldn't sit still. I tried three more times to call MJ, but never got an answer.

At seven o'clock sharp, I heard Jake pull into the driveway. I stood up and took several deep breaths to calm my nerves. He knocked and I crossed the room and opened the door.

There he stood, incredibly gorgeous. I felt like chopped liver in my new jeans and blouse. My heart was in my throat and I could hear the blood pound in my ears as I held my breath. I suddenly exhaled and when I tried to suck in another breath, I began to choke. Jake immediately stepped through the door and grabbed my arm, "Are you okay?"

I nodded my head and waved him off as I choked and tried to catch my breath. When I had recovered and looked up, he grinned and leaned against the open door frame. He knew the effect he had on me and the son-of-a-bitch liked it! I scowled and pointed my finger at him. "Don't you dare say a word."

He raised his hands in surrender. "Not me."

I narrowed my eyes and scowled harder as I grabbed my purse and walked by him. "And wipe that stupid grin off your face. It isn't funny!"

"Yes, ma'am," he said as he locked and closed the door, chuckling as he followed me to the truck.

We drove in pregnant silence to the little Italian restaurant around the corner. When we pulled into a parking space right in front of the restaurant, he asked, "Feel like Italian?"

I smiled. "Yes, definitely, and I'm half-starved." Half starved, but I'd probably throw up the minute food hit my stomach. Maybe a glass of wine would help.

"Good. Let's go."

Jake asked the hostess for something private and we were seated in a small booth toward the back of the restaurant. After ordering a bottle of wine and looking over the menu, we placed our food order and sat for a few minutes, looking at each other and holding hands across the table. Finally, Jake leaned forward and said, "I've missed you this week, Katie."

I nodded. "I've missed you too." We sat, silently gazing into each other's eyes, until our food arrived. I was about as worked up as a dog in a Frisbee factory and it was all I could do to keep myself from shaking and spilling my wine all over my new jeans.

The arrival of our food seemed to break the mood and the ice, so we chatted lightly through dinner and shared what the boys had done that week. I told Jake that Dustin was upset about being excluded from dinner and he assured me Tyler was every bit as annoyed.

When the hell is he going to tell me what we need to talk about?

The chit-chat was making me crazy. It was like sitting in a lawn chair in the middle of a tornado, discussing how windy it is outside.

After dinner, Jake poured out the last of the bottle of wine and came around the booth to sit next to me. He put his arm around me and pulled my head onto his shoulder. As I leaned against him, all the tension and panic of the week drained from my body and I relaxed in his arms. We sat for a few minutes before either of us spoke again.

Finally, Jake cleared his throat as he began, "Katie, there are some things I need to tell you and I think we need to clear the air. It's been awfully strained since we were out at the ranch and it's not fair to you."

I sat up straight and turned to face him. "Yeah, it has been a pretty tense week. I figured you needed some space and we'd straighten it out when you were ready."

He nodded and stared at his wineglass for a minute before he spoke again. "You've been there with me pretty much all the way through this divorce thing and you've been terrific. You've never asked for more than I could give." He took a deep breath and continued, "I love you, Katie, I really do love you, but I'm so confused right now. I tried so hard for so many years to hold my family together and now it seems like I've lost so much. I miss Nikki. Tyler misses Nikki. My family's been torn apart and it hurts. It hurts us all—me, Tyler, Nikki—all of us."

My hands turned clammy. I didn't like the direction this seemed to be taking and my heart leapt to my throat as I sat rigid, listening carefully to every word he said…and every word he didn't say.

Jake continued, "I met you and fell in love with you right away. I fell in love with you and I fell in love with Dustin. My family loves you, my friends love you. What's not to love? I just…" He swallowed and took a deep breath before he continued, "I'm not sure I'm ready for all this. It's all happening so fast."

The bottom dropped out from under me and my heart fell to my feet. I couldn't breathe.

I began to shake and worried I might hyperventilate as I struggled not to scream.

Oh, my God! Happening too fast? What! Is this it? Is he breaking it off?

I could feel Jake's eyes on my face as I stared at my wine and measured each breath with the blood that pounded in my ears. I took my hands off the table and put them in my lap so he wouldn't see me tremble.

"Katie, I'm not asking to break this off. I don't want to stop seeing you. Honestly, I'm not trying to end our relationship. I love you, but it's all moving too fast for me. My family and friends want me to marry you. Tyler wants me to make Dustin his brother, but he wants Nikki to come home, too. I'm so torn. You've been extremely patient, but I feel so guilty all the time. I feel like I should offer you more, but I can't right now." Jake drew in a deep breath and leaned in toward me as he swept my hair back over my shoulder. "I just need some space. I need to slow things down—you know, back off a bit.

I need time to think things through and make some decisions."

I forced myself to breathe in and out…in and out…in and out, as my brain shrieked and railed against what he'd said. When my head begin to clear, an unexpected calmness slipped over me as I realized what it was he hadn't said.

I turned and looked at him. "Jake, I don't think you're telling me everything. I think maybe this all has something to do with Brenda's boyfriend dumping her. I don't know if you're seeing her again or if you're considering reconciliation or what, but I think it has something to do with Brenda. Can you tell me it doesn't?"

He looked into my eyes and shook his head. "Katie, I don't know what to do. She wants me back. She's even got Nikki begging me to come back home. I don't want Brenda. I don't love her any more. I want you, but I feel guilty about my family being torn apart. I need time to get it straight in my head and figure out what to do. Katie, I don't want to lose you, but I'm so confused." He hung his head and sucked in a lungful of air as his shoulders slumped over. Then he rubbed his face with his hands as he appeared to have the weight of the world on his shoulders.

My mind was still strangely clear and I was perfectly calm as I thought it through. I'd been part of a family once and I loved it. I still remembered the pain of having it torn apart and the sense of loss when it was gone for good. I knew what he felt. I looked in his face and knew beyond a shadow of a doubt I loved this man and I knew he loved me too and if I asked, he would probably pay the price to be with me. But could I live with the price he would have to pay? And what would it ultimately cost us both? No, I couldn't. I loved him too much to watch him be torn apart. I couldn't ask him to sacrifice his family for me. I didn't want to risk growing old with a man who might become bitter and blame me for his loss. I couldn't do it. These past few weeks had given me a glimpse into the future we would have ahead if I asked this of him. That wasn't a future I wanted for either of us.

Jake recovered a bit and looked at me as he quietly pleaded, "Let's slow it down, back up a bit and see what happens."

I smiled gently and put my hand on his as I shook my head. "I can't, Jake. I love you, but I can't. I've been totally committed for some time now and there's no way I can slow it down. I'd always wonder if you were with her or if you still loved her or when you'd dump me. I love you, but I'm in too far. There's no slowing down for me. It's too late. If I tried to back off now, I'd become a clingy, whiny bitch and then you'd grow to hate me. I couldn't stand to watch it happen."

Jake stared wildly, like a trapped animal. I reached up and stroked his face. "I'm sorry, Jake. I can't do it. I wish with all my heart I could, but what you're asking of me is something I don't have the strength to do, and I believe it would destroy us. You have a family and I know how much you love your family and how desperately you've tried to hold them together. If there's a chance you could mend what's broken and pull your family back together, you don't need me standing in the wings to confuse you. You need to put your heart into it. Half measures won't fix your family and slowing things down won't fix us."

"Are you asking me to choose?" His eyes filled with fear.

"No, I'm not. I'm choosing for both of us. If I asked you to choose between me and your family and you chose me, I'd always wonder if you would grow to regret it. And if you did, I couldn't live with the guilt. I could never live with the guilt of knowing you might have repaired your family, but you didn't try because of me. I couldn't live with the thought those children might have had both their mother and their father with them again, but it didn't happen because of me. I couldn't live with the pain of watching you grow to resent me because of all you'd lost. We'd grow to hate each other."

I took a deep breath. "No, Jake, I'm not asking you to choose. I'm making the choice. I'm choosing to end it." With that, the tears began to roll down my face and I looked away, picked up my wineglass and threw back the last of my wine.

"I can't let you go." His voice cracked. "I love you."

I looked at him with tears flowing down my face and gently replied, "It's not your choice any more." I reached around and picked up my purse and turned back to him. "It's time to go. Please take me home."

He moved like a man drugged as he slid out of the booth, dropped some money on the table, and helped me to my feet. We left the restaurant and headed to my house in silence. As he shut the truck off in the driveway, we both sat, too stunned to move. When he turned to reach for me, I quickly opened the door and got out, heading for the front door as fast as I could move. As I fumbled with the keys and tried to get the door open, I smelled soap and felt him come up behind me. The door swung open and he slid one arm around my waist and pulled me back against him. I stayed there for a moment, tears streaming down my face, hating what I knew I had to do.

"Katie, please, we can work this out."

"No, we can't. It's done. Let me go."

I heard him swallow hard as he whispered in my ear, "I'll always love you."

A sob bubbled up from somewhere deep inside and I fled into the safety of my home, quickly closing the door behind me as the sob wrenched from my throat. I leaned against the door and with my face pressed against it, sobbed as quietly as I could and listened for the sound of the truck as it left.

After a couple of minutes went by and I didn't hear the truck pull out, hope began to rise up from somewhere inside.

Will he refuse to leave? Will he break down the door and declare his undying love? Will he force his way in and insist he can't live without me?

Just as I found myself wondering if I should open the door, I heard the truck. The shock was so great, I almost ripped the door open and ran shrieking into the driveway, begging him to come back.

I'll never know for sure what kept me behind the closed door because I can guarantee it wasn't through my own strength. I've often thought through the years it was the hand of God holding the door closed and keeping me rooted to the spot. In any case, Jake pulled out of the driveway, taking my heart with him, dragging it down the street like an old tire tied to his bumper.

I stood there, shaking, for some time before I finally moved to the couch and crumpled into a heap at one end. I stayed there all night, thinking, wondering. Was he gone for good? Would he ever be back? Would I ever get over him? The phone rang several times and I could tell from the number it was MJ. I didn't answer. I didn't want to talk to anyone.

By morning, I'd cried every tear I had to cry and pretty much resolved things in my mind. I loved Jake, but we would never have been happy together. His family would always have been between us. I resigned myself to the fact that the time we had spent together was the only time we would ever have. It would have to be enough. I knew in my heart Jake would try to put his family back together and he may actually succeed in doing it, but I also believed him when he said he would love me forever.

Sometimes forever simply isn't enough. Sometimes love isn't enough.

Dustin would need healing too and I resolved to be strong for him. I didn't know how we were going to do it, but I knew we'd get past this together.

The next time MJ called, I answered. "Willy told me about last night," she said. "You okay?"

"Not really, but I will be—in time."

"Are you sure you did the right thing, Kat? Maybe if you gave him some space for a little while, he'd sort it all out and you'd be okay."

"No. It's better this way, MJ. I won't spend my life living with guilt and wondering if he blames me. He's too much in love with his kids. In time, he'd grow to resent me. No, this is something he has to do without me."

"Oh, Kat, I'm so sorry. This must be so hard for you. I can't believe it's going to end this way. You two were perfect for each other and I know how much you love him. Willy's beside himself. He said he talked to Nell this morning and she's pissed as hell. Is there anything I can do for you? Do you want me to come over?"

"No. I want to be alone for a little while. I talked to Mark this morning and he's going to keep Dustin for a few days. I just need a little time alone to get things straight in my head. Can you get someone to cover my shifts until next weekend so I can spend some time with Dustin once I get myself pulled together? He and I'll work through this together. Don't worry, we'll be fine. I'll call you later in the week, okay?"

"Okay. But if you need anything, you call me. I love you."

"Yeah, I love you too." I hung up the phone and stared off into space, numb and empty.

I'd be okay. One day I'd be able to look back on this time in my life with fondness and hold my head up high because I'd done the right thing—I'd taken the high road. I loved Jake and I knew he loved me. But he'd never loved me with his whole heart. There was always some piece of himself Jake had held apart from me, always something he hid, something he couldn't give. This wasn't the relationship I wanted for myself and my son. I wanted a man who was on solid ground and would always be there for us, a man who was free to love me with his whole heart, a man who could put us first, a man I didn't have to fix. Someday I would be able to recall Jake's face, his grin, his kiss, his arms around me or his lips on my neck, without the pain I felt today.

I will be okay.

Chapter Eighteen

The phone rang in the kitchen as I ran from the backyard to reach it. I answered and heard a man's voice say, "Hey, Sis, how ya doin'?" It was Willy.

A few months had passed since my breakup with Jake and Willy and I hadn't talked a whole lot during that time. I think he felt bad about how things turned out and felt a little responsible. But it wasn't his fault and I knew in time that we'd all get back to normal. Things like that just take time.

"Hey. Hi. I'm great. How are you?" I couldn't help but wonder what was up.

"I'm doing great. I was thinking I'd come by. You gonna be home for a little while?"

"Yeah, I'll be here. Come on by. MJ with you?"

"Nope, just me. I'll be there in a couple minutes." He hung up and I just stood with the phone in my hand.

Huh. What's going on?

About ten minutes later there was a knock on the front door. I went to the door and opened it, and there stood Willy with a cockeyed grin on his face. "Hi."

"Come on in," I said. "You want a beer?"

"Yeah, that sounds good." As I pulled a beer out of the refrigerator, he added, "You'd better have one too."

I turned and stared hard at him as I handed it to him. He shrugged. "Your choice, but I'd highly recommend it."

I reached back in the refrigerator and grabbed another beer, popping the top as we headed out to the backyard. When we were each settled in a lawn chair, I looked over at him. "Okay, spill it. What's up?"

Willy examined his beer can as he said, "I came by to tell you Jake's planning to get married."

The bottom dropped out of my stomach and I prayed I wouldn't throw up. "Brenda?"

He nodded as he watched my reaction.

I turned my attention to my own beer can and took a couple of big gulps as I considered what he'd said. After a couple of minutes went by and the lump in my throat subsided, I found my voice. "Well, I guess I'm not surprised," and as I looked up at Willy with tears in my eyes, I asked, "When?"

"Next Saturday."

I took a deep breath. "Well, I hope they make it. It's what Jake really wanted and it's best for the kids."

Willy watched me closely. "He asked me to come talk to you." I looked into his eyes and he continued. "He wants to come by and see you one evening this week, before next weekend."

My heart thumped in my chest.

What the hell? Come by here? Talk to me? Hell no!

I stared at Willy, dumbfounded. "Why? What does he want?" I was almost afraid to breathe.

"I'm not sure, but I think he wants you to talk him out of it. Katie, he doesn't love Brenda. It's been three months since you two broke up and he's still in love with you. I think he wants to see if you still love him."

I took another deep breath and a big gulp of beer. "Willy, I can't. I can't be responsible for breaking up his family. I can't do it." Tears spilled down my face and the sobs welled up from deep inside.

Willy set his beer down and reached for my hand. "Katie, this is a mistake. You two love each other. You belong together. Brenda cheated on him once, she'll do it again. His whole family hates her. David threatened to kick his ass for hurting you. His mom's pissed as hell he's back together with her. Nell's been after me to come and talk to you and beg you to take him away from Brenda. Everyone thinks you belong together. Kat, you've got to talk to him."

"No," I said firmly and gulped for breath. "Willy, if I came between him and Brenda right now, he'd give up everything he's worked to build over the last ten years—for me. He may think it's what he wants now, but someday he'd come to regret it and blame me for it. I couldn't stand it. I can't do it, Willy. He's getting married next Saturday. He's got no right to ask to come here. Just tell him I said no."

Not only no, but hell no!

Willy stared at me for a few moments and then patted my hands and nodded his head as he got up to leave. I followed him to the door where he turned and hugged me. "Sis, I'll tell him what you said, but I sure wish you'd change your mind. It's not right."

"It <u>is</u> right. It's the <u>only</u> thing that's right, Willy. This doesn't have anything to do with love. It's simply one of those things that couldn't end any other way." My heart felt like it was being run through a wringer.

Willy shook his head and walked out the door, got in his truck and left as I returned to the backyard to cry my heart out. Some day, I told myself, it wouldn't hurt so badly—some day.

* * *

The week went by slowly as I waited for Saturday to come and go. School was out for the summer and Dustin was spending a month with Mark. I was grateful he wouldn't be exposed to my pain, but I also wished he was here to give me some of those little boy hugs that always put the world right again. Every night I waited. Each night I lay in bed and listened. Part of me hoped Jake would show up anyway and declare his undying love. Part of me expected he couldn't do anything less. He loved me, didn't he?

Friday night, there was a knock on the door about eleven o'clock. I jumped out of bed and flew into the front room, expecting to open the door and find Jake standing there. When the door opened, I stared for a moment, trying to get my mind around it.

I stepped back and Willy walked in and sat on the couch. "I'm here to try one more time. Nell and I want you to come to the wedding."

Like a fish on a line, I stood there with my mouth open. "Are you crazy?" I half screamed. My mind reeled. How the hell could he ask this of me? What the hell were he and Nell thinking?

He shook his head. "No. Jake's making the biggest mistake of his life and we've got to find a way to stop him. I want you to go as my date. It's not too late. Maybe seeing you will bring him to his senses."

"No!" I said firmly. "I won't do it. Jake has to make his own decision on this. I won't take responsibility for his choices. I won't be responsible for him losing his family. I won't do it! Willy, this isn't some movie where the 'other woman' shows up at the church and the groom declares his undying love for her and leaves the bride at the altar. You go to his wedding because you're his best friend, and you wish him well because you love him. You won't take me to confuse him."

Willy looked at me and shrugged. "I told Nell you'd never do it, but she said we had to try. She'll be awfully disappointed. She sure loves you, and she hates Brenda with a passion."

"I'm sorry, Willy, I truly am. I love you all and I know you mean well, but Jake and I have made our choices and there's no going back. We'll all have to adjust and life will go on." A sob escaped my throat and I sucked in a lungful of air as I put my fingers to my lips. "Tell Jake…tell him I wish him well." I broke down and began to sob.

Willy leaned over and put his arms around me and held me as I cried. When I again regained control, he let go of me and nodded. "I will. I'll tell him what you said." Then he stood and moved across the room. At the door, he turned and asked, "Do you want to know?"

I stared at him helplessly and nodded. He turned and left, closing the door behind him. God help me, I did want to know.

* * *

Sunday morning, the phone rang and I answered it, knowing it was Willy, and dreading what I would hear. "Hello."

"Hi. You said you wanted to know."

"Yeah," I replied, holding my breath as I waited for confirmation of what I already knew.

"It's done. He went through with it. No one can believe it, but he did."

"He married her?" I asked, still not able to come to terms with what Jake had done, still not ready to believe he was gone to me.

"Yeah. You okay?"

"Yeah. I will be. I'll talk to ya later. Thanks for calling. Bye." I hung up the phone and dropped into a chair as my heart was filled with emptiness. Despair settled over me like a dark blanket. It was done. Nothing to do now but let it go and move forward.

I cried for hours and woke sometime in the middle of the night to find myself on the couch, unsure how or when I'd moved there. I got up and moved to the bed, where I stayed pretty much for the next day and a half.

On the morning of the third day, all cried out and having consumed almost two gallons of ice cream, I got out of bed and took a shower. Clean, for the first time in two days, I dressed and emerged from my bedroom. I went to the back door and opened it, stepping out into the sunshine. As soon as Obleo spotted me, he barreled across the yard and waged a full-blown assault. He was so excited, we wound up in a heap on the patio before all the jumping and yelling was done. Sitting on my butt on the patio, I found myself laughing. It felt good, so I let it come. I just sat there and hugged Obleo as I laughed uncontrollably.

In that moment, I knew I would be okay. I'd loved and lost, but I'd lived through it. It wouldn't be the life I'd dreamed of, but I'd find a way to make it good. The sun would come up each morning, the pain would fade and, in time, I'd be good as new.

In time, I'd find a new dream.

Chapter Nineteen

About three months after Jake's wedding, I was at the kitchen table on a Saturday morning with a cup of coffee and a newspaper when there was a knock at the door. I got up and went to the door and when I opened it, David grinned back at me. "Hi, Slick. Can I come in?"

Stunned, I stepped back and said, "Oh, sure. Sorry. Come on in." Just inside the doorway, David reached out and grabbed me, wrapping me up in his long arms and hugging me close. I was overwhelmed at how good it was to see him again and I hugged him back. But why was he here?

As he stepped away, a pain shot through my heart as I caught a whiff of soap. I steadied myself as I closed the door and turned to look at him. I took a deep breath. "Wow. It's good to see you again. Would you like something to drink?"

"A cup of that coffee I smell would be great." He smiled as he followed me out to the kitchen. "Where's Dustin?"

"He went fishing with his dad this weekend. He's missed Jake and Tyler, so Mark's been trying to keep him busy." I poured a cup of coffee and handed it to him.

He nodded his head and I could see his jaw clench as he took the coffee and turned to look out the Arcadia door.

"Would you like to sit out back?" I asked. "It's nice and still kinda cool in the shade."

He looked at me and nodded, his eyes sparkling as he smiled.

We went out into the back yard, moved a couple of chairs into the shade, and sat. The birds sang in the trees and we sat quietly for a couple of minutes before either of us spoke.

Finally, David cleared his throat and asked, "You okay?"

"Yeah. I am okay. We heal a little bit more each day. We're gonna be just fine."

He nodded and looked directly into my eyes as he leaned forward and put his hand on my arm. "Katie, I don't want an answer right now, but there's something I want you to think about." I watched him quietly as he continued, "I've never made any secret of the way I feel about you. You know I've been crazy about you from the first moment I laid eyes on you. I didn't pursue it out of respect for my brother and because you made your preference clear. But I came by to ask you to reconsider."

As I blinked and opened my mouth to reply, he held up his hand. "No, don't say anything. I don't want you to answer me today. I just wanted to say my piece and I'm going to ask you to take a week or two to think about it. Then I'll come by and take you to dinner and we can talk it over."

I shut my mouth and nodded as he continued. "Katie, I know you love Jake and I do too. But he's made his choice and I believe it frees us both from any obligation to him. I know Jake and I think, ultimately, he would want you to be happy. I want you to be happy. For Christ sakes, Katie, I want to be happy too…and being happy to me means having you at my side."

He continued as he rubbed the inside of my arm. "Oh, Jake might be pissed for a while, but he'll come around when he realizes he doesn't have any right to hang onto the past. We could be good together, Katie, and I know in time, you could learn to love me. Maybe not in the same way you love Jake. It'll probably be a different kind of love, but I promise I'm steady and faithful and I'll always be there for you. I'm a patient man and I can wait. I love kids and I'm crazy about yours. All I'm asking is for you to think it over. I'm not asking for a commitment, just to give it a try, give me a try. Let's see if we can't bring something positive out of all this."

I sat there and stared into his eyes. He looked so much like Jake, it was hard to trust my feelings. Finally, he drank the last of his coffee and stood up, taking my hand and pulling me to my feet. As I stood, he stepped close and put his arms around me. I leaned into him. It felt good. It felt like Jake…it smelled like Jake. It would be easy to get lost in this man's arms, but was it fair?

He stepped away and headed for the front door, pulling me after him. At the door, he turned and took me into his arms again. This time the embrace was more intimate, possessive. When I turned my face up to look at him, he put his lips on mine and kissed me—strong and passionate, his lips moving over mine like a man coming home after a long absence.

My heart leaped and my stomach did a flip as it responded eagerly to this man that was so like his brother. I wrapped my arms around his neck and fell into the moment. I didn't want to think about what I was doing or if it was right.

When the kiss ended, David again looked into my eyes and smiled. "I've waited a long time for that." After a moment's pause, he continued, "Think about it. I'll call you next weekend. Give Dustin a hug for me." Then he kissed me on the forehead and turned for the door. At the door, he stopped and looked back over his shoulder and winked. Then he turned and was gone.

I was stunned. What just happened? I'd kissed the brother of the man I loved…and I liked it. What the hell was I thinking? Could I fall in love with this man? Should I fall in love with this man? What would Jake's reaction be? Would he think I was trying to get even? Was I? Could I trust my feelings? Could David trust them? Could I trust David?

There were so many questions and they all ran through my head so fast I couldn't think. I shuffled across the living room like a zombie out of an old late-night thriller and rolled up into a ball against the arm of the couch.

The next week was going to be hell as I sorted through all the questions and tried to come up with answers. Would I take the high road? Was there even a high road here? Well, I had a week to figure it out.

* * *

It was about ten o'clock Saturday morning and I was at the kitchen table with a cup of coffee again. Dustin was in the living room with cartoons when there was a knock on the front door. I heard Dustin jump up to answer it and I moved quickly to be there when the door opened.

As I rounded the corner, I heard David's voice. "Well, hello, young man. How are you?"

Dustin squealed with delight, "Mom, it's Uncle David! Mom, come quick. It's Uncle David!"

I walked in and smiled as David stepped through the door, scooped Dustin up into his arms and turned to give me the heart-tugging grin he shared with his brother. "Hi. I decided to drop by instead of calling. Hope it's okay."

I nodded and laughed as Dustin babbled away at David, totally monopolizing the conversation. I fixed David a cup of coffee and we continued in that vein for the better part of an hour before Dustin finally settled back down to watch cartoons again. David and I were on the couch and suddenly found ourselves in close proximity to each other in the midst of a deafening silence.

He reached out and stroked the side of my face. "How you been?"

Afraid to look at him, I kept my eyes on Dustin. "Good. One of the regular daytime bartenders was sick, so I took all her shifts this week. I was pretty busy and I'm glad Saturday finally came. How's everything at the ranch?" I finally looked at him.

"Fine." He smiled. "Mom said to tell you 'Hi'. Oh, by the way, she said to tell you she took your advice and she's dating old Roy now."

My heart leapt as I exclaimed excitedly, "She is? Oh, how wonderful! I told her I thought he'd be a great catch."

"Well, she must've agreed with you because they've been dating for a couple of months and I think it's starting to get hot and heavy." He smiled and rolled his eyes. "It's not really something a man wants to think about when it concerns his mother, but she sure seems happy to have him around now. In fact, there's a bit more spring in his step too. I wouldn't be surprised if we see a wedding soon."

I laughed at the image of old Roy and Nell at the altar. "Well, they both deserve to be happy. I hope it works out for them. They're great people and I'll bet they'd be great together."

David smiled and rubbed the inside of my arm as he said quietly, "Yeah, like two other people I know."

My face flushed hot and I tried to avoid his intent gaze. He didn't say anything, just appeared to watch my face for some sign.

"Well, what time do I pick you up for dinner?" he finally asked.

Dustin's ears perked up and he turned around and asked, "Dinner? Are we going to dinner?"

David laughed. "Yeah, if you can help me talk your mom into it."

Dustin immediately jumped to his feet and begged me to go to dinner.

I threw my hands in the air. "Okay, okay, I know when I'm beat. Dinner it is."

Dustin jumped up and down and did a high-five with David as I scowled at both of them. Then he plopped back down in front of his cartoon again and David looked at me sheepishly and shrugged. "Hey, I didn't say I was above using every tool at my disposal."

"Yeah, I can see that." I shook my head and chuckled.

David stood up and said, "How about I pick you two up at six and we can go for pizza?"

"Yeah, I like pizza. Six will be fine," replied Dustin over his shoulder, as if it was his decision to make.

David and I looked at each other and laughed. "Six it is," he said as he took my hand and pulled me after him out the front door.

On the front porch, he turned and wrapped his arms around me as he burrowed his face into my hair. "I've missed you so much this week. All I could think about was that kiss and getting back down here to see you again."

My nostrils filled with the fresh smell of soap and my stomach jumped as David leaned in to kiss me. This time, it was a soft and gentle kiss, very sweet and very romantic as he pulled me against him and his tongue explored my mouth like he was trying to memorize every inch of it. Butterflies zinged through my stomach like I was a freshman being kissed for the first time.

When he pulled back, his eyes smoldered as he reached out and ran his hand over my hair. He smiled and winked as he stepped away, walked down the driveway, and pulled away from the house.

Now what? I had thought about this situation all week and wasn't sure I was any closer to a decision. David was a wonderful man and I couldn't deny I had feelings for him…I always had. He was an exciting man and he was steady and dependable, exactly the kind of man Dustin and I needed in our lives. But could I ever learn to separate him from his brother in my mind? Could I love him for who he was or would I always be drawn to him for who he was like? Well, I'd better make up my mind by six o'clock.

At six sharp, I heard David's truck pull into the driveway. Dustin did too and he dashed for the front door. When I entered the living room, my breath caught in my throat. David wore a black felt hat and a black t-shirt with white lettering on the front, perfect-fitting jeans, and boots. The outfit was so similar to the outfit Jake had worn the first time he came over for a date that for a moment, he looked like Jake.

Then the blood returned to my brain and I forced myself to breathe again. David hadn't missed my reaction and he raised one brow as I smiled, but he didn't say anything. He lifted Dustin up and asked, "Well, buddy, you ready for pizza?"

"Yeah, and can we go to the place with all the video games? I love video games. Mom says it keeps me busy so I don't talk her ears off.'

David threw his head back and laughed at this incriminating piece of information and then winked at me. "Well, then by all means, that's where we'll have to go 'cuz I kinda like your mom with her ears on."

After we'd consumed most of a huge pizza, we were all stuffed like Thanksgiving birds. David handed Dustin a handful of tokens and told him to knock himself out on the machines. Dustin, delighted at the size of the pile of tokens, squealed and took off for the nearest machine.

David excused himself to go to the men's room and I sat there alone with my thoughts. What in the hell would I say when he pressed me for my answer? As David returned from the men's room, I watched him closely and was amazed at how much he looked like his brother. They even moved the same, and they used the same brand of soap. How could I ever get past the similarities?

David smiled as he sat next to me and took my hand in his. "Alone at last." He kissed me on the cheek and wrapped his arm around my waist, pulling me against him as he buried his nose in my hair.

"Yeah, well, don't get used to it. You'll be amazed at how fast he can go through a stack of tokens."

"Never fear, I've got a pocket full of fives and I spied a token machine that takes five dollar bills. I can keep him going all night." We both laughed.

When the laughter died and he stared into my eyes, I knew the moment of reckoning was close at hand.

He took a deep breath. "Would you like another soda?" When I nodded, he got to his feet and picked up the glass.

I smiled. "Thanks, Jake."

We both froze. Neither of us dared to breathe, as we considered the implications of what I'd done. His face turned to stone and his eyes went black as night as he calmly turned and strode to the counter to get another soda.

I sat there mentally kicking myself for making such a stupid mistake.

How could I have done that? Oh my God, it was about the worst thing I could have done!

David took his time at the counter and returned slowly to the table, seeming to measure every step. When he sat across from me, I looked up into his eyes and said, "I am so sorry."

He raised his hand as he shook his head. "No, don't worry about it."

In a split second, I knew what I had to do and my heart fell. In the back of my mind, I'd hoped David would rescue me from the pain of losing Jake. But in that single moment, it became clear it wouldn't happen. I had to let David down gently so he could move on with his life. I still loved Jake and it wouldn't be fair to ask his brother to live in Jake's shadow. They were so much alike, I didn't think the wounds could ever heal. I would always compare David to Jake and, although David was at least Jake's equal in every way, he wasn't my first love…and he would come up short of what he deserved.

As I looked into David's eyes and the tears began to fall, I saw he knew it too. His eyes welled up with tears also and he took a deep breath and coughed as he looked down at the table. "If I'd only met you first, our lives might be so different."

We sat there in silence for a few minutes before he took my hand and looked into my eyes. "My brother's a damn fool and he'll never know what he almost had. If you ever have a change of heart and think maybe there's a chance, you know where I'll be."

I nodded but didn't say anything as we sat there quietly, holding hands and saying our silent good-byes.

When we could no longer stand it, we rounded up Dustin and David drove us back to the house. Dustin hugged David goodnight and went inside to get ready for bed as David took me by the hand and led me back out to the front porch.

He took me into his arms and I laid my head against his chest. "David, I'm so sorry. You're a wonderful man and in my own way, I do love you.

But you deserve a woman who loves you with her whole heart and mine's too fragmented right now."

"I know," he replied as he held me in his arms and stroked my hair. "I just don't want to imagine life without you and Dustin. I wish it could be different."

"Me, too," I replied, "me, too."

He pulled back and looked into my eyes as he kissed me…a soft, chaste, haunting kiss. Then he turned and walked to his truck. As the truck started, he sat there for a long moment and looked at me. Then he gave me that heart-breaking grin and drove out of my life.

After putting Dustin to bed, I lay down on my bed and cried my heart out. How could this happen to me? How could I love two men and not be able to have either one? I lost the first one to his old love and the second one to my old love.

Out of one relationship, I'd not only lost two good men, I'd lost an entire family. This was the second family I'd lost, and I'd lost them twice! How could I even begin to get my mind around it? I cried myself to sleep that night and many nights after. Eventually, the tears dried up and I could cry no more. Then life went on.

Chapter Twenty

I woke from a deep fog. I'd been sleeping hard and dreamed about someone pounding on my door. After a couple of minutes, I realized someone really was pounding on my door. I looked over at the clock. It was after midnight. Who could be at the door at this time of night? Dustin was off fishing with Mark for the weekend and if something had happened, they surely would have called.

I bolted from the bed, pulled on my robe, and ran for the front door. Without thinking, I unlocked the door and jerked it open wide, afraid there was some emergency afoot.

As the door opened, I froze. It was Jake. We stood like that for a few minutes, staring at each other. My breath caught in my throat, but there was no cramp in my belly, no knife through the heart. Finally, I got my wits about me enough to ask, "What are you doing here?" It had been almost a year since I'd seen him last.

"Can I come in?" he asked with a grin.

I opened the door wider and stood back, indicating he could come inside. He entered and as he walked by me, I caught the sharp scent of his cologne. I watched him as he crossed the room and sat on the couch. I closed the door and took a deep breath. Was he still with Brenda? Had they split up? Why he was here?

Is it what you want? What will you do if he's come back for you?

I took a moment to remind myself I'd spent the last year trying to get my life back on track. It had been sheer agony at times, but I'd finally gotten myself to the point where I could think of him without pain…and now here he stood in my living room and I'm asking myself if I want all that back?!

I turned and looked at him sitting on my couch like nothing had ever happened and I softly asked, "Why are you here, Jake?"

He looked at me with complete composure, not a hint of what he was thinking. "I wanted to come by and see you, that's all."

I stared. He'd put on a couple of pounds and seemed shorter, not quite as striking as I remembered him. "You look good," I said. It wasn't a lie—he was still a good-looking man, but he'd lost some of the fire I remembered.

"Thanks. You look great too. It's been a long time."

"Yeah, it has." I took a deep breath and plunged in, "How's the family?"

He hesitated a minute. "They're fine. We're going to have another baby, a boy. We'll name him James, after Brenda's father."

I was stunned as I got my mind around what he'd said. For some reason, it had never occurred to me he was actually sleeping with Brenda and I asked myself why it hadn't.

Did you think he was remaining celibate, saving himself for the day he could return to you? Did you think he's a saint?

What the hell had I been thinking?

As I worked through these thoughts, I was surprised at how calm I felt. He'd just told me he was still with her, they slept together, and they had conceived another child together...and I felt fine. There was no pain, no clenching in the pit of my stomach, no tears welled up in my eyes. Slowly, the lights came on in my mind. I was finally over him. I was finally free.

Mechanically, I made my way to a chair and sat down as I replied, "Oh, congratulations. I'm happy for you."

He watched me, assessing my reaction.

When I'd worked through everything in my mind, I nodded. "I really am happy for you, Jake. I know how badly you wanted to keep your family together. I'm happy it's working for you."

He nodded. "Tyler's getting big. He's playing baseball. Sometimes he still asks about you and Dustin."

I looked at him and smiled. "I'd ask you to give him a hug for me, but it probably wouldn't be a good idea."

"She knows," he said, "Tyler told her all about you and she gave me the third degree. She knows all about us."

I nodded. "I hope it didn't cause any problems for you."

He smiled. "Well, it did at first, but she got over it. We've actually managed to put things back together pretty good. We moved to Tucson and I run the marketing end of the ranching business from there. We live in town now. It makes her happy and it makes things easier for me. I've got the kids all together, which makes me happy. It was a big compromise and I sometimes miss the ranch, but it works better this way. It's not perfect, but it's good."

"How's your mom?"

He chuckled. "She's fine. She married old Roy, ya know—a couple of months ago."

"She did?" I exclaimed, "That's wonderful! Roy's such a great guy. I'll bet they're terrific together."

"Yeah, they are. He's real good to her and she takes good care of him." He grinned. "She told me it was all your idea."

"Well, I just dropped the hint. They did all the heavy lifting."

There was silence for a moment before he continued, "David still lives out at the ranch. He almost got married last month to one of the local gals, but he called it off at the last minute. I'm not sure why. He just said she wasn't the right one and it would have been a mistake."

I looked up at the mention of David and found Jake watching me very closely as he talked. I nodded at the news of the broken engagement. "Do you think he's okay?"

Jake shrugged. "Yeah, I think so." He watched me for a moment and then added, "He told me he came by here to see you after Brenda and I got remarried."

I stared at him. Where was this going?

He held my gaze as he said, "I didn't realize he'd fallen in love with you too." He paused, apparently waiting for some reaction. When he got none, he continued, "I thought at first he was jealous of what we had. I don't think any of us really understood at the time how bad he had it."

I blinked as I slowly digested what he'd said. When I didn't respond, he again continued, "You know, a lot of time has passed and I've moved on, and I think you have too. I don't know how you feel about David, but if you were interested…well, I think he still cares for you. I…well, I thought I'd mention it…just in case…well, in case you might be interested."

Stunned, I sat and stared at him for a few minutes before I grinned and asked, "Are you trying to fix me up with your brother?"

He smiled and shrugged his shoulders as he looked at the floor. "Well, I guess it does sound like it, but it's not exactly what I came here to do." Then he looked into my eyes for a moment before he said, "Katie, I will always have a special place in my heart for you and Dustin. In my own way, I will always love you. But I've come to terms with my life. You were wise to refuse to see me again. I've always respected you for having the strength and courage to stand firm and hold to your principles. Things are different now and I'm happy with my life…and with my wife. But sometimes I feel like you and David might have paid a high price for my happiness. I've always wondered if the two of you could have fallen in love if I'd been honest with you and stepped aside in the beginning. Mom and I were talking a few weeks ago about David breaking off his engagement and we both think it's because he's still in love with you. The gal he was engaged to is pretty and she's nice enough, but she doesn't have your passion or your heart. In the end, she simply couldn't measure up."

My mind reeled as I stared at Jake. I didn't know what to say. I had loved this man, lost him, and gotten over it. Now he was in my living room pleading his brother's case. Very weird.

"I'm not sure what to say. What is it you want me to do? It was a long time ago, Jake. I loved David, but I was 'in love' with you. Am I supposed to waltz back into his life and say, 'Hey, heard you were still available...and oh, by the way, I'm not in love with your brother any more.' You don't think it would be a tad bit strange?"

Jake had watched me intently and when I finished, he laughed. "You always were one to cut through the crap and come right to the point. Yeah, maybe you're right. Maybe it is a little strange, but then maybe it's the right thing to do. You'll never know until you try. Let me help you."

I stared stupidly. Then I took a deep breath and stood up. "I need a beer. You want one?"

Jake chuckled. "Yeah, I'll take one."

I went to the refrigerator and returned with two beers. Handing Jake one, I sat and opened mine, taking three big gulps to settle my nerves.

I looked at Jake. "You're serious, aren't you?" My mind was reeling like a Ferris wheel at the fair.

He nodded.

"Did Nell put you up to this?"

"No. This was my idea. In fact, I hadn't even fully worked it out in my mind before I came by. I just knew I needed to talk to you and then as I sat here, it all fell into place."

I blinked at him and took two more gulps of beer.

"Look, you and David are both alone. At least, I think you're alone. Wow, never thought about that...you are alone right now, aren't you?"

I nodded.

He blew out a sigh. "Whew, that's good. Well, like I said, you're both alone right now and I believe he's still in love with you. He's a terrific guy and he could give you everything you ever wanted or needed. You two always got along great and he'd be wonderful with Dustin. I really think you should consider it."

I took three more gulps of my beer and found it empty. "I need another beer…you need one?" I asked Jake as I headed for the kitchen again.

He laughed and said, "No, I've only had mine for about three minutes. I think I'll pace myself, but you go ahead."

I grabbed another beer and took two gulps before I sank back in my chair and stared at Jake. Call me crazy, but his suggestion actually seemed to have merit. Maybe it was the beer. I'd been attracted to David and if I hadn't been so in love with Jake, we might have had a chance at something good. But Jake had always been there—between us. Now things were different. I was over Jake and, apparently, Jake was over me. Would it make a difference? Maybe. Should I take the chance?

Jake watched me as he took a sip of his beer and cleared his throat. "Well, Kat, whaddaya think?"

I took a deep breath and two more gulps of my beer, and shrugged. "I don't know. I don't know what to think. One part of my brain says it's not such a bad idea, while another part of my brain is shrieking, 'What the hell are you thinking?'"

Another gulp of beer and I continued, "I can't begin to imagine the logistics of the whole thing. David and I don't exactly run in the same circles, so I'm not likely to bump into him at the grocery store."

"Well, I might have an idea," Jake offered. "David's thirtieth birthday is next week and mom's having a barbecue out at the ranch. Everyone in town's been invited and I know she'd love to have you and Dustin come. You could show up and surprise him. He'd love it."

"I don't know. It might be too uncomfortable—with us all in the same place at the same time—wouldn't Brenda mind?"

Jake shook his head. "No. Brenda and I don't spend much time at the ranch. She hates it. Whenever there's a big event up there, we generally go for the day and then we either spend the night in Prescott or drive home the same night. The kids go up quite a bit, but mom and Brenda have never gotten along. Besides, we can't make it next weekend. We have a previous commitment with Nikki. That's why I'm in town tonight. I went up to the ranch this weekend to wish him a happy birthday and explain why I'll have to miss his party. Since we won't be there, you'll be able to spend some time together without it being too uncomfortable, kinda feel it out."

"Seems pretty obvious," I said as I thought about it. "It feels kinda odd and a little bit pushy."

Jake took a deep breath and rolled his eyes. "Kat, you're over-thinking this. I'll call mom and tell her you're coming. When you get there, she'll tell David she called and invited you, and you accepted. It's simple. He'll either take it from there…or he won't. My guess is, he will. But either way, you'll know. Come on…give it a shot. Besides, mom and Roy would love to see you and Dustin again."

Taking three more gulps of my beer as I shook my head, I replied forcefully, "No, I won't take

Dustin. I'll go, but I won't involve Dustin until I know which way the wind blows. It hurt him bad when you and I split up. I won't put him through that again until I'm certain."

Jake winced as if I'd poked him with a hot stick and looked at the floor as he shuffled his boots. "Yeah, I feel real bad about it. I knew he'd been hurt and it's been eatin' at me over the last year. I think that's one reason why I'd like to see you with David now." Jake's voice cracked as he added, "If I couldn't be his step-father, I'd want David to be."

I took another gulp of my beer as I digested his response and considered his motives and what obstacles we might face. "Okay, call Nell and see if she wants me to come. Call her now, before I lose my nerve."

Jake raised one brow and shrugged, "Okay. She's probably asleep, but she'll forgive me when I tell her you're coming. Can I use your phone?"

I reached over and picked the phone up. Hesitating a moment to wonder if it was the right thing, I finally shrugged and tossed it to him.

He dialed the number and waited. When she answered, he said, "Hi, Mom, it's me. Sorry to wake you up, but I've got some good news for you and it couldn't wait until morning." He listened for a moment and rolled his eyes. "No, Mom, Brenda hasn't left me. Sorry to disappoint you."

I took the last gulp of my second beer when his response struck me so funny, I laughed and snorted beer out my nose. Then, as I coughed and my eyes watered, Jake tried not to laugh.

I heard him say, "No, Mom, that's not Brenda. It's Katie snorting beer out her nose."

"What?"

"No, I'm not back with Katie. I just stopped by to talk to her."

"Yes, Mom, I know it's after midnight."

"No, Mom, I'm not up to anything fishy. We're just talking."

"Mom, stop. I came by to see if she would come to David's birthday party next weekend."

"Yeah, she said she would. Is it okay with you? No, mom, she's not coming as my date. I already told you I can't be there. No, she's coming to see David and you and Roy."

"Okay, hold on." Jake held the phone out to me. "She wants to talk to you."

I took a deep breath and held out my hands for him to throw the phone. He tossed it, but I missed and it hit the floor with a thud. I looked up and he began to laugh. With a scowl, I bent to retrieve the phone, but when I put it to my ear, there was nothing but dial tone. I looked at him and said, "It hung up on her."

At this, Jake began to howl with laughter and when he finally stopped, he wiped his eyes. "Man, I'd forgotten how much fun you were."

I continued to scowl and hold the phone out to him until he took it and re-dialed the number before handing it back to me. When Nell answered again, I apologized and told her Jake had dropped the phone and disconnected the line. He stared at me with his mouth open.

Nell was beside herself with excitement, but disappointed to hear Dustin wasn't coming with me this time. "You know, Nell," I explained, "Dustin was hurt pretty bad when Jake and Tyler disappeared from our lives. It took a long time for him to heal and I don't want to get him all excited again and then have him hurt if it doesn't work out. You do understand, don't you?"

"Yes, Katie, I do," she replied. "I'm sorry he had to go through that before and I sure hope maybe you and David can work something out. I'd sure love to hug the little rascal again. I've missed him. But I don't blame you for being cautious. I would be too."

"Thanks. I appreciate your understanding."

"No problem. Do you want me to send Roy to Phoenix to pick you up? I know he wouldn't mind."

"Oh, no, don't worry about it. My truck's running good right now. I can drive up."

'Okay, honey, but I want you to spend the weekend up here. We'll put you in the downstairs bedroom and we'll have a great time. In fact, if you can stay longer, we'd love to have you." She thought for a second and then asked for my phone number and told me to get hers from Jake. She instructed me to call her when I was ready to leave so they could watch for me.

I promised her I would call before I left.

We were about to hang up when she said, "Katie, I'm so happy you'll come, but I have to ask you something." Then she took a deep breath and asked, "Are you still in love with Jake?"

I quickly replied, "No. That's behind me."

She hesitated for a moment. "Good. I know it must've been hard for you. I'm sorry. I guess he was dumber than I realized."

I laughed. "Yeah, I guess so."

Nell continued, "Well, Roy and I will be happy to see you…and…well, I know David will be thrilled."

"Oh, yeah, I heard about you and Roy. Jake says you two got married. Congratulations! I knew there was something there."

"Thanks. Yeah, you were right. He's a mighty fine catch, and he keeps my feet warm at night, too."

We both laughed.

"Well," she said, "we'll see you Friday night, then."

I hesitated a minute and said, "I thought the birthday party was Saturday."

Nell replied, "Well, it is. But I think maybe you should come up Friday night. It would give us more time to visit and it would give David a chance to adjust to the idea…you know, privately, without a whole crowd of people around. You know, it's gonna be a bit of a shock for him."

I considered it for a minute. "Okay. I'll be there Friday night."

"Good," Nell replied. "You call us then when you're ready to leave and we'll watch for you. Oh, honey, it will be so good to see you again."

"I'm looking forward to seeing you too, Nell. I've missed you all. Well, I'll call you Friday, then."

"Okay. Bye."

"Bye," I said as I put the phone down.

I stared at Jake for a few moments, until he said, "Thanks." He nodded his head as he said, "I think this will be good."

I realized I'd been holding my breath and I exhaled. "I hope so. I'm not sure I'm up for another round of heartache."

Jake nodded as he stood to leave. "Well, I guess I'd better get back on the road if I'm gonna make home before morning."

I got up and followed him.

At the door, Jake turned and looked at me. He smiled and put his arms around me and hugged me. When he let me go, he said, “You’re a real treasure. You know that, don’t you? Sometimes I wish I’d met you first, before Brenda.”

I nodded as I replied, “Yeah, but you didn’t.”

Jake nodded and chucked me under the chin as he turned to leave. I stood in the doorway and again watched this man walk down my driveway. But this time there was no pain, only the fleeting wish things could have been different. But there was also hope this time, hope that I might have a second shot at an opportunity missed.

Chapter Twenty One

Friday had arrived at last. I'd been a wreck all week, worried about seeing David again. Dustin was off fishing with Mark and I was packed, dressed and ready to go. It was the witching hour and I was more nervous than a long-tailed cat in a room full of rocking chairs.

I picked up the phone and dialed Nell's number. It rang twice and someone picked it up. I heard a man say, "Hello." It was David! I had been expecting Nell to answer. I wasn't prepared for David. I froze.

He repeated himself, "Hello. Is anyone there?"

Then I heard Nell in the background. "What are you doing in here? That's my phone. Give it to me."

David replied, "Wow. Okay. All I did was answer it for you. I didn't order any magazines, I promise."

Nell's reply was muffled. "Oh, that's okay, honey. I didn't mean to snap at you. I just didn't expect to find you in here. I was expecting a call. Uh...uh...why don't you go find Roy and tell him dinner's gonna be ready in a few minutes."

I heard David say, "Okay," and then I heard him mumble something about everyone being touchy.

After a minute or so, Nell came on the line and said, "Hello."

"Hi, it's me, Katie."

Nell lowered her voice and almost whispered, "Oh, Hi, honey. I thought it would be you. Sorry. I didn't know David was in here or I woulda made sure I got to the phone first."

"It's okay. He took me by surprise, is all. I couldn't think what to say, so I just sat here...quiet. Kinda dumb, huh?"

"No, no. That was smart. We want it to be a surprise, don't we? Are you leaving now?" Nell asked.

"Yeah. Nell, are you sure this is a good idea?" I was rethinking our plans and feeling a knot of panic settle in my stomach.

"Honey, it's the only good idea Jake's come up with in the last year. You come on ahead. We'll watch for you. If you have problems, you call us on your cell phone. If you're not here in about three hours, we'll send out the search party."

I chuckled. "Okay, here I come. See ya in a bit. Bye."

Nell replied, "Bye, honey. You drive safe."

"I will," I promised her as I hung up the phone, grabbed my suitcase, sent up a prayer this was the right thing to do, and headed for my truck.

The trip went smoothly and just under three hours later, I pulled into the driveway at the ranch. I'd almost forgotten what a beautiful place it was. Everything looked the same, except the trees had grown a little bigger and there was a new storage shed out back. I pulled up to the house and parked, turning off the headlights and sat back to take a deep breath before I got out.

As I opened the door and my feet hit the ground, Nell and Roy came out the back door to meet me. Nell trotted toward me with her arms open wide and Roy followed with the biggest grin I'd ever seen on his face.

Nell grabbed me and we hugged for the longest time. When she released me, we both had tears in our eyes. Roy shook his head and wrapped me in a big, warm bear hug. When he turned me loose and stepped back, we heard the crunch of gravel from the direction of the barn. I turned and saw David walk out of the barn. I was thankful the area next to the house was dark, so I could see David in the light from the barn, but he couldn't see me well enough to recognize me.

I looked over at Nell and whispered, "He looks older, not so much like Jake now."

Nell put her mouth close to my ear and whispered, "Honey, he never did look as much like Jake as you thought he did."

I looked back at David and wondered if she was right. Had my feelings for Jake clouded my vision? As he got closer, I saw realization set in. He slowed and hesitated for a moment. Then I saw him take a deep breath and smile as he continued toward me. I turned to Nell, looking for support, but she and Roy were headed back into the house. Apparently, I was going to face this alone.

As I breathed deep and turned to face David, he spread his arms wide. "Hey, Slick, how the hell you been?"

I put my arms out and stepped into his embrace. As we hugged for a few moments, I caught the smell of soap and my stomach did a little flip. Jake hadn't smelled like soap when he stopped by the other night. He had smelled like cologne...after-shave. I chuckled as it dawned on me that Brenda had marked him—she'd branded him just as surely as if she'd used a red hot branding iron. He was hers and it was okay with me.

This man, however, had remained constant. He still smelled like soap and, for some strange reason, this stupid little fact gave me hope and my heart soared.

As he released me, I stepped back and smiled. "Hi. How are you? You look great!"

He shook his head as he stared at me. "I can't believe it's you. What are you doing here?" A look of pain flashed across his face. "You're not seeing Jake again, are you?"

I smiled and said, "No, dopey. I'm here because your mother invited me to your birthday party. I came to see you."

He blinked and stared at me with his mouth open.

After a moment or two, it struck me funny and I began to laugh. Once I started, it kept getting funnier and funnier. Before long, we were both laughing. About that time, the back door opened and Nell and Roy peeked out at us.

We finally pulled ourselves together. But when Nell asked what was so funny, we looked at each other and busted up all over again. When we had laughed ourselves out, David looked at me and then looked over at Nell and said, "I don't have a clue. It's just so damn good to see Slick here again." Then he put his arms around me and we hugged one more time.

Nell decided to take things in hand as she herded us all into the house and sat us at the table for dinner.

David sat at the table and shook his head. "Well, now I understand the whole dinner thing." As he looked over at Nell and raised one brow, she shrugged and turned back toward the stove. He looked at me and continued, "Mom sat us down about three hours ago and fed us a bowl of soup. When I asked where the rest of dinner was, she said the soup would hold us for a few hours 'til we ate our real dinner later. Roy seemed okay with it, so I headed back out to the barn to wait. I figured maybe they had a fight or something. I was starting to think I'd have to scrounge up some crackers and milk back at my place."

We all chuckled and started in on Nell's wonderful dinner. She had baked homemade rolls, roast beef, carrots, mashed potatoes and gravy, snow peas, and salad. Dinner lasted for almost an hour and at the end of the hour, we were all stuffed like ticks on a hound. When Nell got up to clear the table, we all got up to help. David and I sent Nell and Roy to the living room to pick out a movie while we did the dishes and cleaned up the kitchen.

I washed the dishes while David dried and put them away. We talked the whole time and it was a warm, easy conversation. I'd forgotten how comfortable David was to be around. I filled him in on what had been happening with us and then he brought me up to speed on things at the ranch and told me about his broken engagement.

When I said I was sorry it hadn't worked out for him, he stared for a moment and then looked away. "It was never meant to be. We weren't right for each other. I think I'd fallen in love with the idea of being in love and tried to make the peg fit the hole. It simply didn't fit."

He had his back turned to me, putting a pan away in one of the lower cupboards, as I laid my hand on his back. "David, you deserve to find the one woman who's perfect for you. Don't ever settle for less."

I felt him take a deep breath as he stood and looked over his shoulder at me. He didn't say anything, just looked into my eyes for a moment and then turned and walked out the back door onto the porch. I was afraid I'd said something wrong, but decided he just needed some space. So I popped up a bag of popcorn, dumped it into a bowl, and headed for the living room.

When I walked in alone, Nell raised a brow at me. I shrugged and said, "I think David went for a walk. I've got popcorn for the movie."

Roy and Nell looked at each other and back to me. "Is he okay?" Roy asked.

I shrugged. "I think so. I think maybe he just needed to be alone a minute. Let's give him a bit."

Roy nodded and patted the couch next to him. "Okay, honey, you sit down right here next to me with that popcorn."

I smiled and plopped down next to him as we fired up the movie.

About fifteen minutes later, David came back into the house and when he finally joined us in the living room, he had another bag of popcorn. "Refills, anyone?" he asked as he held up the popcorn bag.

We all smiled and clamored for more as David folded his long body into the recliner on the other side of me. When he noticed me looking at him, he winked and leaned over to kiss me on the cheek. "You know, you're still the prettiest girl here."

I shook my head and smiled as I told him how absolutely incorrigible he was. Everyone laughed as we settled in to watch the rest of the movie.

The stress of the event and the long drive to the ranch had been too much for me and somewhere near the end of the movie, I fell asleep. When I woke up, I was alone. The house was dark and I was on the couch with a pillow under my head and a blanket over me. I sat there for a minute to orient myself and remembered Nell saying she was going to put me in the downstairs bedroom. So I got up off the couch, picked up the pillow and blanket, and headed off toward my room.

When I flipped on the light, I found everything exactly as it had been the last time I'd been here. It was exactly as I'd remembered it. I quickly changed into my nightgown and turned off the light. As I headed for the bed, I decided to open the curtains so I could look out at the stars as I drifted off. When I pulled the curtains back, the light was still on out in the barn and there, framed in the light, was David. He stood with his hands in his front pockets, looking out across the pasture to the west. As he stood and looked out at the night, I stood in my dark room and looked out at him.

He looked pretty much as he had a year ago, but older. He'd aged considerably in a year's time, but he was still an incredibly handsome man. His face had hardened some and the lines were etched a bit deeper, but it only served to lend his face strength and make him even more attractive. He still had an infectious laugh and a smile that could light up an entire room.

As I watched, him, I wondered how I could ever have thought he looked exactly like his brother.

He had a gentler, kinder face and, although there were many similarities and they both had the same shit-eatin' grin, there were many differences also. As I continued to watch him from my dark room, he turned back toward the barn, switched out the light, and headed down the driveway toward his house. I watched until the light came on in his kitchen and the door closed behind him. Then I watched some more, until the lights went out in his house and I could no longer see his shadow on the shades.

I wondered what this weekend would hold. I wondered what I wanted it to hold. I wondered what he wanted it to hold.

Chapter Twenty Two

The sun was up early the next morning and so was I. I showered and dressed quickly and then headed out to the kitchen in search of coffee. Nell was in the kitchen, hard at work with breakfast, and she called out a good morning as I entered.

"Good morning," I replied. "How are you today?"

"I'm doin' good. It's a beautiful day for a birthday party, don't ya think?" she asked.

"Yes, it certainly is," I replied. "Where's everyone at?"

She told me Roy was out in the barn and she hadn't seen David yet this morning, but she expected him at any minute. "Just takes a little bit for the smell of the coffee to drift down to his place," she added.

We both chuckled and looked at each other as the back door opened and David entered right on cue. He looked from me to Nell and back again and then asked, "What?"

We laughed again and Nell answered, "Oh, nothing, honey. We were talking about things that never change."

David scowled, suspicious he'd been the brunt of a joke, but didn't pursue it as he headed for the coffeepot.

I sat at the table with my coffee. David poured himself a cup and sat across from me. "How are you this morning?" he asked with a smile.

I smiled back at him. "I'm great. Sorry I fell asleep on ya all last night. Guess I was more tired than I realized."

"Don't you worry about it none," Nell replied. "You had a long trip up here. I hope you slept well."

"Oh yeah. I slept like a rock. Must be the clean air up here."

"Good. I'm glad to hear it," she said. Then she turned to look at David. "I told everyone to be here between noon and one. Thought we'd eat about two."

David nodded and took another sip of his coffee. "Okay. I've got a couple of stalls to muck out this morning and then I'll head to the house to get cleaned up." He looked at me out of the corner of his eye and looked back at Nell as he added, "I told Jeannie I'd pick her up a little before noon."

My stomach twisted as bile rose in my throat.

Jeannie? He's got a date? Dammit, I knew this was a bad idea.

Nell turned to look at him with her eyes wide and exclaimed, "What? You invited her? What were you thinking?"

He shrugged as he rose and moved toward the coffeepot for a refill. "She called me late last night, crying. Her feelings were hurt because she hadn't been invited, so I told her we'd been busy and it was an oversight. She made a big production out of it and before I knew what had happened, I'd agreed to come pick her up. I don't like it any more than you do, but…well, it just worked out that way."

"I swear, you'll never be rid of her if you keep on being so nice. I thought at first she just needed to be let down easy, but now I'm starting to think she's got a plan." As she talked, Nell shook a wooden spoon at David while her face turned red.

David walked over and put his arm around her, smiling as he said, "Don't worry. It'll work out okay. I'm only going to pick her up and drop her off. It's not like it's a date. She knows it," he assured her.

Nell scowled and thumped him on the back with the spoon as she said, "I'm not so sure it's gonna be that easy." Then she looked at me and asked, "What about Katie? She came all this way to see you. How can you spend time with her when Jeannie's tagging along?"

Aw crap!

"Don't worry about me," I interjected. "I'll be fine. I know a lot of the people that will be here. I won't have any problem mingling."

I didn't like the direction this conversation was going. David clearly had made a date for the party and now I felt myself becoming the fifth wheel. Panic began to set in. I had to find a way to rescue my pride and not let David know I had come up here thinking to rekindle some old flame.

Stupid, stupid girl. You should have listened to your gut.

"Besides," I continued, "David and I are just old friends. I only came up here to see everyone and to wish him a happy birthday." As soon as it came out of my mouth, I regretted it, but there was no taking it back now.

David stared at me with his jaw clenched. The muscle worked in his jaw and I knew I'd somehow injured him.

Stupid girl!

He looked away, picked up his cup, and moved to the door. "See, mom. Katie and I are <u>just friends</u>. There's no problem." The door slammed shut behind him as he left.

I sat there for a minute, stunned. What had I done? When I looked at Nell, she shook her head and turned back to the stove. "You two are gonna screw around and botch this whole thing up again…I just know it!" Then she looked over her shoulder at me and waved the spoon in the air. "What were you thinking?"

"I don't know," I confessed. "I thought he had a date and I didn't want to be in the way. I was embarrassed. Nell, I don't know if I can do this. I've still got some very strong feelings for David and…well, there's so much history. I don't want to get hurt again. I guess I panicked."

Nell sighed and shook her head as she watched me. "Honey, you've both got feelings for each other and neither one of you wants to be the first to take a chance. One of you will need to make the first move, and it might have to be you. You rejected him once for his brother. You might have to be the one to push the door open this time. He might be too gun-shy to do it. Jeannie still wants him. He doesn't love her. But you gotta remember he's a nice guy and nice guys sometimes do stupid things when they're pressured by a woman. Don't let her get her hooks into him again—fight for him."

I sat there, quietly listening to her lecture. When she finished, I blew out the breath I'd been holding. She was right. It was my turn to take a chance. If I wanted this man, I would have to do the asking, and I'd have to do it before Jeannie pushed him into a corner. I took a deep breath and screwed up my courage as I got up from my chair. "Okay," I said to Nell, "When you're right, you're right. Guess there's no time like the present," and I headed out the door toward the barn. I had no clue what I'd say when I got there, but I had a few hundred feet to work it out.

Roy spotted me as soon as I entered the barn and raised one brow. I walked over and quietly asked him where David was. He pointed to his left, toward the back of the barn and said, "He's down there, but I'm not sure he's in any mood for conversation."

I shrugged, turned in the direction Roy had pointed, and said, "Well, it's too bad because I am."

Out of the corner of my eye, I saw Roy grin and turn toward the house as he made his escape from the vicinity of the barn before the proverbial "stuff" hit the fan.

As I walked through the barn, I heard a shovel scrape the dirt floor. The closer I got to the sound, the madder I got. David wasn't a stupid man. He had to know I'd come all this way to see him. He was determined to be a jackass and force me to ask. Well, okay…I'd ask, but I'd give him a piece of my mind, too! He wouldn't get off that easy.

I rounded the corner to the last stall and found David, shirtless, shoveling out the stall. He worked with a vengeance and had already worked up a sweat. For a second, I was breathless as I watched him work the shovel. I'd never seen him without his shirt and was surprised at how muscular and tan he was. David was beautiful, as the muscles in his back and shoulders flexed and the sweat glistened on his skin. As I noticed how broad his shoulders were and how his strong back tapered down to a narrow waist, a shiver ran through my body. Spellbound, I could only stare as he worked, like a snake following a charmer's flute.

He somehow sensed I was there and without breaking his rhythm or looking up, he growled, "Did you come to take a picture or do you have something to say?"

Flustered by my physical reaction to him and embarrassed at being caught staring like a besotted school girl, I jumped and began to stutter. "Well, yes…I mean, I…well, I…yes, I do have something to say." I tossed my head and threw my shoulders back to pump up my courage and continued, "I…well, I…oh, hell, David, why are you being such a jackass?" It wasn't the best start I could have chosen, so I opted to plow forward and hope he wouldn't pick up on the jackass comment. "Well, I wanted to say I'm…well, I'm here because your brother wanted me to come. Well, no, I mean, your mom invited me and…well, it's your birthday and I thought it would be nice to see everyone again and…well, no, that's not right…I'm here because…"

David threw the shovel into the corner of the stall and turned to face me with his hands in the air and yelled, "What? What is it? What the hell do you want from me, Katie? Are you here because of my mom? Or Roy? Or because maybe you thought my brother would be at the party? Which one is it? Tell me. I can't wait to hear it!"

When he yelled, it tripped a trigger deep inside and all my frustration and anger from the last year gushed to the surface. I was furious. I stared at him for a moment and then I exploded, "You are a Grade-A Jackass, you know that? I came up here for your birthday party because I thought maybe we both had healed enough to give things another shot. You told me once you'd always be here for me, so I thought...well, I thought maybe there was a chance. Then I get here and as soon as I show up, you make a date to bring another woman to your party. Well, that's rude. It's rude...and...well, it's just plain mean. You're a mean man and I don't know what I ever saw in you!" I knew what I was saying wasn't fair, but I was on a roll.

David stood like he was frozen in stone and watched me yell, with something like shock on his face. As I finished, he reached for me, but I'd worked up a good head of steam and wasn't about to let him touch me or have the last word. I spun on my heel and started to stomp off as fast as I could move. Unfortunately, I didn't see the rake leaned up against the side of the stall as I rounded the corner. So when I stepped on the bottom of it, the rake sprung up and cracked me on the side of the head to send me sprawling on the floor.

David was at my side in a heartbeat and grabbed me before I hit the floor. "Are you okay?" he asked with concern in his eyes.

I was angry and my pride was in the toilet. Now I'd been a klutz in front of David, which only served to add embarrassment to the mix. David pulled me to my feet and brushed me off as he tried to look at my head to make sure I wasn't hurt. He struggled not to laugh, which only threw fuel on the fire.

I wrenched my arm away from him and spun on my heel as I snapped, "Keep your hands off me," and headed for the house.

David called after me with a chuckle in his voice, "Katie, come back here. I'm sorry. Please, let's talk."

I was not in the mood any more, so I kept stomping toward the house. Without a backward glance, I raised my right hand and gave him a one-finger salute over my shoulder, just to make sure he knew where he stood.

He called after me, "Oh, now that's real mature!"

I saluted again as I entered the house.

Nell and Roy were at the kitchen table and looked up as I came in. Roy grinned and Nell said, "What happened? You're bleeding. What did you do?"

"Nothing," I growled as I stomped past them. "The man's a jackass!"

As I went through the doorway into the living room, I heard Roy say, "Well, I'd say that went well, wouldn't you?"

I heard a smack, followed by an "Ow, what'd you do that for?"

I headed upstairs to clean up and maybe pack my bags.

* * *

I took a long, hot shower and cleaned the straw and blood out of my hair. There was a small cut on my temple where the rake had hit me. It wasn't really any more than a large scratch, nothing compared to my wounded pride. When I was cleaned up and cooled off, I could see I'd handled things very badly and had made a tremendous fool of myself. I wanted to crawl into a hole and die or sneak home to lick my wounds. But Nell had gone to a lot of trouble to have me up for the weekend and she'd be hurt if I left. So I took a deep breath and resolved to buck-up and act like nothing had happened. I'd go to the birthday party and try to have a good time. I'd stay away from David and his date and then tomorrow I'd go home and put it all behind me.

The thought of David with a date wrenched my heart and I felt like I wanted to cry again, but the tears wouldn't come.

What the hell is wrong with me? What is it about the men in this family that I always seem to fall in love with one of them, and end up crying?

I sat down heavily on the bed as the truth hit me. I was in love with David, and I'd been in love with him for a long time. It was different than it was with Jake. That had been fast and furious, born of a whirlwind attraction to a man who'd lied to me and whose priorities had always lain elsewhere. Jake had been the easier man to be in love with…safer. He was already injured. The nurturer in me had been drawn to a man who needed me, drawn to him because of my need to fix broken things. Maybe, on some subconscious level, I recognized he was a man who could offer no commitments—and expect none.

This time it was different. This time it was David.

David, who had always been there for me each time Jake wasn't.

David, who'd always picked me up whenever Jake pulled the rug out from under me.

David, who had always been consistent and steady, who never changed.

David, who had said he would always be there for me if I ever changed my mind.

Now I had, but was it too late? Could I take the risk? Did I have the guts to love a man who didn't need me, someone who loved me simply for who I was? Did I have the guts to swallow my pride and let him know how I feel, at the risk of being rejected?

Overwhelmed by reality, I curled up on the top of the bed and lay there, staring out the window. I lay there for a long time, hurting and re-playing scenes in my mind as the tears fell again. Eventually, exhausted, I fell asleep.

I woke to the sound of a knock on the bedroom door. "Katie, it's Nell. Honey, are you alright? Sweetie, open the door so we can talk. Please."

I got up and stumbled to the door, opened it, and returned to flop back on the bed as Nell came to stand over me. She put her hands on her hips and looked at me for a moment before she said, "Oh, my, this isn't good. You look awful. From the looks of you and the mood David's in, I'd guess you two had a fight." Then she remembered the blood on my head when I came in earlier and asked, "You were bleeding when you came in. Are you hurt?"

I shook my head. "No. It's only a scratch. I was stupid. I stepped on a rake and it hit my head."

Her eyebrows shot up and her shoulders shook as she suppressed a chuckle. "Stepped on a rake? Oh, well, I'll bet that did hurt."

"Not as much as my pride. Oh, Nell, I've made such a mess of things. David's furious and he'll probably never talk to me again. What am I going to do?" I looked up at her with tears in my eyes as I confessed, "I finally admit to myself I'm in love with David and now I've gone and messed the whole thing up. I can't go through this again."

Nell sighed and sat on the side of the bed as she patted my shoulder. "Katie, my boy may not realize it yet, but he's still in love with you, too. It might take some time to straighten it all out, but if you hang in there, I think he'll come around. He's not stupid."

I looked at her with one raised brow. "I've heard that before."

She chuckled and shook her head. "Well, it's not possible for a woman to have two sons that stupid. We have to get lucky sometime."

At that, we both fell on the bed laughing and didn't quit until we were flat on the bed and gasping for air. It felt so good to laugh it all out!

Nell was the first to recover, so she stood and pulled me up after her. She walked me to the mirror and said, "Now, the ranch hands' wives have all arrived and are getting the food ready. Our guests will be here in about a half an hour. You take a good, hard look at yourself and see what you can do to repair the damage you've done. I'll get you some ice cubes to take the swelling out of those eyes. You'd better get to work if you're going to be 'the prettiest girl around' in time for the party."

Hearing her use David's words gave me hope and I took a deep breath. Looking at myself in the mirror, I groaned. "Oh my God, there's absolutely no hope!"

Nell laughed. "I've got faith in you. You'll figure out a way to fix it." Then she headed for the ice tray in the kitchen and returned a few minutes later with a cup of ice cubes. "Here you go. Put these on your eyes before you do your makeup. I think about fifteen minutes oughta do it." I hugged her and she patted my back and left me to do major repairs.

The ice and some eye drops did the trick and within minutes, my eyes were clear and the swelling had gone down enough that it probably wouldn't be noticed. I took special care with my makeup and then hit the closet to find something to wear. It was going to be a cool day, so I opted to wear my red sweater with some jeans and a new pair of red boots I'd bought to go with the sweater. I added some red hoop earrings and a matching bangle bracelet. As I stood back to survey the results, I heard a car coming down the driveway. The guests must be arriving. I looked pretty good and, knowing red was David's favorite color, thought I might have a chance to catch his eye. So I took a deep breath, put on a smile, and headed for the door determined to put things right.

Chapter Twenty Three

As I stepped out onto the porch, David got out of his truck with a pretty blond girl right behind him. She looked a few years younger than David and was short, with a pouty look. As he turned to help her out of the truck, she batted her big baby blues and flashed him a smile full of straight white teeth. I hated her.

As she turned and moved toward the porch, David spotted me over the top of her head and he stood for a moment, staring at me. I smiled and waved like nothing had happened. He blinked several times and started forward to intercept Jeannie as she headed straight for me. He was too late. She walked right up to me, held out her hand, and said, "Hi. I don't believe I've met you. I'm David's fiancée, Jeannie."

Stunned at hearing her introduce herself as David's fiancée, I forced a smile and held out my hand to shake hers as I said, "Hi. I'm Katie. I'm a friend of the family."

David scowled at Jeannie. "We're not engaged anymore," he growled. "I told you to stop telling people that."

She looked back over her shoulder and flashed him a huge, white smile again as she said, "Oh, honey, don't be silly. You know it's just a matter of time before you change your mind again."

My stomach clenched and I was overcome with the fear I might throw up right there on my new boots. I turned and moved off the porch, leaving him to deal with Miss Over-Confident. I'd find a better time to talk to him. As I stepped down onto the lawn, Nell watched me from across the yard. She arched one brow and I smiled and waved to let her know I was okay. Then I spied the beer coolers and decided that was the ticket. A beer would calm my nerves and my stomach nicely.

As I opened my first beer, I heard a familiar voice call my name and I turned to find Mac grinning at me. "Hey, Mac, how you been?" I asked as I hugged him.

He replied, "Well, I've been mighty fine, but I'm surprised as hell to see you here again. Good Lord, girl, you're prettier than ever! Don't tell me that flea-brained Jake finally came to his senses?"

I blushed and stammered out, "No, Mac. Uh...well...uhmm...I'm not here with Jake." As the surprise registered on Mac's face, I bolstered my courage and continued on, "We decided to make this a civil arrangement. Jake gets custody of his family every other weekend and I get them on alternating weekends."

As Mac threw his head back and guffawed, I felt a hand on the small of my back and turned to find David standing next to me, laughing. "Very funny," he said. Then he leaned close and whispered, "I'd like to talk to you. Have you got a minute?"

Taken by surprise and not yet ready to have that talk, I bolted like a scared colt, making some lame excuse about having to help Nell in the kitchen and leaving Mac and David standing there with their mouths open. So much for the courage I'd bolstered.

Apparently, not enough beer for stupid girl.

By the time I reached the safety of the kitchen, I was kicking myself for being such an idiot. That was the perfect opening and I'd blown it. I gulped down the last of my beer and checked the refrigerator to see if there were any more beers hiding in there. I got lucky and found one lurking behind the pickle jar. I quickly polished it off and headed outside to find another. I was in desperate need of courage, even if it came from a bottle.

Why was I so freaked out over this? Was it David? Was it Jeannie? What the hell was it? The answer popped into my head as if someone had handed me a cue card.

It's the fear of losing again.

As soon as the thought flashed in my brain, my heart clenched with a missed beat.

I've lost so much the last few years—my parents, my marriage, Jake. Now I'm going to lose another person I love if I don't pull my head out soon.

As I popped the top on my third beer, I spied David across the lawn having what looked like a heated discussion with Jeannie. She was gesturing wildly as he shook his head and stared at the ground. The people around them were tactfully drifting away to give them some privacy. For a split second, I wished I were where I could hear what was being said—but only for a split second. Then I reminded myself I had just fled from David in a complete act of cowardice. Who was I kidding? I probably couldn't handle overhearing their conversation. I needed to talk to him, but now wasn't the time. I'd never get him alone long enough.

I'll wait, give them time to hash it out. Maybe she'll get mad and leave.

I turned away and went in search of Nell. I couldn't find her, but I did find Roy with Mac and Annie. When I walked up, Annie squealed with delight and ran to hug me. I'd missed seeing her and, apparently, she'd missed me too. It warmed me to know everyone remembered me and I'd been missed. We stood around and chatted for a while. About fifteen minutes later, I heard a truck pull out fast. We all turned to see David's truck headed toward the road with Jeannie sitting in the middle, next to David.

My heart fell to my feet. He was leaving…with Jeannie. Where were they going? I swallowed my fear and turned back to the group, trying to make myself sound nonchalant. "It's a little early for a beer run, don't cha think?"

Mac chuckled. "They're probably headed off somewhere to make up in private."

My breath caught in my throat as I struggled to hold onto what little composure I had left. From the corner of my eye, I saw Roy's expression turn to one of sympathy as he watched my reaction. I straightened and silently pulled in a lungful of air to try and stave off my panic.

If they're going somewhere to make up, there's nothing I can do about it now. I just need to hold it together…and find a quiet place to think and drink, not necessarily in that order.

I excused myself and crossed the yard toward the coolers when I suddenly found my path blocked by Chance. I hadn't seen him since Annie's birthday party. He smiled a rather smarmy smile as he waited for me to recognize him.

"Hello, Chance," I said. "It's been a long time."

He continued to smile. "Well, if it isn't the beautiful Miss Katie. I'm surprised to see you here. Is Jake here with you?"

My stomach turned at the thought of having to explain my presence to this creep. "No, Chance. I'm sure you've heard Jake is back with his ex-wife. I just came to wish David a happy birthday."

Chance raised one brow and smirked. "So, you and David are close now. Thought you were a woman who didn't switch horses."

I smiled sweetly as I replied, "Well, sometimes the horse dies and when it does, you get off. I came up to see the McAllisters and to celebrate David's birthday. We have remained friends—nothing more, just friends."

"Oh," Chance said as he winked and flashed another of his smarmy smiles. "Well, then, may I volunteer my services as a dance partner?" Moving closer to me and lowering his voice to what I'm sure he thought was a seductive tone, he continued, "Like I said before, you won't find a better partner, either on your feet or off."

My face must have registered my horror at Chance's suggestion because he flinched like he'd been punched.

"Thank you, but I'll have to decline your offer, Chance. I'm not in the mood." Then, to discourage any further disgusting suggestions, I stepped around him and continued in the direction of the beer coolers.

I grabbed two beers, took a couple of steps and stopped. Two might not do it. I was sort of a light-weight when it came to drinking and was already starting to feel a buzz, but this situation called for more than two beers. I fully intended to throw one hell of a pity party for myself. So I turned back to the cooler, grabbed a third, and headed around to the back of the house, hoping I could sneak out to the barn without being seen.

When I got to the barn, I sat on a bale of straw outside Cody's stall. He immediately came over looking for a handout. "Sorry, boy," I said, "I didn't bring any carrots." As I stroked his nose, my heart constricted and the tears began to fall again. Feeling exposed crying in the middle of the barn, I looked around for a more secluded place to hide. Finally, I dragged the bale of straw into Cody's stall, sat on it with my back against the wall, and let it all out. As I cried quietly, Cody put his head in my lap, seeming to know I needed comforting. Funny thing about animals, they can sense when you need a friend. They never try to "fix" things. They just listen quietly, which was exactly what I needed right now.

I'm not sure how long I sat there crying and hugging a sympathetic Cody, but by the time I finished, I'd polished off all three beers and was a bit drunk. Well, maybe more than a bit…very drunk, actually. As I considered the wisdom of sneaking up to the house to get another beer, I heard the crunch of boots in the gravel at the entrance to the barn. I had company and I wasn't in the mood to share my space, so I remained very quiet, hoping whoever it was would go away.

Someone flopped down on the bale of straw in front of the next pen over and I heard the clank of beer bottles. Praying I wasn't the silent witness to a midnight rendezvous, I quietly scrunched up in the corner to wait it out. Then a thought struck me and I silently prayed it wasn't Chance. It definitely would not be good to be caught alone out here with him after he got a few beers in him, especially given the shape I was in.

Some time went by and the only sound I heard was the occasional clanking of bottles. There was no conversation—probably someone else nursing a broken heart and looking for a place to drink alone. Unfortunately, I was out of beer and had to pee. I couldn't hold out much longer. Hearing the sound of someone opening another beer, I knew I'd have to make an exit soon. I'd have to risk it might be Chance.

So I stood up, smoothed out my clothes, and walked out of Cody's stall just like I belonged there. The sun had gone down and it was dark in the barn, but I recognized David's long legs as soon as I stepped from the stall. I wasn't sure if I was relieved or not.

Startled by my presence, David jumped to his feet, eyes wide, and dropped his beer. It didn't break, but rolled across the floor and bumped against the toe of my boot. I bent to pick it up and, to bolster my nerves, I took a big gulp of beer as I watched him over the top of the bottle. David, clearly stunned, stared at me. Then he leaned over and looked into Cody's stall, as if to confirm I wasn't hiding a man in there.

With my heart pounding and my head spinning from all the beer, I was scared to stay and scared to run. I seemed rooted to the spot. David moved quickly, before I'd had a chance to decide on a course of action. He took two steps and cornered me against the door of Cody's stall with an arm braced on either side of me. He towered over me and looked into my eyes with an intensity I'd never seen in him before. I could hear my heart pound in my ears.

As I sucked in a lungful of air and moved to one side, he stepped in close and pinned me gently against the stall door. I could feel his body along the entire length of mine. I caught the faint smell of soap, mingled with the smell of beer. He was probably as drunk as I was.

Against all rationality, my body responded to his with a tremendous shudder and I thought I might drop as my knees gave way. But his warm, firm body held me in place, trapped like a bug in a spider's web. As I stood there trembling, David leaned forward and kissed me hard on the lips, his tongue slipping inside mine, demanding, consuming. Then his lips were moving across my jaw and down to my neck as his hands slid up under my sweater and around to my back, one hand skimming slowly across my bare skin to grasp the back of my neck. His warm, work-roughened hands scraped along my skin as goose bumps skittered along behind his hands. My breath caught in my throat and my heart became a jackhammer.

I'd lost control of my body and my back arched as David continued to kiss my neck and throat. As his mouth moved down over the top of my sweater to pluck at the tip of one nipple, I moaned and moved to take him in my arms. Just as my arms went around his neck, I felt him go rigid. He seemed to struggle for a moment before he took a deep breath and stood straight, backing away from me a half step, but still holding me by the shoulders and searching my eyes intently.

"I'm sorry," he whispered, "I shouldn't have done that. Are you okay?"

My entire body shook with the effort to regain control and my brain was so fogged with beer and my desire for him, it was like I was swimming in mud. Suddenly, my stomach muscles clenched and I knew I was going to be sick. I pushed him away and ran for the door, but didn't make it. After two or three steps, I stopped, bent over, and threw up on my new boots. As my head spun and my gut wrenched, I thought with horror I was going to fall forward into my own vomit. But before that happened, an arm snaked around my waist and steadied me down onto a bale of straw as a bucket was set in front of me.

David's voice was soothing against my ear as he said, "That's okay. It's all right, Slick. You sit still and you'll feel better in a few minutes." Then I heard him chuckle as he stroked my hair. "I don't think I've ever had anyone react to my advances quite that way before."

When I'd vomited up my last toenail, I put my face in my hands and leaned forward with my elbows on my knees. David handed me a cool, wet towel and I wiped my face while he cleaned up the mess I'd made. When the sickness had passed and I felt better, I looked up to see David leaning against Cody's stall, silently watching me. I closed my eyes and buried my face in the wet towel, certain I'd just blown my last chance with him.

I was embarrassed and feeling defensive, so I took the only logical course of action as I went on the offense and asked, "Where's your fiancée?"

I heard the shuffle of David's boots as he thought about his answer. "She's not my fiancée. I took her home and told her never to call again." His boots scraped again as he moved around to sit on the bale beside me. Then I felt his arm around my waist and his breath on the back of my neck as he asked, "Are you okay?"

"I've been such a fool," I cried as I leaned against him. "I should never have let you go, and now it's too late. I'm so sorry." My heart ached like it was skewered on a platter.

He simply held me quietly and let me cry. At some point, I either fell asleep or passed out—I don't know which.

* * *

When I awoke, I was in my bed, and I was naked. I panicked for a moment and jerked upright as I looked around the room and patted the bed to make sure I was alone. No one in the room but me. I flopped back on the bed as the room began to spin and lay there stock-still until it quit, trying to piece together what had happened last night.

The last thing I remembered was crying into David's chest as he quietly stroked my hair. Try as I might, I couldn't remember anything beyond that point. Finally, I gave up and rolled into a ball on my side as I fell back asleep and stayed asleep until I heard the door open.

I opened my eyes to find Nell standing beside the bed with a cup in her hand. "Wow. You really tied one on last night! Your head must hurt something awful. Here, I brought you something for the hangover. Drink this."

"What is it?" I asked as I took the cup.

"Better you don't know until later." She grinned. "You just drink it and I guarantee you'll be good as new in about an hour."

I drank it and thought I might gag again. It was awful, but I choked it down because I dearly wanted to be "good as new" sometime in this century.

She took the cup and patted my arm. As she turned to leave the room, I said, "Uh, Nell, who put me to bed?"

She turned and arched one brow as she said, "I don't rightly know. If it wasn't you, it must've been David. He's the one who informed me you'd drank too much and gone to bed early. Why?"

"Oh, no reason. Just wondered who to…uh…who to thank." I replied softly as Nell smiled and turned to leave.

I fell back asleep and must have slept a couple more hours, judging by the light coming in the window. Pleasantly surprised to find my head fairly clear, with the faintest trace of a headache, I decided a shower was in order. So I scrubbed down real good, washed and combed my hair, brushed my teeth twice, and pulled on some jeans and a t-shirt. Then I put on some socks and my old boots and headed out to the kitchen with my hair still wet. As I poured myself a cup of coffee, I heard the back door open and turned to find David with a half-grin on his face.

"You okay?" he asked.

"Yeah, I'm okay," I told him as I quietly seethed inside. "Nell says you're the one who put me to bed last night."

He nodded as he carried his cup over to the coffeepot to pour himself another cup.

I didn't move out of his way, but stayed where I was and leaned back against the counter next to the coffeepot, forcing him to reach around me to get his coffee and put the pot back on the burner. As he reached past me, our eyes met and I calmly asked, "Who took my clothes off?"

He blushed and grinned that bone-tingling grin as he turned away. "I did."

I gave him a soft kick in the butt as he took a sip of his coffee. "You smug son-of-a-bitch!" I accused. "Was it good for you? 'Cuz I sure as hell don't remember it! What did you do after you got my clothes off me?"

He slammed his cup down on the table, spilling coffee everywhere, and spun back on me with fire in his eyes. Just like the night before, he took two steps and pinned me against the counter as he dropped his voice and said, "I didn't do anything. You'd been sick and you were a mess. I couldn't stand the thought of putting you to bed like that, so I got your clothes off you and cleaned you up a bit. Dammit, Katie, I love you! I'd never do anything to hurt you. Can't you get that through your thick skull?" Then he spun on his heel and was out the door before I could blink twice.

It took a minute for what he said to sink into my brain. Holy hell, I'd done it again! He'd just told me he loved me. I'd accused him of doing something unspeakable and he'd said he loved me.

What the hell am I doing? This is madness. He loves me and I love him, yet we keep doing this nightmarish dance of anger. It's got to stop.

The pieces suddenly fell in place in my mind.

Yes, I do have the guts to love him. Dammit, this time he's not getting away!

Chapter Twenty Four

I was headed for the barn when I heard a door slam down the road. He'd gone home instead of to the barn. So I turned and headed down the road, determined to end this madness now.

I got to his house and tried the doorknob. It was unlocked.

Should I knock? Hell no!

I opened the door and let myself in. As I entered his kitchen, David was at the counter and spun around to face me. I didn't say a word. I simply walked across the kitchen, put my arms around his neck, pulled his head down, and kissed him squarely on the lips.

Too stunned to react, he stood there looking like I'd hit him between the eyes with a two-by-four.

I stepped back a half step and put my hands on my hips as I said, "Well, if what you say is true, then it would seem we're both in love with each other and we've been acting like a matched pair of jackasses. What do you suppose we ought to do about it?"

He seemed to stop breathing as he said, "I don't understand. What are you saying?"

"I'm saying I love you, you big idiot, and I'm asking you what you're going to do about it."

As I spoke, he'd moved slowly toward me and as soon as I finished what I had to say, he pulled me into his arms. He hesitated a moment, searching my eyes as if he wanted to make sure I was serious.

Then he groaned deep in his chest as his lips gently touched mine.

But I needed more. I needed consuming, I needed to know I was his. There would be no restraint this time, not for me. I slipped my arms around his neck and pressed my body against his as I deepened the kiss, demanding more. As I gently pulled at his lower lip with my teeth, passion exploded white-hot and he groaned as his tongue delved into my mouth and he lifted me off the floor. His kiss was deep, possessive. He'd staked his claim and I know in that moment I was his as surely as if I'd been branded.

I was on fire as he set me back on the floor. He was kissing my face and my throat. His hands were under my shirt, on my back, on my belly, caressing my breasts. I couldn't catch my breath. I tugged at his shirt and fumbled with the buttons until he suddenly scooped me up in his arms and carried me into the bedroom. Breathing raggedly, he gently set me on my feet next to the bed. He stared into my eyes as he removed my shirt and bra. Then he bent to gently plant a kiss on the top of each breast and slowly circled one nipple with his tongue before taking it into his mouth.

I arched my back like a cat in heat and fumbled like a schoolgirl as I struggled to get his shirt off. We were skin to skin from the waist up and I was on fire from the waist down. I was working at his belt when he kissed me again and gently laid me back on the bed. He unbuckled my belt and removed my boots and pants, leaving me completely exposed as he stood back and looked at me.

"You are so incredibly beautiful," he whispered and his voice cracked as he leaned over to kiss my belly. I moaned and arched my back as his hand slid between my legs. He stood again and began to remove his pants when suddenly a loud siren split the air.

He threw his head back and groaned, "Oh, God, not now!" Then he took a deep breath and looked at me as he began to put his pants back in order. "I've got to go. That alarm means there's a fire somewhere on the ranch. I'm sorry." He turned and bolted for the door, buttoning his shirt as he ran.

I lay there panting for a moment, stunned at the sudden chill in my bones at his absence. When my wits returned, I jumped up and dressed quickly, following him down the road and out to the barn, where smoke billowed and horses bolted out the door. Someone was apparently inside the barn, releasing horses. I looked around and didn't see David anywhere, so I sent up a quick prayer he remained safe. As I surveyed the scene and tried to decide what to do amidst all the confusion, Roy ran out of the barn. He threw an armload of halters and lead ropes at my feet and told me to get someone to help me catch the horses and get them into the front pasture, up by the road.

I grabbed a young ranch hand and told him what we were supposed to do. He helped me move the halters and lead ropes out into the open where we would be out of everyone's way. I spotted a number of horses milling about in the driveway up by David's house and I was afraid they'd get out onto the main road and then we'd have problems of a different sort. I pointed to the horses and told him we needed to start with those. He nodded and told me to run and close the gate so none of the horses got out while he caught and saddled a couple of horses for us to use to round up the rest. I nodded and took off up the driveway with an armload of halters and ropes. As I approached the gate, I could hear a fire engine off in the distance. Certain they were coming here, I kept the gate open so they could get in quickly and stood in the gateway to prevent escape until they were through.

The fire truck came through the gate and horses scattered everywhere. I closed the gate behind the truck and set out to catch horses. Just as I got my second horse caught and secured to the front fence line, the ranch hand I'd commandeered showed up on horseback with another saddled horse in tow. I looked at the horse and smiled. It was my old buddy, Cody. It took me a minute to get up on him, but I got it done and we set about trying to herd all the horses into the front corner. We ended up herding a small group of horses forward, opened the gate and drove them through, and then going back for another small group.

Within fifteen minutes, we had most of the horses in the front pasture. At this point, we decided to tie our mounts up and catch the couple of remaining stragglers on foot. Another ten minutes and we had them all secured in the pasture. The flames had fully engulfed the barn, but the firemen had the fire under control so it wouldn't spread to the house and other outbuildings. The barn could be rebuilt, so I guessed we'd probably be in fairly good shape if we'd managed to get all of the equipment and animals out.

I dropped onto an overturned bucket and looked around, trying to find David in the crowd. Nell came up behind me and shoved a bottle of water into my hands. I took it gratefully, guzzled half of it and squirted the other half over my head. Then I asked her if she'd seen David. She smiled and pointed. As I followed in the direction of her finger, I saw David off to the left of the barn, sitting on a bucket similar to mine, with his head in his hands.

I jumped up and ran toward him. At my approach, he looked up. When he saw it was me, he smiled and stood up with his arms wide. I ran into them and he kissed me on the top of the head. "Are you okay?" he asked.

"Yes, I'm fine," I answered. "You okay?"

He nodded and pulled me close again. We stood that way for a long time, watching the firemen work on the fire. The ranch hand that had helped me round up horses earlier headed down the driveway to re-open the front gate. A short time later, a paramedic's truck rolled into the driveway.

I turned to David. "Was someone hurt in the fire?"

He shook his head. "I don't know. I didn't see anyone get hurt, but we've probably got plenty of minor burns and they should probably check everyone for smoke inhalation."

We waited until the truck came to a full stop in an open area up by the house before we started in that direction. Paramedics jumped out and began to process the scene and triage injuries quickly and efficiently. We were surprised to see how many injuries they were able to find on people who had insisted they were fine, including both David and me. David had some second-degree burns on both hands and a small one on his back where a burning timber had dropped on him as he was releasing horses from the barn.

I had rope burns on the palms of my hands and my sprained wrist was beginning to swell and bruise.

Once our injuries were cleaned and bandaged, we were sent up to the house where Nell had set up a comfort station of sorts and had mobilized the wives of the ranch hands to cook and serve meals. David and I sat quietly at a table under a tree in the front yard as we rested and ate. We were just finishing up when Mac's truck pulled into the driveway and we both jumped up and went to meet him.

Mac got out of his truck and looked at the barn, shaking his head. Then he looked at our bandaged hands. "You two okay?"

We both nodded and David responded, "Yeah, we're fine. But we've got a handful of horses injured." We led him across the driveway to the pen where the ranch hands had isolated the horses with visible injuries. A couple of the boys jumped up and ran over to give Mac a hand working on the horses.

Mac waived David and I off. "You two have done enough and you look like hell. You go up to the house and take a nap, both of you—doctor's orders!"

David frowned. "Hate to tell you this, Mac, but you're not a doctor. You're a vet."

Mac laughed. "Since when did it ever make any difference to you?"

We all laughed as Mac continued, "Seriously, I'll radio back to the ranch and get Pete to round up a relief team for your boys. When they get here, you two are gonna need to be fresh in order to get them organized and working on what needs to be done while your crew rests up. The smart thing for you to do is get some rest now, while the professionals are still in charge of the scene. I'd pick out a couple of your lead guys, and send them to bed for a couple of hours, too."

Mac's advice was sound and we both nodded our agreement as David shook Mac's hand and said, "Thanks, Mac. I really appreciate the help."

"No problem," Mac responded. "You two get off your feet for a while. I'm thinkin' it'll take Pete four or five hours to organize a relief crew, round up equipment, and get them all transported out here. So you've got that much time to get some sleep and clean up before they get here."

We nodded and turned back toward the house. David explained the situation to Roy, Nell, and a couple other ranch hands. Then he sent them all off to their beds to rest up for the next shift. With that done, he took my hand and tried to lead me down the road to his house. When I pulled back, he turned and raised one brow.

"I don't think it's a good idea for me to stay with you," I told him. He scowled and opened his mouth to protest when I held up my hand and continued, "I don't think it would look right. No one knows about us yet and it would look like we just jumped into the sack together. Besides, my clothes are all here and I've got some calls to make. Remember, I'm supposed to be back in town tonight. I need to make arrangements for Dustin and call my boss to let her know I won't be there to open the bar in the morning. She'll have to get someone to fill in for me."

David took a deep breath and nodded his head as he turned to lead me back toward Nell and Roy's house. He walked me into my room and closed the door behind him. Then he took me in his arms and kissed me softly, sweetly. "I'm almost afraid to let you out of my sight," he said. "It seems like every time I do, things get all screwed up."

I smiled and stroked the side of his face. "I know. We have to trust each other more. David, I love you and I'm here for you, not for Nell or Jake or anyone else. I'm here for you, for as long as you'll have me."

He kissed me and held me for the longest time before he finally pulled away and turned to leave. At the door, he stopped and turned back as he asked, "Can I ask you something personal and stupid and very, very childish?"

"Sure," I said as I smiled.

"Did you ever sleep with Jake?"

The question stunned me and I blinked a couple of times before I grinned and replied, "No. You've already gotten further than Jake ever did." Then I wiggled my eyebrows up and down for effect.

He blushed as he grinned and dropped his eyes to the floor for a minute before looking up. "Okay. Sorry. I know it was stupid, but it kept niggling around in the back of my mind. I know this isn't a contest and it doesn't really matter either way, but I…I don't know…I just wanted to know."

I walked over to him and put my arms around his neck as I kissed him. It was a deep, passionate kiss, designed to let him know how I felt. When it ended and I pulled back, we were both breathing hard and I could see the desire in his eyes. He smiled and said, "Okay, that shower's gonna have to be a cold one now."

I chuckled, shooed him out the door, and headed for a cold one myself.

Chapter Twenty Five

Five hours later, we were all rested up, showered and back on the job. Mark had agreed to keep Dustin a few more nights and my boss said to take whatever time I needed.

The relief crew arrived and we sent our tired ranch hands home to rest up for the night. They were told to get a full eight to ten hours sleep and be back for their regular shift in the morning.

David then gathered the relief crew together and told them it would be a fairly light evening for most of them. "It's almost six o'clock now and it'll be dark soon. We need to get all the animals bedded down for the night. I'll need a couple of you to set up and fill some water barrels for the horses in the front pasture. We rescued a bunch of barrels and hoses, but you'll have to look around to find them. Make sure you clean 'em out good before you use 'em. We don't want a bunch of sick horses because we got in too big a hurry."

As David looked around at the relief crew in front of him, he continued, "I'll need another couple of guys with doctoring skills to check on the injured stock in the back pen. Make sure no one's bleeding or having problems. Make sure they've got enough bedding to keep them warm through the night so we don't have any of them going into shock. I'd like it if the guys working with the injured animals could stay the night out in the bunkhouse and check on the animals throughout the night. There are a couple of them with more serious injuries and they could bear watching. Who here's got experience doctoring animals?"

Three of the guys raised their hands as everyone pointed at one of them and agreed, "Tyler's the best. He can heal anything."

"Okay. You three will do." David pointed at Roy and said, "Roy here's my foreman and he's the best damn doctor around, next to Mac. You three will be taking orders from him. Nell over there is my mother and she's chief cook and supply officer. She'll see you men have food, coffee, and any bedding or personal supplies you might need to stay the night. She's the one you don't want to piss off." As the men all laughed, David continued, "Make sure your wives know you won't be home 'til morning." All three of the men chosen nodded and followed Roy off toward the back pen.

David turned toward the rest of the group and continued, "We'll need the rest of you to sort out all this equipment. We've got tack and equipment everywhere and it all needs to be sorted and cleaned. This gal here next to me is Katie. She and I will be taking inventory and working with you to help prioritize the work so we're focused on the most critical equipment. You boys will want to keep in mind that Miss Katie is spoken for—by me. So there's no need to go hittin' on her."

I looked over at David with raised eyebrows as the boys all laughed again.

David shrugged and quietly said to me, "Just kinda breaking the ice and saving time and misunderstandings."

I rolled my eyes. "Yeah, sure." Inside I felt all warm and fuzzy that he wanted to make it public knowledge.

David turned his attention back to the crew. "Okay, let's get going. I think most of you will be off by about midnight. Our focus will be to get the animals situated and the equipment we need to run the ranch tomorrow identified, located, cleaned, and ready to go. Once that's done, we're done for the night. Okay, a couple of you go set up the water barrels and the rest of you sort this equipment into piles. Katie and I will work up a list of the equipment we think we're going to need for tomorrow. Then we'll take inventory and identify what needs work. Let's go."

A couple of the boys peeled off, grabbed a couple of water barrels, and headed for the front pasture. I headed to the house to find some pads of paper and pens, while David set one of the crew members to work setting up emergency lighting so we could see to work after dark.

We spent the next four hours sorting and cataloging equipment, identifying things we would need the next day, and assigning priorities to the remaining items. By about eleven o'clock, all the equipment had been inventoried and prioritized, and the critical items were checked, repaired, cleaned and ready for use.

The animal care crew reported all of the injured animals were settled in for the night and looked good. A couple of horses had been cut out of the herd in the front pasture and moved into the hospital pen because they had injuries previously undetected, mostly sore muscles or coughs that needed to be watched. Roy reported that he was comfortable with the skill level of his crew and everyone had what they needed to get through the night.

David told the boys food had been set out for them in the front yard. He suggested everyone eat a bite before they headed home or off to bed. So everyone headed for the food. We ate and saw everyone off before we headed into the house ourselves. David and I collapsed on the couch, while Nell and Roy said their goodnights and headed off to bed.

As I sat there with my head on David's shoulder, the whole world seemed right. Even with the excitement and loss of the fire, there were no major injuries and it felt good to work beside the man I loved. Strangely, it seemed like it had been the perfect day.

"You did good today." David took my hands in his and kissed the inside of my bandaged palms. "You're very organized and you've got a good head for prioritizing work. Where'd you learn to do that?"

"I don't know. Guess it comes from being a working single mother. My life's all about priorities these days."

"Well, I gotta tell you, it felt so right working side by side with you tonight." He looked into my eyes for a moment before he continued, "Did you notice there were times when neither of us had to say anything—we just knew what the other was going to say?"

I nodded. "Yeah, it was like we'd both tuned into the same wave length. It was kinda fun."

David chuckled and shook his head as he stretched and sat forward with his elbows on his knees. "What are your expectations from this relationship?"

I looked at him and blinked, not fully understanding. When I couldn't formulate an answer, I said, "I'm not sure I understand what you're asking."

"Well, what is it you want out of this? Are you looking for a long-term dating relationship, marriage, what? Are you a love him and marry him kind of girl or are you a gal that wants a long engagement?"

"Are you asking me to marry you?" I asked him pointedly, with a grin.

He blinked at my blunt question and said, "Well, yes, I guess I am. I know this isn't very romantic, but I've known you a long time. I've seen you at your best and, I think, at your worst. I've seen you under pressure and I know everything I need to know about you. I love you. I love your son. I want you both in my life and in my home. It's as simple as that."

"But I realize women have different needs than men and I don't want to pressure you or rush you. I just want to cut through the crap and know what you expect from me so we can take the shortest route to paradise." Then he leaned against me and lifted my hands to kiss the backs of them. "Because I won't be truly happy until you're my wife."

I took a deep breath and tried to swallow the lump in my throat as I smiled up at him. "McAllister, that was probably the most romantic proposal I've ever heard. I'll admit it started out a bit shaky, but you really brought it home there at the end."

He smiled. "Is that a yes?"

I smiled and nodded. “Yes. Yes, that’s a yes. Definitely a yes.”

He took me in his arms and kissed me gently. When he pulled back, he pressed on. “Okay, now we’ve got a goal. So what’s the plan? Do you want a long engagement and a big wedding, short engagement and a simple wedding, or a Justice of the Peace tomorrow morning?”

I laughed. It was clear the third option was the one he truly hoped I’d go for. I thought for a minute. “Well, the Justice of the Peace tomorrow morning is out. Dustin would never forgive us.” David frowned as I continued, “But the good news is, the long engagement and big wedding is also out.” He perked up a bit, so I continued, “What about getting a preacher out here to the ranch next weekend or the weekend after and we can combine the wedding with a good, old-fashioned barn-raising?”

David stared with his mouth open. When he didn’t respond, I gave him a questioning look and asked, “What?”

He shook his head and smiled. “You are absolutely the most surprising woman I’ve ever met. Do you mean to honestly tell me you would willingly share your wedding day with a barn-raising?”

“Yeah, I would. I want our family and friends to be here for our wedding and I’d rather have a party than a stuffy old reception. There’s a lot going on right now and we’ll need to re-build the barn before winter hits. Seems like a good opportunity to kill two birds with one stone. What’s wrong with that?”

David shook his head again as he looked into my eyes. “I don’t think you can ever know just how much I love you right at this moment.” Then he pulled me to him and kissed me again. This kiss was more passionate than the last and it led to another and then another, as David leaned back against the arm of the couch and pulled me up on top of him.

When we finally came up for air, we were fast approaching the point where clothes would start coming off if we didn't rein it in.

"I'd like to do this right, Katie," he breathed heavily into my ear. "We're not alone and I don't want to put either of us in a compromising position, so I think it would be wise to wait. A week or two isn't so long. Is that okay with you?"

I nodded.

"Okay." He sat up and moved me back onto the couch next to him. "When do we do it?"

I looked at him in surprise. "What?"

He chuckled. "I mean when do we tie the knot? Think you can you get your plans in place by next weekend or do you need two weeks?"

I thought about it for a minute before I responded, "Well, given that next weekend would only give us three or four days to get things in place, I'm thinking we may need to do it the following weekend. It gives me time to call everyone and invite 'em and it would give you time to get the clean-up done and the new building materials delivered."

David nodded as I spoke, agreeing the following weekend would be best. "Okay, the following Saturday it is. Do you have any objection to a sunrise service so we can get an early start on the construction work?"

"None," I answered. "I think a sunrise service would be beautiful."

"What about a honeymoon? We should go somewhere to be alone for a few days. Once we get the framing done, Roy can oversee completion of the barn and we could leave on Sunday or Monday."

David thought for a second before he continued, "Katie, I don't know how you feel about working, but I'd sure like to have you here, working beside me at the ranch. How would you feel about quitting your job?"

"You wouldn't have to ask me twice. I'll call the boss with my two weeks notice tomorrow so I can be completely free by the time I come up for the wedding. Then I'll start the paperwork to get Dustin transferred up here for school and we'll bring the dog with us when we come back up. We'll do a quick relocation and then move the rest of our stuff and decide what to do with my house after we get home from the honeymoon. We can probably let Dustin stay here and dig in at the ranch for those few days we're gone—if Nell and Roy don't mind watching him."

David threw his head back and laughed. "Oh, Slick, you amaze me! We burn down a barn, fall in love, get engaged, plan a wedding and a honeymoon, end your career, and plan a major move all in the space of a day. You are never going to be a boring woman to live with, are you?"

I laughed with him. "Well, I figure I'd better move fast if I want to hang onto you. I finally know what I want, so why screw around? We've already discovered you and I seem to get our signals crossed when we have too much time to over-think things."

David chuckled at my answer and pulled me into his arms, where we stayed for a few more minutes before we agreed it was time to turn in. He walked me to the door of my room and gently kissed me goodnight.

Alone in my room, I opened the curtains and watched him walk down the driveway to what would soon be "our" home. The world took on a warm glow as it settled into place and everything felt right. What would Jake think when he heard the news? I hoped he'd be happy for us.

* * *

The time had come. It was two o'clock and my last shift was done. MJ had agreed to work the last few hours for me so I could get on the road early. She and Willy would come up later, after she got off and they would spend the weekend at the ranch helping Nell with the wedding cleanup. It was finally time to say my good-byes at the bar, pick Dustin up from Mark's house, load the truck, grab the dog and head north to our new home. My stomach was full of butterflies. It was exciting and terrifying, all at once.

I'd left Nell in charge of all the wedding arrangements out at the ranch. She'd ordered flowers, invited all the neighbors and David's family, and enlisted what we were starting to refer to as our "Wives Corp" to help with the shopping, equipment rental, and food preparation.

MJ and I had found a beautiful new outfit for the wedding ceremony. It was one of those trendy, yuppie cowgirl outfits with the fringe on the jacket and the skirt. It was a little over the top, but it would be fun for a casual country wedding. I sent my new red boots out to be professionally cleaned after my night of over-indulgence at David's birthday party and they came back beautiful—they looked perfect with the dress.

Dustin was beside himself with excitement. He had talked with David by phone a number of times over the last two weeks and they were still in negotiations over what Dustin should call David after we were married. David had suggested Daddy wouldn't be appropriate because it was Mark's nickname. They had both agreed Father David was out of the question, which relieved me tremendously. There were still several other options on the table, but the negotiations were still on-going and probably would be for some time.

David said Nell had made the boys put up a dog run for Obleo so they could keep him safe until he got used to being at the ranch. The building materials and tools were delivered yesterday and everything was ready to go.

Our honeymoon would be three nights and four days at a friend's upscale but secluded cabin near a wooded lake up in Colorado. It would be cold, but not cold enough for snow, just cold enough to cuddle up under a blanket in front of a fire. Puuuurrrrfect!

When I got home with Dustin, we found Willy leaned up against the front porch railing. "Hi. Thought I'd come by and give you a hand loading up."

I smiled and hugged him. "Oh, how sweet! That will save me so much time. Thanks!"

As we walked into the house and Dustin headed to his room to finish his last minute packing, I turned and looked at Willy, suspicious. Raising one brow, I asked, "Everything okay?"

He smiled. "Yeah. Just came by to help. No messages to relay or anything this time, just big brother volunteering his services as a pack animal to help little Sis load her truck as she heads out to find her Prince Charming."

I laughed as I hugged him again and pointed to the stack of boxes in the middle of the living room. "Okay, animal…pack!"

He laughed as he hoisted two boxes and headed out the door.

When we were all loaded up and the dog was settled in the backseat of the pickup truck, we said our good-byes to Willy and told him we'd watch for him and MJ later that night. As Willy pulled away from the curb, I locked the front door and got behind the wheel of the truck, looked over at Dustin and said, "Well, you ready to do this, Bucko?"

He gave me a thumbs-up and said, "You betcha, Slick!"

I laughed. "Where did you come up with that?"

He giggled and told me, "David. He said you'd love it if I called you Slick."

I laughed and ruffled his hair as I told him, "Okay, I'll have to have a talk with him. He's teaching you bad habits already." I loved that the two of them were so bonded. Made it feel like a real family already.

We both laughed as I backed up to the end of the driveway and stopped. We sat there for a minute, saying goodbye to our old lives. Then we took a deep breath, looked at each other, smiled, and did a thumbs-up as we headed down the road to find our new ones.

Chapter Twenty Six

We arrived at the ranch about seven thirty, in the midst of sheer chaos. The driveway was full of delivery trucks and pickup trucks of all shapes and sizes. There were building materials stacked everywhere out behind the house, there were tables and chairs set up on the front lawn and a whole host of people moving in and out of the house.

David spotted us as soon as we pulled up and quickly headed our way. I managed to get out of the truck without releasing the dog, but Dustin wasn't quite as quick. Obleo escaped from the passenger side and made a beeline for the tables in the front yard. Tables usually meant food and he was ready to eat. Obleo's a very sweet dog, but he's got a bit of a problem—he doesn't answer real well when you call him. In fact, he *never* comes when you call him, unless he's otherwise motivated by food or attention. Right now, he was in search of food and no amount of attention or calling his name would bring him back.

At its peak, the pursuit consisted of at least a dozen adults and a couple of kids chasing one blond Cocker Spaniel under tables, across the porch, and through the house. Barreling through the kitchen in a frantic search for the food he could smell so well, but couldn't find, Obleo almost bowled over the woman who was putting the finishing touches on the top tier of the wedding cake. At that point, Nell joined in the chase with a huge wooden spoon in her hand.

Some of the ranch hands also joined in the chase and tried to herd the dog into the back part of the house where they could trap him in the laundry room. Every time someone would get close to Obleo or he would get close to the laundry room door, he always managed to run through a pair of legs, duck under something, or do a double-back and elude everyone.

Eventually, the chase moved back outside, where Obleo must have decided the delivery trucks held the key to his epicurean bliss, as he jumped in and out of countless delivery trucks. When the dog gave up on the trucks and leaped back onto the porch, he found the kitchen door closed, preventing any entry back into the kitchen.

It was David who came up with the collar, literally, when he snagged Obleo mid-air as he dove off the porch and onto the nearest table in the front yard. They fell to the ground in a heap, with David holding tight to a wiggling, whining Obleo. I ran to rescue David and clipped a leash onto the dog's collar so he couldn't take off again. When Obleo finally jumped free of David and realized he was still caught, he flopped to the ground and whined as he dropped his head on his paws. David got up, dusted himself off and shook his head as he looked at me. "Wow. So that's the side of Obleo you warned me about."

I laughed and Dustin said, "Yeah, he's just like the kid who was the only one in the land of point with a round head."

I continued to laugh as David ruffled Dustin's hair and said, "Yeah, I can certainly see how that relates. It would appear the dog run was a really good idea." Then he scooped Dustin up in his arms and swung him around as he hugged him. "Man, you've grown a foot since the last time I saw you! Are you as excited as I am about tomorrow?"

Dustin nodded his head vigorously. "Yeah, I've never seen anyone raise a barn up before."

David's eyebrows shot up as he laughed. "What about the wedding? Are you excited about that too?"

Dustin shrugged. "Oh yeah, that's cool too," but he didn't seem nearly as enthusiastic about it as he had been about the barn.

David chuckled as he put him down and wrapped his arms around me, whispering in my ear, "That's the part I'm excited about!" When he kissed me on the neck, the tingle shot all the way to my toes.

As we walked around the house to get Obleo settled in his new dog run, I looked around at all the delivery trucks. "Holy cow, it looks like Nell mighta got a bit carried away."

"Ya think? She's been having a ball with it. I told her I didn't care how much she spent, as long as it met with your approval. You might want to get her to fill you in all the details while there's still time to change what you don't like."

I shook my head. "I'm sure it will all be perfect. As long as you're there, it's all I really need. I just hope she doesn't blow a bunch of money when the barn needs rebuilding."

"Don't worry about it, Slick, there's plenty of money to cover both projects," he assured me.

"Oh, and while we're on the subject," I said, "what's up with telling Dustin I'd love it if he called me Slick?"

David sputtered and laughed as he looked down at Dustin and held out his hand. Dustin gave him five and they both did a really weird version of a happy dance. I watched and let them have their fun. I loved the relationship they were developing.

When they were finished with their little bit of fun, we introduced Obleo to his new home and made sure he had plenty of food and water. Then we headed out to the truck. David looked at the load in the truck and asked if everything was to be unloaded at Roy and Nell's or if some of it was going down to his house. I thought a minute and said, "Well, the suitcases in the back seat should stay here, but the rest of it probably goes down to the house. If there's anything Dustin needs while we're gone, he can get one of the boys to help him carry it up."

David nodded and removed the bags from the backseat. Then he took the keys and tossed them to one of the ranch hands, instructing him to drive the truck down to his house and very carefully unload the boxes from the back of the truck and put them in the garage.

With our suitcases in tow, we headed into the house. Nell met us at the back door, still holding her wooden spoon, and there were hugs all around. Dustin found Roy right away and started in asking a million questions about the fire and the new barn. Roy chuckled and took him by the hand to take him out and show him what they were doing. Nell sat me at the kitchen table and ran through all the plans she'd made, while David quietly slipped out the back door.

Coward!

It took about an hour for Nell to fill me in on all the details. I gave her a kiss on the cheek and thanked her for all the work, assuring her it was absolutely perfect. She beamed at me and then her expression changed as she asked, "Did David tell you Jake and his family are coming?"

I looked at her and said, "No, he didn't mention it. Are they staying over tonight?"

She nodded as she added, "They'll stay out in Jake's old house. I sent some of the gals down this morning to dust the place and leave fresh linens. They should be here any time. You ready for it?"

I took a deep breath and nodded. "Yeah, I guess so. We might as well get it out of the way now. I think much of what happens will depend on Brenda and how she reacts. It should certainly be interesting."

Nell blew out a deep breath. "Yeah, I'm not sure interesting is the word I woulda picked, but…well, we'll see. Maybe she'll surprise us." As she turned away, I saw her roll her eyes and had to fight to keep from laughing.

I stood up and excused myself to go find David. It might be better if we were together when Jake and his family arrived. It might reinforce the image of me with David, rather than the one of me as Jake's ex-girlfriend.

I found him out by the site of the new barn, talking to Dustin and Roy about the plans. He smiled and put his arm around me as I walked up. "Well, did mom fill you in? Everything meet with your approval?"

"Oh, yeah. She's been busy, but she's come up with some great ideas and it looks like she's enlisted enough help to keep herself from over-extending. Everything will be perfect. We'll just have to watch and make sure she doesn't wear herself out."

Roy cleared his throat. "Oh, don't worry about her. She's in her element. She's been orderin' stuff and bossin' people around for two weeks now. This isn't work for her…it's her idea of fun."

As we all chuckled over Roy's observations, a van turned into the drive. I felt David tense up next to me and I turned to look at his face to see what was wrong. He looked into my eyes and said, "That's Jake's van."

I nodded and leaned into him. "Well, maybe we oughta head over and greet them."

Roy started for the house as David pulled me around to face him. "You're sure about this, aren't you? I mean, you're sure you're over Jake and you really want to marry me?"

I stared up at him, surprised at the question, as I stroked the side of his face. "I have never been more positive about anything in my entire life. I'm completely, totally and helplessly in love. You are the man I want to spend the rest of my life with, the man I want to help me raise my child. I don't take that lightly. Tomorrow's just a formality. I've already made the commitment in my heart. Don't you know that?"

David took a deep breath as he nodded and answered, "Yeah, I know it, but it seems too good to be true sometimes. I can't help but worry something will go wrong. I guess I just needed a little last-minute reassurance."

He leaned over and kissed me. It was a very sweet and warm moment—until we headed for the house and he playfully reached down and pinched me on the butt. My eyebrows shot up as I looked over at him and he winked and gave me a thoroughly roguish grin.

He was so cute. Life with him was going to be fun, not the tense, difficult life I would have had with Jake.

I am one lucky girl.

Jake and his family were out of the van and on the front porch when we walked up. Jake smiled and waved as he said, “Well, there they are now. Hey, little brother, how are you?” After hugging David, Jake turned to me and smiled as he reached out to hug me. “You look wonderful. I guess life with my brother agrees with you.”

I smiled and hugged Jake, then turned and offered my hand to his wife. “You must be Brenda. It’s so nice to meet you.” She shook my hand limply and mumbled a rather unfelt “Pleased to meet you.”

Well, this is going well...so far, no hitting, pinching, or hair-pulling.

When I turned to meet the children, Tyler beamed at me. I shook my head. “Why, Tyler, I think you’ve grown two feet since the last time I saw you.” I held out my arms and he jumped into them. I swung him around in a circle and put him down, adding, “…and I think you’ve gained a ton too. Man, you’ve gotten so big, I’m not going to be able to pick you up very much longer.”

Tyler was clearly delighted with my response and he laughed and hugged my neck so hard I thought he’d break it. When he turned me loose, I asked him if he would introduce me to his sister. He turned and said, “This is my sister, Nikki. Nikki, this is Aunt Katie.”

I was delighted with the title he’d already bestowed on me, even though I noticed Brenda tense up out of the corner of my eye. I held out my hand to Nikki and told her how pleased I was to meet her. She smiled openly as she shook my hand and said, "You're very pretty and nice too. I'm glad Uncle David found a nice girlfriend. I didn't like his last one."

I smiled and leaned close as I whispered conspiratorially, "Good. I didn't like her either." That earned me a big smile from Nikki.

With the introductions completed, I stepped back into David's waiting arm and sensed, with that move, my position in the family was cemented. As we turned for the house, I overheard Brenda snap at Jake that he'd forgotten her overnight case out in the car. Jake sighed and simply said, "Yes, dear," as he headed for the car.

David and I exchanged a knowing look as we continued into the house.

The rest of the evening passed quickly and Brenda insisted she and Jake needed to turn in early if they were to be up in time to be properly dressed by the "un-Godly hour of seven o'clock." They had agreed to let Tyler and Nikki spend the night up here at the main house. The rest of us smiled and wished them pleasant dreams as they headed down the lane toward Jake's house.

When they were gone, everyone breathed a sigh of relief. I sat up straight and looked around the room. "Well, I think that went well. She didn't punch me."

Everyone looked at me, stunned, for a moment and then they all collapsed in laughter. David shook his head and kissed me as he pulled me up off the couch. "Come on, let's find those kids and make sure they get tucked in safely." Then he lowered his voice and turned his head so only I could hear the rest, "...before I take you to your room and tuck you in safely."

I rolled my eyes and said, "Oh, you talk tough, but when push comes to shove, you'll chicken out."

He swiveled his head to look at me out of the corner of his eye, with one brow raised, as he whispered, "We'll see who chickens out, missy!"

Before we could get out the door to search for the boys, MJ and Willy walked in with bags in hand. We sat and visited with them for a few minutes and then left them with Nell to show them to their rooms and help get them settled in.

When we finally found the kids out on the porch, Nikki was more than happy to stay at the house where Gramma was cooking up a storm and the wedding preparations were being made. But she rolled her eyes when the boys jumped up and down, high-fiving and belly-bumping each other because it meant they would get to stay together.

But David rescued her from the boys when he said, "I'll tell ya what. This is the night before my wedding. I think a bachelor party would be in order for us guys. Why don't we leave the girls to their wedding planning and we can go down to my place and party the night away."

Well, I'm sure the boys didn't have a clue what a bachelor party was, but they must've figured anything with the word "party" in it must be a good thing because they repeated the belly-bumping routine.

I laughed and asked David, "Just what did you have in mind? No naked broads jumping out of cakes, I hope!"

He pulled me close and kissed me. "Well, I thought maybe I'd take the boys up to my place and we'd party, maybe something involving a movie and popcorn, perhaps some candy?"

I shook my head. "Okay, but if you want to get any sleep at all tonight, I'd skip the candy."

David smiled. "Okay, no candy, just lots of popcorn."

The boys disappeared and were back in a flash with their pajamas in hand. When I frowned and told them they needed toothbrushes too, they looked to David for confirmation.

He nodded. "Yep, toothbrushes are definitely bachelor party equipment." So off they went in search of toothbrushes.

As Nikki said goodnight and headed inside, I snuggled up to David and said, "See, you did chicken out, after all."

He flashed me an incredulous look and said, "Oh, no. I might sneak back up here after they're asleep and surprise you."

I laughed. "Don't you dare leave those boys down there all alone. You made your bed, Mister. Now you're gonna have to lie in it."

He frowned. Caught in his own trap.

"Oh, by the way," I said, "just on the off-chance you hadn't made any big plans for what to wear to the wedding tomorrow, I bought you something." From the stunned look on his face, I could tell he hadn't given it a single moment's consideration. He looked so surprised, I couldn't help but laugh as I nodded and said, "Oh, yeah…I thought so." I went to my room and pulled out the new red, white and black striped shirt, white Wranglers, and black felt hat I'd bought him.

When I returned with his new clothes, he whistled and said, “Wow, I like those.”

“They’ll match the dress I bought and they should fit because I called Nell and got the sizes.”

He shook his head and kissed me on the cheek. “Thanks. What would I do without you?”

“I don’t know, but we’re not going to find out.”

Ever.

He smiled and tapped me on the end of the nose with his forefinger. “Sorry I didn’t think about clothes. There’s been a lot going on around here. But I did do one thing right. I told you I’d get a ring and I remembered that.”

I smiled. “Good. Then you’re forgiven.”

He laughed as he reached into his pocket and pulled out a small jewelry case. While I held his clothes, he got down on one knee, took out a ring with the biggest diamond I’d ever seen, and looked up at me. “Katie, will you do me the honor of being my wife?”

Stunned, I just stared. I’d expected a simple wedding band. This ring looked like the Hope diamond! I took a deep breath, smiled and stuck out my ring finger, while still holding onto the clothes hangers with my other hand, and he slipped the ring on my finger. The ring was beautiful, but I couldn’t take my eyes off the man as he stood, wrapped his arms around me, and pulled me into a lingering kiss I will never forget.

“This probably qualifies as one of the shortest engagements in history,” he whispered into my ear as I hugged him tight and whacked him in the back of the head with a hanger.

So much for a romantic moment! It was just as well, as the boys were back with jammies and toothbrushes, so we shooed them out the door. I kissed David goodnight, handed him the hangers, and sent him off after the boys, telling him I would see him bright and early tomorrow morning. He turned and waved as he followed the boys down the driveway.

I turned and went to my room to pull the curtains and watch both my boys head home. I sighed as I saw the kitchen light go on and the back door closed behind them. I turned and fell into bed fully clothed. I was asleep right away and dreamed most of the night about weddings and happily ever-afters.

Chapter Twenty Seven

Five o'clock came early, but I figured it would take me a couple of hours to shower, dress, and do all the last-minute things. Nell figured the guests would begin to arrive about six o'clock, so she and the Wives Corp put out fresh baked rolls, coffee, and orange juice to hold everyone over until the food was served after the ceremony.

MJ was in my room, helping me dress and do my hair. I'd just stepped out of the shower and was standing there in a towel with MJ rubbing lotion on my back as I protested it wasn't necessary. "We'll get married," I told her, "and then we'll build a barn. I'm going to get dirty again, which means I'll need another shower this evening before...well, before anything sexy happens. So the lotion is a waste."

"Oh, shut up," she said, "and quit wiggling, will ya? You never know what David might have planned—maybe a little quickie in the closet. I want to make sure you're ready when it finally happens."

I looked at MJ as my eyebrows shot up and I squeaked, "A little quickie in the closet? Are you kidding me?"

"No, I'm not," she boldly replied. "At this point, I say whatever it takes! You two have the worst timing I've ever seen and we're not taking any chances today. You are going to be ready from your head to your toes for whatever that hot, sexy man of yours has in mind."

I laughed and shot her a look that said she was absolutely incorrigible as I crossed the room in my towel to find my underwear. She shrugged and said very emphatically, "Trust me!" Then she turned away as she muttered under her breath, "If this marriage doesn't get consummated today, it won't be because I didn't try."

"I heard that!" I shouted across the room and we both laughed. "Seriously," I said, changing the subject, "I'm so glad you and Willy are here today. Do you think this is awfully uncomfortable for Willy, with him being Jake's best friend and all?"

"No, not at all," she replied. "We talked about it last night and he's good with it. He says Jake had his chance and he blew it. You know Willy loves you like a sister. He only wants what will make you happy. He grew up with the McAllisters and he loves them all. I think he's looking forward to us being able to come up more often to hang out with you and David. So you'll have to invite us up."

I put my arms around her and hugged her tight. "Oh, MJ, you know you don't ever need an invitation. You two are welcome up here any time. In fact, Jake's old house is empty most of the time. Willy oughta talk to Jake and get him to give you guys a key so you've got your own place to stay whenever you come up." I wiggled my eyebrows as I added, "Give you a little more privacy, ya know?"

MJ's mouth fell open and her eyes went wide as she drew in a big breath. "Oh, wow, what a great idea! It'd be like our own little cabin in the pines!"

We laughed and continued to make plans as we worked to prepare me for the big day. I hadn't been nervous until now but it was starting to sink in I was actually getting married again. This was forever.

Strangely, even knowing now how horribly a marriage could end, I still wasn't as scared as I'd been the first time. I believed it was because I trusted David more than I'd ever trusted Mark. Funny how we instinctively know things sometimes, but either we don't listen to the warning voices or we make excuses. I'd made a lot of excuses for Mark. Come to think of it, I'd made a lot of excuses for Jake too.

About five thirty, there was a knock on the door and we found Nikki standing outside, all dressed up and ready to go. She smiled shyly at MJ and asked if we needed any help. MJ threw the door open wide, exposing me in my underwear to anyone who might pass by, as she said, "You betcha! Come on in, kid. We can use all the help we can get!"

"Just shut the door, will you?" I squealed as I sprung to crouch behind the dresser, in fear Willy or Roy might happen by at any moment.

Nikki came in tentatively, giggling at my expense, and we spent the next hour doing "girl stuff".

By about six forty-five, we had bonded like the Three Musketeers. I was all dolled up and ready to go, and we were all very pleased with the overall effect. The dress was white with some red beadwork. We stuck a white flower in my auburn hair and the leather on my boots matched the color of the beads. I was truly color-coordinated from head to toe.

David would wear white Wranglers with a striped shirt that picked up the color in my dress. The black felt hat and his black boots would pick up the black stripes in his shirt. The overall effect would be very striking and I was extremely pleased with my efforts.

Nell had picked up on my color scheme with red ribbons and white flowers. Everything was absolutely beautiful. There would be no attendants. It would be a very simple ceremony. We'd exchange vows and rings, then we'd kiss, and that was it. The rest of the day would be taken up with eating, drinking, and building a barn. It sounded like the perfect day to me.

MJ and Nikki and I spent a few minutes downstairs in the living room, greeting family and friends and taking pictures, but they were very careful not to let David and I get a glimpse of each other. This was to be a traditional ceremony and tradition demanded the groom not see the bride before the ceremony on the day of the wedding.

Just before seven o'clock, Nell bustled into the living room to shoo everyone out and tell me the guests were ready and it was almost time. I kissed MJ and Nikki and thanked them for their help as Nell herded them out the door and turned to look at me. Suddenly, it was all far too real. I was frozen like a deer in headlights, as it dawned on me it was time. I could feel myself start to shake and my breathing became very shallow and erratic. Nell ordered me to sit down for a minute, but I refused, "I'll be damned if I'll wrinkle this dress five minutes before my wedding," I insisted.

Nell came over and put her arms around me, hugging me close as she smoothed my hair. "Katie, I know your folks are gone and I know no one can ever replace them in your life. But Roy and I want you to know how much we both love you and Dustin. We hope you'll think of us as parents and allow us to fill the gap for you."

"Oh, Nell," I replied, "I love you both so much. I'm not just marrying a man. I'm marrying a whole family. It's so wonderful. I'm so excited about my new life and my new family. It's a dream come true."

Nell smiled again with tears in her eyes as she straightened the shoulders of my dress. "Katie, you're the daughter I've always wanted. I've wanted you in this family from the first moment I met you. I'm so happy for you and for David...well, I'm just happy, that's all." As she leaned forward and hugged me, we heard a man clear this throat from the kitchen doorway. We both turned and found Jake in the doorway with his hat in his hand. Nell frowned as my heart leapt in my chest and my stomach did a flip. What did he want? Panic began to take hold.

Holy crap! I don't need this right now.

I could feel myself begin to take in short, erratic breaths. Why he was here...now.

Nell turned and tried to shoo him outside but he held up one hand and said, "Mom, I need to talk to Katie for one minute. I won't be long, just give us one minute alone. Please." Nell looked at me as I nodded and she reluctantly left the room, shaking her head and swearing Jake had better not screw everything up again.

I stared at Jake, wondering what was about to happen, and hoping it didn't ruin the rest of my life. My heart pounded as I rubbed my palms together to dry the perspiration.

Jake stepped forward and took my hands in his. "I had to see you one last time before you tied the knot. Wow, you look stunning. That dress is incredible." Then he looked into my eyes. "But, then, so are you."

My heart beat against my ribs like a wild bird in a cage. I could feel his breath on my face and smell his cologne. I was starting to get light-headed and had to remind myself to breathe.

This is a lot more pressure than a girl should have to face on her wedding day!

"Katie," he continued, "I wanted to tell you how very sorry I am about how things worked out between us, but I hope you'll be very happy with David."

I took a deep breath and again, I smelled his cologne…and then it hit me again how much this man had changed. He had changed to suit the situation.

The man I was marrying was steadfast and firm, like a rock. My mind immediately went to my rock—the one that sat firm and dry in the middle of the creek, forcing the water to cut a path around it as it refused to budge. Yes, that was my David. He was my rock. He didn't change. Rather, he changed the circumstances around him. This wasn't a decision I would second-guess. No, I had chosen correctly this time.

Jake might have been the man of my dreams once, but he was as shifting and inconstant as my dreams. David was the man who would make my dreams come true.

When I spoke, my voice was steady and a strange calm came over me as I said, "Jake, there will always be a soft spot in my heart for you and for Tyler, but what happened between us worked out exactly the way it was supposed to. David was always the right man for me. I can't imagine my life without him."

Jake nodded and gave me a kiss on the cheek. As he turned to leave, I saw movement out of the corner of my eye. Someone had been standing at the doorway to the kitchen. I wondered who it was and what they'd overheard.

As Jake left the house to join the other guests, I took several deep breaths and headed for the kitchen door, which is where Nell had instructed me to make my entrance.

I stepped out onto the porch and found Dustin waiting, all dressed up to give me away. It was so sweet and so precious, my eyes filled up with tears and I was so overwhelmed I couldn't speak. He looked up at me, adoringly, with those big brown eyes and said, "Mommy, you look beautiful. David's eyes are gonna pop right out of his head!" Then he stuck out his elbow for me to take it. My heart swelled with pride until I thought it might burst and my shoulders shook with laughter as tears rolled down my cheeks.

It was one of those moments in life that takes your breath away and will be forever branded in my heart—a moment so sweet and precious it can never be forgotten.

As I took his elbow, he smiled and walked me around the corner to where David stood with the minister. By the time I arrived, tears were streaming down my face and I was thankful I'd opted for the waterproof mascara.

David smiled and I could see there were tears in his eyes also as Dustin walked me over to him. It was so incredibly cute when Dustin reached up and moved my hand from his arm to David's. I could tell even David was moved as he blinked back the tears. Before Dustin could move away, David reached out and scooped him up in one arm as he held onto me with the other hand. I bit my lips to keep a sob in check as I looked deeply into the eyes of the man I loved, the man who had just made a very public statement he would not only be my husband, but he would also be a father to my son.

The ceremony after that was pretty much a blur. I was so overcome with emotion, I did whatever the preacher told me to do. One of the few moments I remember with any clarity was when the preacher asked who gives this bride and Dustin's hand shot in the air and he shouted, "I do." I'm sure Nell coached him, but it was so sweet and there was a rumble of laughter that made it very special.

The next coherent memory I've got of the ceremony was the kissing part. For some reason, the kissing parts always seem to stay with me. I also remember the camera flashes all around us as the minister introduced us as Mr. and Mrs. David McAllister.

It truly was beautiful. Nell had positioned us so the sunrise would be right behind the preacher. Although it was light out, the sun hadn't cleared the tree line yet, so the sky was full of pinks and blues and yellows. The wedding pictures were works of art. I took it as a sign of clear, perfect new beginnings.

We all ate breakfast and drank our fill of orange juice and champagne. Then, as everyone drifted off to change clothes and start on the barn, David took me by the hand and we snuck around the side of the house to have a quiet moment alone.

Giggling quietly as we ran, we ducked into an opening behind a bush and pressed ourselves up against the house as we tried to catch our breath. I looked up at David and smiled. He moved against me, pressing me to the side of the house as he kissed me. His kiss was warm and passionate as his tongue danced with mine and his hands cupped my bottom and pulled me in against him. I wrapped my arms around his neck as my stomach did flip-flops and I secretly thanked MJ for insisting on the lotion.

"You know they'll be looking for us soon," I whispered between kisses.

He groaned. "Yeah, I suppose this isn't a good idea, is it?"

"No, probably not," I agreed, breathing heavily and arching against him as he nuzzled and kissed my neck. When he moved his hand up under my blouse to cup one breast, my breath caught in my throat. "I thought you didn't want to put us in a compromising position."

He lifted his head and grinned. "You're my wife now. There's no compromise, just a little embarrassment. I can live with it."

I giggled as I shifted underneath him, making him groan and drop his head to my shoulder. He lifted his head and looked into my eyes hungrily. "Woman, whose idea was this damn barn-raising, anyway?"

"Mine," I said as I trailed one finger down the back of his neck, "and next time I have an idea that stupid, lock me in a closet, will you?"

"Gladly," he croaked in my ear as he took a deep breath and pushed himself away. We stood there for a minute or two, bodies apart, his forehead touching mine, staring into each other's eyes and breathing deeply as we struggled to gain control over our emotions and our bodies.

Finally, he straightened and took a deep breath, exhaling slowly as he shook his head. "You are a wicked, wicked woman. You know that, Mrs. McAllister?"

I laughed. I loved the way my new name sounded.

He twirled a lock of my hair around his finger and raised one brow as he continued, "But I promise you, I will get even—tonight!" Then he leaned close to my ear and whispered, "Tonight's the night. No more stalling, no more backing off, no more last-minute reprieves…tonight is the night."

"Ooooh," I crooned. "I seem to remember the last time you made a threat like that, it was all talk and you chickened out."

His eyes grew round and he gave me a shit-eatin', lop-sided grin. "Okay, the challenge has been issued and accepted. We'll see who's talkin' tough and who's not. You wait. Tonight's the night, baby."

Then he leaned in and gave me a quick, deep kiss before he spun away and walked back to the front yard, leaving me there, on fire and wanting so much more.

Chapter Twenty Eight

A couple of the guests packed up and left, but most stayed to help. The men worked on the barn while the women cooked and cleaned and ran whatever errands needed to be run. David wasn't particularly interested in sitting through the opening of the wedding gifts, so I opened them as the women all ooooh'd and aaaah'd.

It was a beautiful day. Although it had been chilly enough for sweaters and light jackets in the morning, the afternoon warmed up and it was very comfortable in the front yard under the shade trees.

As the day progressed, I was impressed with how quickly the walls of the barn went up. It looked like the exterior shell would be completely erected by the end of the day and the roof would probably be done also. The new barn looked to be almost twice the size of the old one, so it was very impressive to see it come along so fast.

We broke for lunch in shifts and ate quickly to avoid losing precious time. Everyone agreed they wanted to work straight through until it got too dark to see clearly, so dinner would be timed for just after sunset.

As the sun went down, the last sheet of metal was bolted onto the roof. They had accomplished what they'd planned to do that day and as the hammers and other equipment were lowered to the ground, a cheer went up. We had the shell of our new barn.

When the food had been set out and everyone had washed up for dinner, David gave the blessing. He thanked God for the food, the friends, the new barn and his new family. I silently thanked God also—for my new family and for this incredible man. Then we all sat down to eat. It was wonderful. As I looked around, I realized these were my new friends and family. I was overwhelmed at how truly blessed I was to find this man and to have him love me as much as I loved him.

When he looked up and caught me staring at him across the table, he put his fork down and stared back with just a hint of a smile on his face. We stayed that way for a long time, gazing into each other's eyes and enjoying the noise of friends and family around us. Then he got a bone-melting grin on his face as he leaned forward and mouthed the words, "Tonight's the night." As I blushed and looked around to see if anyone had noticed, he laughed and shook his head.

Although it had been a long day and everyone was tired, the neighbors had arranged for one of the local bands to come out at eight and play one set before they headed to their gig in town, so everyone could dance a little. It was fun and seemed to energize the crowd a bit. Nell and Roy broke out the beer and the party was on.

Jake came around and said his good-byes. He and Brenda and the kids would drive into Prescott for the night and get an early start from there the next morning. The kids both hugged us and told us what a great time they had. I thanked Nikki for helping me get ready that morning and she blushed as she said,

"You're welcome. You were so pretty. It was the most romantic wedding ever."

David and I smiled and told them they would both have to come back soon and spend a few days with us. Tyler and Dustin said their good-byes and promised each other something secret about toads that I was certain I was better off not understanding. Then David and I walked out to the driveway and saw them off.

We were standing in the driveway in one of those moments where it's just the two of you alone in a crowd, when David took me in his arms and said, "I've got a confession to make."

I lifted one brow and said, "Oh? Well, spill it."

With a serious look, he told me, "I saw Jake go into the house right before the ceremony and I followed him. I overheard the two of you talking."

My stomach lurched and my heart thumped as I said, "Oh?" How much had he overheard and what would his reaction be?

"I didn't hear all of what Jake said to you, but I did get there in time to hear what you said to him. Did you mean it?"

I looked into his eyes for a long moment before I replied, "Yes. I meant every word. I truly believe you and I were meant for each other. What I had with Jake was very, very pale in comparison to what you and I have. You are truly the love of my life."

He pulled me close and kissed me with heart-stopping intensity. I clung to him weak-kneed as I returned his kiss, matching every twist of the tongue, every moan, and wishing everyone would go home and leave us alone together.

When the kiss ended, we found ourselves in the middle of a cheering crowd. We both turned red as beets when we realized how many people had witnessed our extremely passionate kiss.

David leaned close and whispered in my ear, "I think this is where we're expected to make our exit, and I think it's about high time, too."

My cheeks still felt hot as I nodded and looked around for Dustin. I didn't have to look too far. He was front and center in the cheering crowd. I bent over and hugged him goodnight, telling him I'd see him tomorrow morning before we left for Colorado.

He hugged me back and said, "Don't hurry home, Mom, Roy's gonna show me how to build a door for that raised-up barn." I laughed and ruffled his hair as David picked him up and hugged him goodbye too.

Then David grabbed my hand and pulled me after him as we jumped into his truck and headed down the drive.

Surprised, I looked over and said, "I thought we'd be staying at your house tonight."

He looked at me and raised one brow as he said, "Are you kidding me? Do you have any idea of the kind of hell those people would raise outside my house if they thought we were in there, trying to consummate this marriage? You ever heard of a good, old-fashioned shivaree? Oh, no, we're not risking any interference tonight. I rented us a cottage on the other side of town. You hang on while I fly this thing—because tonight's the night, baby!"

I laughed and laid my head on his shoulder as he drove. "So, did you by any chance, remember to grab us some clothes or toothbrushes for tomorrow?"

He looked at me sheepishly and I knew the answer as he responded, “Guess we’ve got time to stop and buy some toothbrushes. As for the clothes, we won’t need ‘em.” Then he winked and smiled that shit-eatin’ grin.

Note from the Author

Thank you for purchasing and reading this book. I hope you have enjoyed your reading experience. I would very much appreciate you returning to the online retailer where you purchased this book and leaving a review. If you do leave a review, be sure to email me at the address listed below and let me know where you posted the review and I will send you a free electronic copy of my short story, *Midnight On The Double-B.* Best Regards and Happy Reading.

Kayce Lassiter

Contact Kayce

Email: kaycelassiter@yahoo.com
Website: www.kaycelassiter.com

Coming Soon

Loons Of A Feather
(watch for it at your favorite retailer)

55146034R00176

Made in the USA
Middletown, DE
15 July 2019